ΛVENIR ECLECTIΛ

VOLUME 1

Editors: Grace Bridges and Travis Perry
Copyeditors: H. A. Titus, Mary Ruth Pursselley,
Jeff C. Carter, Jeff Chapman, Caprice Hokstad

Contributors: Grace Bridges, Jeff C. Carter, Jeff Chapman, Frank Creed,
Pauline Creeden, Karina Fabian, Joseph H. Ficor, Kat Heckenbach,
Holly Heisey, Greg Mitchell, Keven Newsome, Travis Perry,
Mary Ruth Pursselley, J. L. Rowan, Walt Staples, H. A. Titus, Fred Warren

These stories appeared first at http://www.avenireclectia.com.

ISBN: 978-1-927154-27-4
Published by Splashdown Books, New Zealand
http://www.splashdownbooks.com

AVENIR ECLECTIA

INTRODUCTION

We made a world, and it looks like you're about to step into it. Good choice. I'm really glad you decided to join us.

Avenir Eclectia is a multi-author microfiction project, an online shared world, a story by mosaic. What does all that mean? Well, in March of 2011 the website went live at www.avenireclectia.com, and has been posting flash fiction regularly ever since. All stories are based in the same section of space: an inhospitable planet, an orbiting space station, various moons and asteroids and ships plying the distances. The inhabitants are descended from generation-ship colonists, so they are humans from Earth—however, due to the intervening years, there has been a great deal of cultural shift. They barely remember where they came from; Earth is like a myth to them.

But why did I set up the project in this way? Here I have to give credit to Kristine Pratt of Written World Communications. She told me of a non-fiction book she was publishing—it was to have 100 very short stories from different authors. The collaborative idea appealed to me, and I said to myself, what if we did that with fiction?

I wanted a world where writers of all speculative genres would feel at home. Space settings for the science fiction folks including myself. Planetside for the fantasy people: giant beetles and undersea cities, with sentient oceanic lifeforms, some of which are telepathic, and some of which are evil (to accommodate those of the horror genre). I set up some basic parameters together with early contributors, and we were ready to roll.

The project has taken on a life I could never have expected. All these contributors took a piece of the world and made it their own, mingling with each other's characters and building the picture, piece by tiny piece.

During the site's first year, Walt Staples was a most ardent supporter and contributor. He wrote more than anyone else in that time, and although he never did write a novel of his own, the body of work he created for Avenir Eclectia is so substantial we had to leave most of it out of this collection. But don't panic! He's earned his own book, which we plan to publish in the not-too-distant future. It will be a legacy for a colleague and friend we miss very much.

Several of the contributors in this anthology are also working on Avenir stories to be published in novel form. And the site continues to publish three times a week, so there will be more to come.

This anthology is not really an anthology at all in the traditional sense. The microfiction stories as published on the site built a common world. Some characters mentioned by one author were picked up again by other authors, the same locations were repeated again in increasing detail, in such a way that the entire body of stories eventually formed a single work.

Which is why this collection of short stories has no table of contents listing each individual author's contribution by page. Our intent is that you read this work from beginning to end as you would a novel.

For fans of the site, you will notice that as mentioned above, certain authors have opted to publish their stories separately from this collective whole. Still, most of the authors who were published on the site, including Walt, are represented in this work, even if with only a few stories, or in some cases, just one. You will also notice that the stories are in a different order than originally posted on the site and have been lightly edited, even though early published stories are generally at the beginning while later stories tend to be at the end. We've sought to enhance the reading experience by making sure that in a given character arc there were not too many stories between each author's tales. Also, stories have been put in order to build to a climax that is optimistic without being sugary, deeply spiritual without being dogmatic.

We've also had the opportunity to include some of the artwork from the site, along with articles on specific topics addressing the conditions of the world orbiting 94 Ceti. And more. You may want to peruse the "Inside Avenir Eclectia" information section at the back before diving into the stories, to familiarize yourself with the basic situation.

As much as Grace has been surprised and pleased at how the story website she launched has taken on such a life of its own, I've been pleased that my basic idea of rearranging the order of the stories for this work has turned out so well. It's been my pleasure to have taken the lead in editing this collection of stories—stories that would not have existed at all without Grace's vision and the website she founded.

So now, dear friends, we gladly present to you Avenir Eclectia.

Grace Bridges and Travis Perry
September 2012

1. COOL, SMOOTH METAL
GRACE BRIDGES

Cool, smooth metal met Ave's fingers as she slid down the wall to sit in the corner. No one would bother her here in this obscure corridor—not for a while, at least. She concentrated, and felt the distant, almost intangible vibrating of the station. Its comfort calmed her, and she hummed to herself, head down, hair shutting out the world and thoughts of Smith. A good kid, but they were both too young—only fourteen Foundings. And the children—the beggars, the poorest of all beings, who didn't even have a claim to parents—they looked up to her. She must do right, and not be distracted by an obsession for love, as heady as it was. The time was not yet come.

Ave recognised the tune she hummed, and smiled a little: her name-song, and that of the colony. "Arise, Avenir Eclectia; be strong, Avenir Eclectia. Stand firm, Avenir Eclectia; live on, Avenir Eclectia." A rousing anthem that gave her the tingles. Her first carer had given her the name of the entire colony: Avenir, though she went by Ave. She placed her hands on the floor, felt her connection to the huge space habitat and the presence of the planet below, and hoped she hadn't hurt Smith beyond repair. He'd understand, someday. Wouldn't he?

The beings on the planet called to her and she rested in their mental embrace, sensing only the living station through the cool, smooth metal.

2. JOY
MARY RUTH PURSSELLEY

There is no peace under the great domes the strangers come from. Their very walls emanate anguish, animosity, and despair. One can sense it, even from a distance, hanging in the water like blood lingering after a shark's kill. It is my curiosity—the force behind many things I do—that lures me there in spite of all. Curiosity...and pity. I don't understand the unhappiness of the strangers. What has caused it? Can nothing be done to change it?

Or is this bitter aura their nature?

I am inclined to believe not. Today, as I hovered close over the domes, one mind stood apart from the others. It was not angry or tainted like the

1

others. Its touch in my consciousness wasn't septic like the others. Reaching out to listen more closely, I realized why this mind was different.

This stranger was happy. I listened as emotions rippled through her consciousness like bubbles in the deep ocean, and her mind formed peculiarly-shaped thoughts—the words of her language. The shapes, patterns, and rhythms of the thoughts were new and different, and made me laugh at their oddity.

Until one thought formed a shape I recognized.

The word itself, in the stranger's tongue, meant nothing to me. It was the shape of the thought behind the word, the emotion on which the word stood, the precise harmony with which the thought and emotion were fused, that gave me pause.

The stranger thought my name. Her consciousness formed the exact shape and feeling of my identifying thought. But she did more than that. She gave my name a word in her language.

Joy.

3.   APPRENTICE
KAT HECKENBACH

The sight of the boy huddled in the corner stopped Spiner in his tracks. If he were caught following up on the illegal experiment...

He slipped behind a support column. He couldn't chance anyone seeing him, not even a homeless child. But pity tugged at his heart as he watched the tattered urchin pull scabbed knees to a skeletal chest. Tears streaked through grime on the boy's cheeks. Spiner leaned his forehead against the cool metal beam.

"You can come out, sir. It's okay." The boy's voice squeaked mouse-like. He couldn't be more than five Foundings old.

Spiner stepped out into the corridor and walked softly toward the boy. He knelt down as the boy wiped away tears with the back of his hand. "Are you hungry?"

The boy nodded but didn't meet Spiner's gaze. "I won't tell anyone you're here, even if you don't feed me," he said.

"I appreciate that." Spiner reached out and brushed a string of blond hair away from the boy's eyes. "You know what I am?"

"A wizard, sir." He lifted his head, eyes wide. "I'm sorry, I know you don't like being called that, but I mean no disrespect."

Was he only five then? Such a big word for a little boy.

"No worries, kid. I've no apologies for my beliefs."

"I believe, too," the boy said. "I—I want to learn."

Spiner studied the boy's face. Intelligent eyes. The eyes of a survivor. He whispered, "You'd like to be an apprentice?"

The boy's "yes" was barely audible.

Spiner leaned in. "Let's go. Food first, and then some lessons."

One corner of the boy's mouth tugged up into a half-smile as hope sparked in his eyes.

4. DEADLY GEAR
TRAVIS PERRY

Ernsto Mons slid the fifth mini-torpedo into his bandolier, laid out on the stained mattress in a cheap hotel in the deepest part of Zirconia. His weapons included the guided torpedo launcher, wickedly sharp hooks attached to duraflex netting, ten sonic stun grenades, a tranquilizer gun loaded for underwater use, some of its tips poisoned and some not, and a steel curved knife nearly big enough to qualify as a sword. His gear also included his armored dive suit, specially designed to allow him to face the high pressures at depths of six kilometers. But that was stored in the third storage cell on the right from the nearest airlock into the city, the one at the very bottom, one little-used due to the incredible water pressure and complete blackness of the depths outside.

He fingered his five platinum coins—these would bribe the enforcer at the entryway. The other twenty-five were for him to keep, with twenty-five more when he delivered his prey to the wizard up on Avenir.

Ernsto grinned to himself. "Like you said, old man. One angel comin' up your way—dead or alive."

5.   MORNING
GRACE BRIDGES

Tennant gained the rim of the lava sea with a final crunch of his boots and paused for breath. He never tired of this moment, giving colour to his otherwise dreary life: moving from the sealed habitat on the broken planet's regularly curved surface, to this, almost literally the end of the world—a deep, violent crack in the crust of Sheba, moon of Eclectia. The land, such as it was, ended; the cliff dropped off into dizzying space and lava lapped at its distant foot. The fissure's other side rose up two k's away, distant, unknown.

He turned his face straight up and beheld another major remnant of the cataclysm, the rings of cooled lava that threatened to fall on his head. Swathes of rubble danced around it and in the gap between Sheba's halves. If he strained his eyes he might make out Quatermain beyond the littered asteroids. The two had been one moon as recently as two hundred Foundings ago, it was said, and he believed it.

He blew out a breath, fogging his faceplate, and returned his gaze to the task ahead, fighting vertigo. Tennant glanced at his partner, then stepped forward from the volcanic grit into the maze of scaffolding at the edge of the abyss. Precious ore to feed the factories of Avenir, partly present in the crust of the more habitable planet Eclectia that now loomed beyond the incredibly distant horizon ahead.

They attached their harnesses and turned to back down the first ladder. The Avenir station glinted there in the bright light of Ceti 94, and off to the right he spied the lesser glow of its distant twin star before the rock blocked his view.

They reached the tunnel entrance and unhooked themselves in turn. Tennant allowed himself one last, long look over the wild and ever-shifting lava in the canyon still far beneath them, before he spun and entered the mine to begin another long shift.

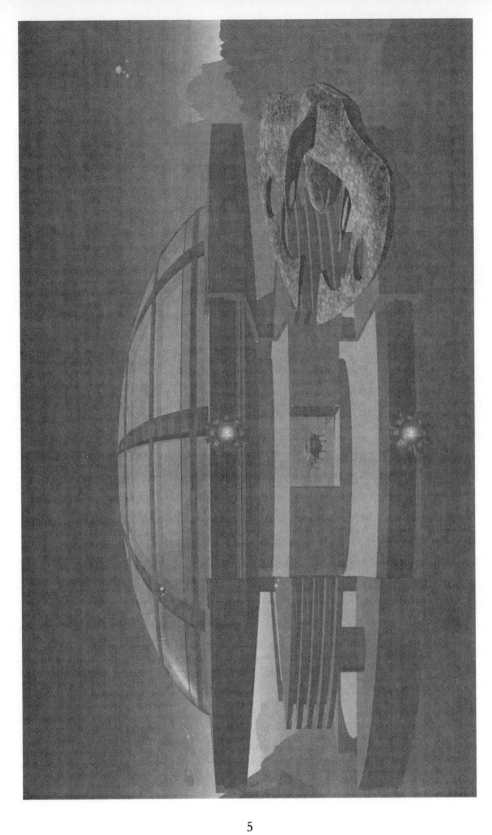

"Stay close, children," Teacher said in her harried voice. "And do not touch."

Katha watched as his classmates grudgingly obeyed—until Teacher's eye was off them. Then they went back to the usual stupid tricks: shoving and horseplay. Gras stayed close to Teacher, but that didn't keep the bullies from snide remarks. The popular crowd looked bored except when flirting with each other, or what they thought passed for flirting. Only a handful actually paid attention. No wonder Teacher was harried.

Katha trailed behind and fought real boredom. He came here all the time. He knew so much more about these creatures than even Teacher, and yet every time he visited, he discovered something new about this fascinating species behind the glass. If he could just get away from the class! The creatures were their most uninteresting when a crowd watched them because they tended to turn and watch back. Boring!

Not to mention how stupid his classmates got. Like now, as Teacher turned her back to consult with their tour guide: Tourra started trying to engage one in a game of chase by racing from one end of the glass to another to see if any would follow. How original. Next someone would lick the glass, or worse, stick his open mouth on it—yep, Bourz. Figured.

Teacher turned around and shouted, "Quash! Quit banging that glass! How would you feel if someone banged on your house? Come along—time for the next exhibit."

The class grudgingly moved on, Katha with them. As he gave one last glance, he saw one of the creatures wave. He raised a fin and repeated the gesture, pleased that no one else had gotten to see.

When he grew up, he was going to devote his life to the study of these strange creatures who came from the Above and built their tank homes in his world.

7. PALLBEARER
WALT STAPLES

The old man shuffled down the corridor, slowed by his burden. His friend had put on weight towards the end. He glanced down at his own paunch and grinned ruefully. His friend wasn't the only one packing it on of late. He thought about his burden. Friend? No, much, much closer than a mere friend. Almost a lover. What was that ancient word? Bunkie—the one you ate, slept, shared a blanket with, and died with if worst came to worst. Yep, his bunkie.

The disposal tech looked up as the old man entered. "Yes, sir? Can I help you?"

"A disposal."

The tech looked at the shroud-wrapped burden. "Why didn't you just put it down a disposal chute? Why lug it here?"

The old man smiled slightly. "Biological."

The tech raised his eyebrows and tilted his head. "Okay." He pulled up a form on his display. "Weight of object to be disposed of?"

"Five kilos."

"Description?"

"My bunkie."

The tech looked at his display, then leaned closer to it. "I'm not seeing a listing for that. Could I take a look?"

At the old man's nod, he unwrapped the shroud on the end nearest to him and stopped. After a moment, he looked back up, his eyes softened. "Yeah, okay. Tell you what, I've got a document box that should work. Be right back." When he returned, the old man placed his burden in the container and the tech sealed it. He then attached a small reaction unit and a guidance pack to the container. He consulted his display and tapped in the coordinates for the guidance pack's A.I. Then he opened the funerary airlock and placed the container on the track. The container moved in and the inner hatch closed. The tech tapped once and the light above the lock changed from green to yellow to red.

The old man began to ask, "I wonder, when I…"

The tech smiled gently. "I billed your account and made a note of your I.D. When the time comes, if it's within the parameters, you'll be put on the same course." He looked at his display. "Your…bunkie will reach Beta in

162 standard days."

The old man, his eyes wet, sniffed. He wiped a finger beneath his eye. "Thank you, so much."

The tech nodded. "I had a dog once too."

8.   DEEP, DEEP DARK
TRAVIS PERRY

As Ernsto Mons slipped deeper into the inky blackness, his armored dive suit creaked and popped under the pressure. He swallowed hard—he had never been a deep diver; he'd never faced the deepest depths before. But he had been a smuggler and had killed men in cold blood when he needed to; he knew he was tough, so he brushed past his fear.

The movement locator built into his suit—an expensive piece of sonar gear his wizard benefactor in Avenir had paid for, like the suit and most of his weapons—flicked with green dots of movement. Dozens of dots, moving fast, around two hundred meters below him.

He tilted his helmet forward, straining his eyes to see any sign of anything down there. The only image his retinas received was of deep, deep dark.

Ernsto swallowed hard. *This is nothin'*, he told himself, his brow damp with icy sweat.

9.   TSUNAMI
GRACE BRIDGES

Eleon McManus hauled on the ascent lever and threw his vehicle into reverse at the same time, then leapt to the comms unit on the other side of his cockpit and hit the emergency relay together with the tsunami warning button. If he felt the tremors out here in the sea, there could be danger for the land and settlement.

Alerts sent, he returned to steer his submersible. He had been moments away from committing to the docking maneuver when the sea had begun to shudder. Now at a safe distance, he throttled back from the reversing movement and waited to hear back from the harbourmaster.

Meanwhile, his ascent had continued and now the head of the sub broke the surface and a thousand droplets ran down the curved window. Eleon peered out at the harbour buildings, now too far away to make out any movement. He reached out and touched a control, and engines whined as the sub spun to face the open sea. If a wave was coming, he should face it for the greatest safety.

"Mac?" crackled from the speaker. "Reckon we felt that same time you did. All personnel now sealed inside our building, and they're closing the watergates now."

Eleon let out the breath he'd been holding. It might be an everyday occurrence in the life of every person on Eclectia, and a freight driver in particular, but he had long ago decided humans weren't built to take the stresses of a violent seismic planet like this. But it's not like they could up and leave—even its breathable air was a miracle in the unimaginable expanses of hostile, lifeless space. He was lucky to have secure quarters in the undersea city of Zirconia, built to withstand the greatest quakes.

He flicked a switch to take a little more water into the ballast tanks. On the outward journey still, he had no cargo for stabilisation. By now the rock valley leading to the settlement of miners and hunters would be sealed to a height of a hundred metres, the huge metal doors sliding out of their slots carved in the cliffs on each side.

His friends in Adagio would be okay. Eleon faced the oncoming wave and asked the whales to keep him safe.

10.   THE OTHER SIDE OF THE GLASS
KARINA FABIAN

The grouchy man in a lab coat looked away from the scanner he was holding and scowled down at her.

"What's she doing here?" he demanded in a grouchy voice.

Grandmother squeezed her hand. "Gerald, this is Trancy. She came with me to see the angels today."

The grouchy man curled up his nose like she smelled weird, but she'd taken her shower. He scolded her grandmother. "This facility is open twenty-five hours a day, thirty days a month—except for two hours every nine days."

"Which is when the biggest groups of angels gather," Grandmother replied. "This is when they're their most interesting."

"She can watch them on the vids like everyone else."

"She won't bother anyone."

Trancy smiled. She knew that tone. No one said "no" when Grandma used that tone.

And neither did Mr. Grouchy. "She'd better not." He sniffed in her direction, then turned away.

She decided she didn't like him.

Nonetheless, she did her very best to stay quietly at Grandmother's side while she helped the other researchers set up. Now and then, Grandma explained what they were doing, and how elusive the inhabitants of Eclectia's waters had been.

"Elusive?" Trancy rolled the word on her tongue.

"We don't see them much," Grandmother defined.

"Except for times like these!" one man said cheerfully and bent down to point at one end of the window.

She watched the angels, mesmerized, as the researchers started their observations.

"Looks like a school of thirty—a little bigger than lately, but not unusually so. Juveniles and adults."

"I still think we're on the path to some kind of maturation grounds."

"Then why do they stop? Every time?"

"We're a threat."

"We've not done anything to the angels. No, we're just a curiosity—there! Look! The adult directs their attention to us."

"Which holds to my theory that they are training them to recognize us as a threat. See that one, racing from one end of the window to another? Obviously a territorial behavior. Five to one, one of them will press their mouth to the tank in some kind of display! In ten…nine…"

A moment later, Avenir credit chips passed hands. The same thing happened again as someone predicted that one would lash its tail against the tank.

But something else caught Trancy's eye.

"Grandma, we've seen that one before!" She pointed to one angel, whose fins had delicate yellow piping, lingering a ways from the rest.

Grandmother followed her gaze. "Why, I think we have—but not in a school."

Mr. Grouchy growled. "You just want to kill my migration theory! Well, we've got it recorded; we'll check. They're moving on to Crendal's group now.

"Bye!" Trancy waved.

The entire group gasped as the yellow-striped angel waved back.

11.   THE TRADE
KAT HECKENBACH

Jax crouched behind the rock, sweat dripping down his back. His hand twitched around the spear held tight against his shoulder. The familiar *click-click* was getting louder quickly; the bug was close.

He stiffened and adjusted his grip on the spear as he anticipated the appearance of the beast. When it sensed his presence, it would rise up on enormous black legs, giant pincers threatening. But the triangular section of tender underbelly where the accordion lungs rose and fell would be exposed—for one critical moment. Jax breathed deeply to calm himself.

Nothing had quite prepared him for the life of a bug hunter. Back home on Avenir he'd been a businessman. Suits, ties, meetings with people of power. People with the kind of power he wanted, so much so that he'd been willing to do anything…

Even putting his family in danger.

Then that morning came. The enforcers barreled through his front door, and Jax was dragged out of his home, hands and legs shackled. The anger in his wife's eyes had hurt. The fear in his children's eyes had nearly killed him.

He didn't have to think twice about the offer from the government. Tell all about everyone he'd been involved with, every detail of their crimes, and be set free on Eclectia. His death was faked to take his accomplices off his trail. Of course it meant giving up his family, but it ensured their safety.

The clicking intensified, jarring Jax out of his thoughts. Every muscle in his body tensed.

A roar erupted from the other side of the rock. Jax counted, *one, two, three*… He jumped to his feet and aimed as the creature reared up. The spear left his hand, arced over the rock…*whoosh*…and lodged into the exposed flesh. The giant beetle screeched and hissed with escaping air and dropped straight down, shaking the earth beneath Jax's feet.

He stared as the beautiful, dying beast twitched, its legs curling and scraping the rocky ground. Then he lifted his gaze skyward, tears burning the corners of his eyes.

12.   THE BOTTOM
TRAVIS PERRY

Ernsto's feet touched down at the bottom of the sea, six kilometers below surface. The lifeforms that had been beneath him had cleared away as he descended; he never saw any trace of them with his own eyes.

His sonar screen now showed more green dots of movement, seven hundred meters dead ahead. He shuffled forward, deliberately leaving his dive suit floodlights off. He wanted his arrival to go unnoticed until he was ready to strike.

Various types of the creatures called "angels" lived at all depths of the ocean, but the top-dwelling ones contacted mankind often and knew which human beings to avoid. But these bottom-dwellers wouldn't be ready for a man like him.

He would approach the group his sonar told him were clustered together in the dark, net at least one, kill any that resisted, and then jet upward to Zirconia before the aliens could react, a solid, simple plan to exploit the angels' ignorance. The only shortcoming—he didn't know anything much about them either...

His eyes began to pick up a glow coming through the inky blackness of the deep. At first he wondered if he were imagining it, but it kept growing brighter and brighter. *Must be undersea magma*, he thought, but no, the water temperature was far too low. And the color seemed wrong.

At one hundred meters from the movement on his sonar screen, the glow's brightness approached that of the Twin Whale, light rising up from the ocean floor and illuminating little bits of floating debris and odd-looking fish swimming over the light. These fish, he realized with disappointment, were the source of his sonar reading.

But he noticed something else, a bit of a ridge between him and the light. He approached it cautiously, crawling the last few meters to the edge, knowing from experience that crossing a ridge in a danger zone standing up is a good way to get shot—though his experience had been that of the man doing the shooting.

Facemask over the edge, the brilliance below him stung his eyes. It took long seconds to adjust, but he gradually saw the ocean dropped down below the ridge into a massive shining thing, at least a kilometer wide, full of movement.

Shapes with wide fins like wings, lit up with sparking and changing patterns of bioluminescence, mostly white, what must be dwellings, likewise glowing, mostly blue or green. Passageways—no, streets; several hundred meters below him an entire city of angels shone brightly at the bottom of the sea.

There must be thousands of them, he thought to himself, his mouth dry. For a long moment, he almost quit the mission. But no—he had never failed to deliver any cargo he'd been paid to smuggle. He wasn't about to start failing now.

He patted himself down, running his hands over his bandoliered and belted weapons. Then he braced himself to roll over the ridge, down into the Angel City below.

13. LULLABY
GRACE BRIDGES

"Sing us a song, Ave!" The clutch of orphans, around four Foundings old, stared at her with demanding eyes, clustering around their ringleader, a tiny girl with blue eyes and golden hair wrapped in a ragged, patched spider-wool blanket.

Ave adjusted her position sitting against the wall, and forced a grin. "What song do you want to hear?"

Felicia frowned, considering. "The one about Avenir, please." The other little ones nodded.

Ave smiled, for real this time. They always picked that one. She began to hum, and the children hunkered down in their bedrolls. Finally she sang it out, her voice breaking at "Be strong, Avenir Eclectia."

The words of the song echoed oddly from the conduits of the service corridor. Eyes drooped closed, faces grew slack, breathing grew calm. Ave

13

sang the song through twice more, letting it comfort the inner ache that threatened to burst forth and overcome her just as ruthlessly as a sudden vacuum leak. She must be parent to these children and the rest, even though she had no family herself, knew nothing of parenting. *Be strong…*it was her only answer, even when she had no more strength.

What must it be like to have a father? A mother? Longing rushed up from a secret place within her, and her face crumpled suddenly. After a lengthy moment, she sighed and flicked a tear from her eye. It was no use wishing for what could not be.

"Don't cry, Ave." Felicia's small hand found its way into hers, and she snuggled against Ave's shoulder.

Ave kissed the top of the golden head and closed her eyes in thankfulness.

14.   ENYA'S SMILE
FRANK CREED

Motors hummed and chugged in the dim bowels of Avenir station where they kept the cyborgs. Our taskmaster had just programmed the last unit for sleep, walked down the rows of steel double bunks, and closed the door behind him.

Must sleep. I grabbed the jar from beneath my pillow and slid down from my bunk. I knelt on the cold metal floor next to Enya's bed where I worked the smelly white grease into her knee, hip, elbow and shoulder.

Her dead eyes fixed on the underside of my bunk above her.

"Enya? Wife, why don't you look at me?" I brushed grey hair from her forehead with my clean hand.

Her eyeballs flicked toward me, and her lips barely parted as she breathed my name, "Robear…" She smiled—a rare smile that reached all the way to her eyes. In that moment, she knew me. This is why I kept killing time with my power mop and cleansing cloths day after day. Smiling eyes.

I smiled back, and shuffled around to the other side of her bunk to attack the arthritis in her joints with more of the white grease. *Must sleep.*

Her eyes returned to my bunk above her, a wan smile still playing on her lips. Implanting chips and wires in our brains affected her far more than it

14

did me. As long as we remained useful we would be kept in service. What law we had broken to receive such a fate, I no longer remembered. I could only recall my programming and Enya. My programming told me we deserved this and it was just.

"Your knees are bruised. You hand-polished floors all day, didn't you?"

No response. The smile had faded. She was gone again.

Must sleep. I spun the lid back on the jar and climbed back up into my bunk. Wiping my greasy hand on my chest, I closed my eyes and thought of Enya's smile.

15.   MIDNIGHT SONG
KAT HECKENBACH

"Sir, they're singing."

Spiner looked up from his lab table and found the boy staring through the tiny porthole into the pitch black of space. Surely he'd heard wrong…

"Singing, Gavin? What are you talking about?"

Gavin tilted his head to the side, but didn't answer.

Spiner propped his chin on steepled hands and stared at the young apprentice. The boy's freshly cut hair held the slightest curl at the back of his neck. His shirt still hung like a sack on his wiry frame despite weeks of eating four full meals a day. Fortunately he devoured knowledge as easily as he did food and had proven very quickly that Spiner made the right decision by taking him in.

Gavin sighed and turned around. "It's stopped now."

Spiner shook his head. "What—?"

"The sea angels," Gavin said. "The ones Ave told me about, down on the planet. I felt it the other day, but didn't know where it was coming from. But just now, I realized, it's them. Not singing with sounds…" He bit his lip, and searched Spiner's face with his gaze. Finally, his eyes brightened. "They sing emotions. They were singing…joy."

15

16.   BABE
TRAVIS PERRY

Ernsto Mons, on the verge of rolling leftward to plunge over the ridge to the glowing angel city below, caught a glimpse of glowing light in the corner of his right eye. He thrust upright in surprise, jerking upward his guided torpedo launcher.

And there, less than five meters away from him, his eyes rested upon the most beautiful thing he'd ever seen. A shape like a woman, glowing with a dazzlingly brilliant white glow. His eyes hurt to take her in at first, but after a moment they adjusted and he began to see details. Completely unlike the angels he'd glimpsed at the surface as a boy, she had wings like some kind of ocean ray, peacefully rippling as she flapped to hover near him. What would have been a ray's tail was for her much wider and thicker and ended in a horizontal fin. Her body was roughly the length of a human with wide shining wings attached. She had no arms but her almost-human shaped head was adorned with what he'd first thought was hair, but realized were actually long thin dark tentacles on the top of her head, stretching up behind her. Her eyes were as large as his fists and glassy dark and the mouth…was more like an animal's muzzle than a woman's…

Why does she seem like a beautiful woman to me? he wondered to himself. Beautiful in rippling light, yes, beautiful the way a woman is, no.

But beauty poured out of her somehow along with gentle kindness and innocent curiosity about him. The feelings washed through his being. He'd heard angels could do that, could project emotion…but nothing had prepared him for the actual experience. And there was no doubt she was every bit a woman, though he saw no breasts or anything else on her that would mark her as a woman in the way he knew.

His hands released the torpedo launcher and grasped for something else. "Hey, babe," he said, for some reason wondering why he needed to say anything. But it seemed right somehow.

She cocked her head sideways and asked herself in a way he could *feel* what he'd tried to say to her. "I jus' said," he answered, "You're 'bout the most beautiful sight I've ever seen."

Then fast, before she could sense his force of will, he snapped up the tranquilizer gun and shot her. Her pain hit him hard—not the pain of the puncture, which was small, but the horror of betrayal, shock at his cold-

17

hearted violence.

His heart pounded in his chest as she faded to the ground, the brightness leaving her. He lunged forward and caught her in his arms.

"That's how things are, babe," he said to her unconscious form. "Life is tough—and for you, it's about to get worse."

17.   THE WINDOW
GRACE BRIDGES

Ave crept along a Level 14 service corridor, and hoped she wouldn't meet a cyborg. Unregistered persons were not allowed in service areas, and she didn't like being chased any more than the chip-controlled humans liked chasing her.

Ave came alone, slipping away from the small children who liked to cling to her, so she could move quietly above all else. Perhaps this time, too, she would reach her goal, a curiously-built gangway that led nowhere except to a true anomaly—a window.

It was the only place Ave had ever looked Outside. She'd pestered the wizards to tell her what was out there. Now she could recognise the various objects visible depending on the station's spin: Eclectia, sometimes close and ominous, or distantly seething; Sheba and Quatermain, with their shifting seas of molten rock; the great Whale Star, and its distant Twin.

She reached the final junction and looked left and right—no one was about—so she scooted across into the niche, only to scramble to a halt before a towering man-shaped silhouette. *Gulp.*

"I won't hurt you," said the giant.

Ave calmed her breathing and moved around to the left so the light from Outside fell on him. "Who are you?"

He spread his hands as if it pained him, and Ave caught sight of the power mop leaning against the wall behind him.

She drew in a sharp gasp. "You're franked!"

"I am a servant." He turned his face to her. In the Whale's light reflecting from the ring section, she could see the battle in his eyes as with all cyborgs—he hated his programming. But this one was different. He hadn't chased her off, for starters. That small rebellion alone would be earning him a splitting headache right now.

18

Ave wrinkled her brow. "How...?"

"My wife." He forced the words out, wincing, defying the silence stricture. "Also a servant. Must...must care for her."

Ave nodded. "You must love her very much to be so strong. What's her name?"

"Enya." A light came into his eyes as he gazed out the window, and it wasn't just from the Whale Star. "My Enya."

18.   THE FINAL APPROACHING
J. L. ROWAN

As the waves swallowed the pod, Elmerin felt himself a boy of ten Foundings again. The sense of excitement and adventure that had faded with age returned with a force that startled him and left him slightly breathless. He pressed his hands to the glass of the viewport, his eyes narrowed. Perhaps now, after all this time...surely now...But as the Whale grew dim and the waters darkened, the aches and pains of elder years returned, and childish fancy bowed its head to hard-earned experience. He lowered his eyes and shuffled amongst the other passengers to his assigned seat to await the pod's arrival at Zirconia.

He studied the water outside the porthole next to him. *As black as space, and as deadly.* He quashed the thought with a stab of guilt. The seas held something space never would—the sentient creatures he had spent his life trying to reach. Trying, and failing.

And now, there would be no more trying. He'd told his fellow wizards that he was retiring to Zirconia, but that wasn't quite true.

Death had stalked him for months, and his failure at the last Approaching had made it clear that he would never realize his dream. No more Approachings awaited him—none but the Final Approaching, the journey all wizards must take.

So many Foundings, and nothing to show for them. With a heavy sigh, he closed his eyes. It was a foolish thought, coming here to die. If he hadn't achieved contact in the prime of his—

A vision blossomed behind his eyelids, a vision of colors and sensations, of joy and welcoming. He blinked, and saw outside the porthole a school of blue and golden fish that fairly glowed. They moved as one, and when his eyes met theirs, he was enveloped by the greatest peace he had ever known. They hovered beside him, shimmering in the darkness.

Come. The intense feeling washed over him, stronger than mere words. *Come with us.*

His throat closed up, and tears spilled onto his cheeks. Was it possible? After all this time? Their gaze seemed to confirm his deepest dream. A smile spread across his face, and he loosed a soft breath, releasing with it the heartache of years now distant. "I am ready when you are."

19.   NEVER AGAIN
KAT HECKENBACH

Xavia fanned herself with her outspread hand and groaned. "Is it always so hot on this level?" Her jeweled bracelets clinked softly in rhythm with the movement of her arm. She wrinkled her nose as she scanned the marketplace around her. Bare metal, garish lighting. Commoners scuttling around the meatmongers' stands like the beetles whose meat they were there to purchase. "Why did I let you talk me into this, Tomi?"

Tomika rolled her eyes and tucked a tress of long black hair behind her ear. "Aren't you at all curious about what goes on down here? Where things come from? How they get here?"

"Not at all," Xavia said as they shuffled forward with the crowd. "As long as it's on my plate and cooked the way I ask…which reminds me, I need to put in an official complaint about the chef at—"

A scream broke the surrounding chatter, and Xavia clamped her hand onto Tomika's arm. "What's going on?"

The mass of people in front of them shifted, but Xavia could see nothing except their backs.

Tomika pulled free of Xavia's grasp and climbed up on a bench, her high heels ringing the metal seat. She peered over the crowd and then stepped down. "Looks like a gang fight at the other end."

"You're *kidding* me! On our level something like that would never—"

The crowd suddenly surged back, forcing Xavia and Tomika against the table behind them. Xavia reached back to steady herself, and swallowed a scream of revulsion as her hand slid into something firm but…slimy.

She lifted her hand and turned around. A beetle the size of a dinner plate lay on its back, legs splayed. Its belly was pried open, revealing a swell of glistening pink flesh.

"Ugh, oh, Tomi…I knew they were big, but…"

"Xav…" Tomika's voice came from behind Xavia's left shoulder. "That one's just a baby."

Xavia spun to face her friend and narrowed her eyes. "Take me home."

20.   PRESSURE
TRAVIS PERRY

Ernsto slammed his palm into the airlock emergency override switch, flattening the wide red button, mechanical creaking erupting from the door hinges as it swung open, a half-meter of water still in the lock, water pouring into the hallway as he stepped out. The enforcer he'd paid off stood there, his mouth gaping open.

"Whadinell you doin'!" squeaked the man's voice.

Ernsto glanced behind him. The angel was floundering in the draining water. The lip of the lock would keep all of it from leaving, so if it were just a matter of breathing water, he knew she'd be fine. But there was another problem—pressure. Her body was struggling to adapt between the deep ocean pressure she'd spent her whole life at and the one atmosphere of air pressure used by humans living in Zirconia—a near-vacuum from her point of view.He'd brought her into the lock anyway. After all, the reward had been for an angel, "dead or alive." He could ignore the waves of pain from her he could actually *feel*, but he found in some unexpected part of himself that he didn't want to.

"Get me a pressure tank. Now," he barked at the enforcer.

"You didn't pay me for that!" The man's blue eyes set deep into his piggish pink face widened into whites.

Ernsto took three quick steps, still in his pressure suit, but his helmet off. The long knife on his belt he pulled and he held it to the man's throat. "You will get me a pressure tank, or I will skin you alive." His voice rasped in a whisper—he let the keen edge of the knife do all his shouting for him.

The enforcer started to move. "Hurry back or I swear by the depths, I will find you." The man, sufficiently motivated, rushed off.

Ernsto slowly turned back toward the lock and dispassionately watched the angel flounder.

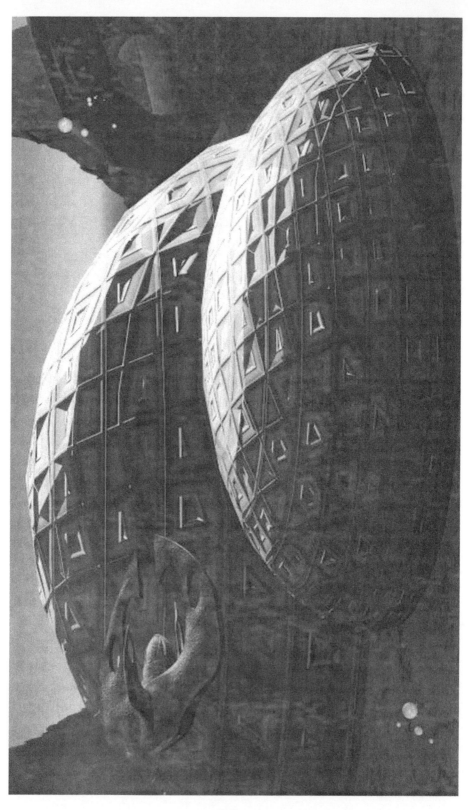

Eleon McManus loped through the lush open area of Zirconia's sector B3. The curved window to his right formed a sky beyond, which glimmered with occasional schools of fish in the murk.

Passing a fruit tree, he longed to snag an orange. But these plants passed down from Earth were too rare, and he didn't want the enforcers to chuck him in the slammer, not when he had some time off tomorrow.

He slipped through the last of this sector's forest and reached the stairs to the residential pods that overlooked it. After climbing up to the third level, he swung onto the walkway that rattled with his steps. He paused a moment, then raised his hand to a buzzer.

Half a minute later, the door unsealed with a whoosh and Gryphon Sylt looked out. "Mac! Sight for sore eyes. Come in!"

Eleon passed through the thick rubber-rimmed frame into his friend's abode. "How's life, Sylt?" He peered at the other man's haggard face. "What's going on?"

Gryphon shrugged, a wild, flailing maneuvre. "System's down again. All the history's inaccessible. And I have no apprentice to help write down what's in my head."

"Can't the system be fixed?"

"It's not graded as essential. There's not enough spare manpower from the IT department."

Eleon didn't know what to respond, so he wandered to Gryphon's kitchenette and poured two lavabush ales from the plastic barrel in the coolstore.

Gryphon sighed. "Maybe they're right. Maybe it doesn't matter, as long as we survive."

Eleon pushed a glass into his hand. "We'll lose our identity if we don't remember where we came from."

"Oh, I'm writing down what I can, never fear. It's not a lost cause. Only almost."

"Well then." Eleon lifted his drink and the two clinked together. He took a sip and grimaced at the slightly bitter taste. "Here's to happy writing!"

A shiver ran down Reichter's spine. The great ship was too quiet. With his visor open, the investigating peacekeeper not only heard his own breathing but that of his enforcers, Cooper and Takai. He considered telling Cooper to stop the whistling; he'd been driving the theme to "For a Few More Credits" into the deck since they boarded the liner. Before he could form the words, Takai spoke up, "Coop? Will you stop whistling that? Or at least change the tune." The outburst was uncharacteristic of the blond giant. Reichter suspected the silence was giving him the creeps too.

"Sorry, Yoshi." He fell silent. It was rare that the small, dark man didn't argue.

Reichter came to a decision. "Coop, Yoshi, if you want to, go ahead and turn your internal channels to some music, but keep it low. Turn up the gain on your external mikes; that should let you hear any faint sounds over the music."

Both nodded and made the adjustments. The notes of the first movement of Raif Von's "In the Fens" quietly purred in his ear as he followed his own order. He breathed a sigh of thanks for the new nanofactories that generated their music players—growing up there had never been enough factories to produce any kind of affordable luxury item. Used to be that whistling was about the only way to make music for yourself...

He mentally ticked off what they had. One—lights, atmosphere, rotational gravity, but no ship's A.I. Two—Avenir Control's last sailing for the liner was fifteen standard years—or twelve Foundings—ago. Three—no cargo manifest or passenger list because it was recertified as a private yacht. Four—the owner and a large number of friends had not been heard from in at least twelve standard years. And five—the biggie—no bodies so far.

They stepped out on a balcony over the promenade deck with its huge pool. Takai remarked, "That's odd."

Cooper looked at him. "What's odd?"

The big man gestured at the pool below. "Most people paint their pools some shade of blue, not purple."

The other enforcer shrugged. "Maybe it went better with his

complexion." He turned to their superior. "What now, sir?"

Reichter glanced around the balcony, then at the deck below. "Coop, you go down and start checking the promenade. Yoshi and I'll check these couple of staterooms," he nodded toward the doors lining the balcony, "then we come down and help you."

"Yes, sir." He turned to the grand stairway. As usual, Cooper ran his mouth. "Pretty impressive. I wonder how many credits the guy was pulling down and whose grandmother's secret he was keeping." Reichter listened with half an ear as he pressed buttons to dilate the doors, occasionally needing to use the pass-pad built into his gloves' index fingers. "Whu-wee! Stinks down here and I ain't even at the bottom yet."

Takai's voice sounded in Reichter's earphones, "What's it smell like, Coop?"

"Like our compartment the morning after you had tacos. Like an egg gone evil. I—" There followed a rattling crash.

Reichter called out, "Cooper! Cooper! Report!" He grabbed Takai's tool belt as the enforcer rushed by. "No! Yoshi, stop!" The peacekeeper's use of his command voice halted Takai. He stood impatiently as his superior hooked a safety line from the peacekeeper's belt reel to his belt's carabiner. "Okay, you lead." Reichter drew his sidearm. "I'll cover you."

"Yes, sir."

They began to descend the stairway. Cooper lay in a heap at the bottom. A red light on the back of his helmet blinked. "Dead light's on," Takai observed matter-of-factly. Reichter knew it was taking all of the big man's willpower to stay professional. He knew from his own experience, the tears would come later.

"Yep."

Takai coughed about the time the stink hit Reichter's nose. The peacekeeper grabbed the banister with his free hand and yelled as he hung on, "Yoshi! Up, up! Come back up the stairs!"

The enforcer's voice was slurred as he spoke between coughs, "It's okay. The smell's gone. I...I smell sweet—"

Reichter dropped the side arm and caught hold of the safety line. He pulled mightily and surged up the steps dragging the bigger man. "Get up the stairs, Yoshi! That's an order!" Takai stumbled along behind. At the top of the stairs, he sat heavily, coughing as tears and mucus ran down his face.

Reichter breathed in and out swiftly, hyperventilating slightly as he flushed his lungs. He leaned over Takai and checked his readouts. "Blood Oxygen," "Heart Rate," and "Blood Pressure" were at the lower end of the green, but rising. "Oxygen Intake" went from yellow to green as he asked, "You feeling better, son?"

The younger man wiped at his blond handlebar mustache as he asked, "What happened?"

The peacekeeper's face was grim. "Something hiding in plain sight and I didn't think of it." He put a hand on the enforcer's shoulder. "Are you okay, now?"

Takai nodded. "I...I think so, sir."

Reichter unclipped the safety line from his reel from the enforcer's rig. He then took a line from Takai's belt reel and hooked it to his own carabiner. "Okay, Yoshi, here's what we're going to do. I'm going to go down and get Coop. When I've got him secured to my line, you'll pull me up while I pull him up. Understand?"

Takai nodded. "Yes, sir."

The peacekeeper smiled at him. "Good. Okay, now you just sit there and rest until I get him hooked up. Then I'll give you the high-sign."

Reichter berated himself as he turned and did what he should have done in the first place—he closed his visor and went on internal atmosphere. He set his sniffer so as to confirm the element he knew he would find below.

Takai broke the silence on the cruiser's bridge as they headed back to Avenir, "Sir, it wasn't your fault."

Reichter smiled sourly. "I doubt, Yoshi, the council will agree with that opinion when we get back to the Cop-Shop. But, thank you all the same."

The enforcer shook his head. "Hydrogen sulfide. Where did it come from, sir?"

"That fancy fish pond on the promenade deck. It was a swimming pool when the liner was in service. Apparently, the new owner decided to turn it into a huge koi pond. After the circulation stopped when the A.I. packed up, things died in it and it turned stagnant. Eventually, anaerobic bacteria had a field day and the hydrogen sulfide was the result. That purple color of the pool was the little critters themselves."

"So the gas killed the people?"

The peacekeeper tilted his head and squinted an eye as he considered. "No, probably not. Water recycling shut down with the A.I. The only food left I found was dry stores. I suppose they tried drinking from the pool; that probably did a number in. It must have been very bad for the last ones—there's all that water sitting there in plain sight, but they know it'll poison them. That's probably why they were huddled in the promenade staterooms." He fingered his beard as he gazed into space.

"Yep, in plain sight."

23.   DELIVERY
KAT HECKENBACH

Mary curled forward and squeezed with every muscle in her body. Her neck strained. A scream caught in her throat...escaped as a grunt.

And then release.

The pressure eased, and her muscles slid from her bones as she rolled back until her head smacked softly on the pillow. The distant cry of her newborn daughter was barely audible over the ringing in her ears.

Movement appeared, fuzzy, in her periphery. The fuzziness cleared and became a smiling, blonde nurse, with a nametag that read *Amelia*.

"She's beautiful, Mary. They're nearly done with the scan."

Amelia barely had the words out when another nurse strode over to the delivery table. The woman's face stretched under the force of severely pinned-back gray hair. She slapped a printout into Amelia's hand and stalked off.

Amelia rolled her eyes, and then gazed at the paper. Her smile broadened. "Perfect, Mary. Not a single significant genetic fault. Your daughter is going to be smart and beautiful. Your husband...would be proud." Amelia's voice quivered, and Mary felt the gentle pressure of the nurse's hand on her shoulder.

Mary nodded, and choked back a sob. Jax would have been proud no matter what. *If only I'd had a chance to tell him he was going to be a father again.*

24. CUSTOMS
BY TRAVIS PERRY

Ernsto fidgeted in the line. He remembered when moving goods up to Avenir used to be a lot easier. But then the Anti-Smuggling Acts had been published...

The pressure tank next to him, roughly the size and shape of a coffin, but rounded and made of burnished steel, was mounted on a robotized wheel cart. The line he stood in was for commercial passengers with oversized luggage.

Some part of his brain picked at the word "CUSTOMS," which had been newly embroidered in bright letters across the armbands of the enforcers standing in this designated section of Zirconia's upper deck. *Somebody must've pulled that out of an ancient dictionary somewhere.* The word meant nothing to him.

"Next!" said the voice and he stepped forward, the robot cart following him with the tank as he'd programmed it to do. "Papers please," said the man in his sharp new black-and-white uniform.

"Sure," said Ernsto, handing over actual printed paper, not digital, not bugshell, supplied to him through a contact of his wizard benefactor in Avenir. Since he could barely read, he could only hope the wizard's man had filled the form out right. The enforcer's eyes widened at this rare form of official documentation. Which was a good sign.

"Well, sir," he said, "All is very much in order...you may proceed."

"Hold it, Smit!" barked the supervising peacekeeper, stepping toward them. He was not wearing any kind of uniform, but his badge hung prominently from his belt.

The peacekeeper snatched the papers out of his subordinate's hand. "Gabril Jons, is it?"

"Yes, sir," said Ernsto, attempting a smile.

The man evaluated him from his toes up to his face. "You look a lot like the image capture I've seen on that smuggler Ernsto Mons." He glared straight into his eyes, looking for any sign of inappropriate response.

"I've heard people tell me that a time or two before," he muttered. "Can't say as I like it bein' accused of criminal activity. I'm Gabril Jons, general merchant, just like the papers say."

"I think you and your cargo need to be scanned," said the peacekeeper.

28

Of course, that would never do. The scan would reveal the presence of the angel in the tank, illegal to transport. And it would also show the weapons hidden under the loose merchant's shirt Ernsto wore.

"The papers don't allow that." He enunciated carefully the explanation he'd memorized, "This cargo may not be exposed to any extreme form of magnetism or ionizing radiation. This is a special delivery to Minister Hobson on Avenir and has been pre-inspected. Just as the papers say." Even as he spoke he was calculating. The peacekeeper and enforcer near him he could kill before they'd realized he had hidden weapons. But the two behind would have time to react, to maybe pull an alarm of some kind, if not actually fire back. And there were more enforcers at the scanning station and the commercial shuttle itself, along with surveillance devices. Plus plenty more on the upper decks of Zirconia. His chances of escaping them all seemed slim, no matter how many he killed.

But he'd known "Forcers" his entire life—he'd known from experience that many of them joined up just to boss others around, to make themselves feel powerful. When given the chance, they could be cruel beyond belief. He was not about to fall into the hands of these dregs—he'd rather die first.

That wizard said it was all arranged! He was angry at the old man. And with himself for having trusted anyone.

The needle gun in his sleeve he'd set up to fire by orienting his arm and squeezing his armpit just so. He turned to the peacekeeper, arm in place, ready to kill. "But officer—"

And then a powerful emotion swept over him, interrupting his plan in motion. It was a deep calmness, slapping away his rage with a shocking coolness, like getting hit on the shore with a sudden surge of the ocean. He gasped.

It showed in the eyes of the lawmen that they felt it, too. Deep, sudden calmness. They probably didn't know where it had come from, but he knew. He recognized the presence behind it. It was the angel in the pressure tank—she had sent this emotion.

The peacekeeper, calmed and perhaps beyond that, perhaps *influenced* somehow, took a second look at his high-class forged papers. "I'm...I'm sorry to trouble you, sir. Officer Smit was right. Everything *is* in order. Please proceed."

As Ernsto moved forward toward the Avenir-bound shuttle, he

wondered why in the name of all Holy-in-the-sea-below-and-the-stars-above would the angel do that for him. *Why did she save my life?*

25. MADDIE'S PUB
BY GRACE BRIDGES

Hinges creaked in the privately-owned building at the edge of the tents of the Palmer Trading Company hunting camp, just outside of Adagio. Maddie glanced up in time to see a bedraggled huntsman drag himself inside. He kicked the door to ensure the rubber seal took properly.

Good. She didn't want more wind-borne ash in here than was absolutely necessary. Only the newbies to Eclectia's harsh land would leave any door or window open. She'd trained her regulars well.

Maddie turned back to the open fire, fueled by scrubby brush—the only stuff that grew well here. She poked at the meat stew in the cauldron, and its pungent aroma released into the room. She frowned. If only she had a potato to put in it—that would make a dish fit for a wizard. However, no wizard had ever set foot in her establishment, and potatoes only grew in the underwater gardens—out of reach for any grit-breather unless he was filthy rich, but the rich folks didn't live here. Here, they had to make do with the bitter leaves and seeds of the lavabush—both for bread and ale—and the third-grade meat plentiful in a hunting village.

She ladled stew into a bowl and made her way between the tables to plunk it before the hunter. "Here you go, Jax. Good hunting today?" He stared blankly at the food for a moment, then nodded with the weariness of one who had speared a giant beetle and hauled it back to town. Maddie knew that look very well. She gave him a friendly whack on the back, waited till he let a small smile slip out, then headed back to her kitchen across the room.

The earth rumbled and the building shook, its flexible mortar and light ashblock walls absorbing the shocks. Maddie clutched at the counter to prevent herself from falling. Her guests looked up from their meals. The quake settled and the murmur of conversation started up again.

Maddie bowed her head for a moment before going to pour a lavabush ale for Jax. She thought she might need one, too.

"Quiet!" he hissed.

The shuffling behind ceased.

Derin reached a hand out to the translucent polymer dome that held the water at bay.

"She's beautiful."

"Sir, how can you tell the gender?"

"I just know," he said.

He stepped closer to the dome wall, watching as the angel hovered outside. Large fin-like arms flapped in slow-motion, keeping the angel in a stationary position. Its long body ended in a split fin with bones strong enough to walk on land for short distances, according to prior research.

The angel tilted its aqua-blue head and watched Derin as he took another step.

"Are the speakers on?"

"Yes, sir."

"Hello there," he said to the angel. The sea creature mimicked his mouth movements. "Can you understand my words?"

The creature blinked and tilted its head the other direction.

"My name is Derin. I'm a wizard of Avenir here to study your kind. This underwater facility is my home now, I hope you don't mind. I'm not like the others. I believe you have... something, that I want to learn. I promise to never hurt you or your friends."

Derin took more steps until his nose almost brushed the polymer wall. The angel rotated its arms and floated toward him.

From inches apart, they stared into each others' eyes.

"Will you... teach me?" Derin put his hand to the dome surface. "There are things I need to know, questions I need answered. Will you help me?"

The angel leaned its head to Derin's hand. For a moment, he could feel its small nose press into his palm through the polymer membrane. In that moment, something slid through his body, warming his blood and numbing his muscles.

He smiled.

A siren sounded. Derin's skin flinched, and the angel jerked back. With a flurry of motion, the creature flipped backwards and flew along the ocean floor, disappearing into the cloud of disturbed sediment.

"Sir, we have a black water warning."

Derin stared after the angel. "How close?"

"Half a kilometer."

"Standby to activate the ion fence. But first, send out a bot and collect a sample."

"But, sir, the last two never returned."

"Try again."

"Yes, sir."

Derin heard the movement of feet behind him as the assistants and crew prepared to carry out his orders. But he stayed long after they had left, staring after the angel.

27.   WORDS
KAT HECKENBACH

Gavin stood next to the wizard—*gotta stop thinking that…he says he don't mind, but if I slip up and say it out there he could get busted*—who wiped his hand on his already smudged lab coat. Thick, black bangs hung in his eyes as he peered into a bubbling test tube. *And he keeps tellin' me I need a haircut.*

The table in front of them was covered with odd-looking equipment that whispered with ticks and whirs. Shiny steel and tarnished brass competed for dominance between modern technology and—*what's that word Ave told me once…oh, yeah*—Victorian.

"Dr. Spiner, tell me again why you use this old stuff? It looks archaic."

The man peeked out from behind his bangs and gave the strange smile he always did when Gavin used older people's words.

"Newer isn't always better, son. Especially when you're studying things of such antiquity." The wiz—*scientist* winked and looked back at the table, then reached for a spindly metal contraption without further explanation.

Antiquity was the kind of word no one but Ave would use when speaking to him, at least not without patting him on the head and giving him a dumbed-down definition. But Dr. Spiner had trusted him to understand. Gavin bit his lip to stop the grin that wanted to push his cheeks out with pride.

And then, as he climbed onto a stool for a better view, he realized Dr.

Spiner had used another word no one had ever spoken to him before. A word that made his eyes burn pleasantly with tears.

Son.

28. THE WIZARD
TRAVIS PERRY

Two clean-cut burly men stood outside the entryway; the one on the right held his arms crossed over his chest and eyed Ernsto with contempt. They wore good suits with the appropriate slight bulges under the arms and at the small of the back—obviously high-paid security types.

The blond-headed rightie spoke with disdain, "You must be Mons."

Ernsto stopped walking and the robotic cart hauling the pressure tank behind him halted, too. "I must be. You gotta problem with that, handsome?"

The man's pale blue eyes bored into his own. His dark-haired partner on the left reached under his jacket—Ernsto raised his right hand, making visible to both of them the needle gun he palmed there. "Nice and slow, sugar. These are poison."

At that moment the metal door in the hallway slid open. A man with a genial twinkle in his eye, a balding forehead and a gray ponytail appeared, wearing a white loose-fitting shirt and trousers. "Mons! Come in, my boy, come in!"

"You sure I'm welcome?" He eyed the security men.

"Of course! Rolf, Nasir, stand aside."

Within minutes he'd entered the room, passed by numerous shelves lined with books and notebooks, walked through a lab with transparent containers holding body parts of all kinds of sea life—including one vial filled with eyes large enough and of a shape that could have been those of angels. The next room held a giant pressurized clear tank and before he knew it, Ernsto found himself helping the man empty the contents of his mobile tank into the larger version. The angel floundered briefly and he felt her pain, but it didn't last long.

Inside the tank, the fine hair-like tentacles on her head covered her eyes. "My goodness," said the man with a chuckle. "That will never do. Lights, dim ninety percent." The light in the room faded abruptly. "Would you like to work for me full-time, Ernsto, my lad? I could use a man with your talents."

His eyes adjusting to the dimness, Ernsto asked, "How did ya get me to help with the angel without askin' me?"

"Oh, it's just one of those things a wizard learns to do," answered the man, his voice low.

In the dimness, Ernsto saw the angel's dark wide eyes watching the wizard. And he felt from her revulsion. And fear.

29. JUST A MYTH
PAULINE CREEDEN

Zana Black stepped inside the darkness of the pub to a greeting of silence. A gasp went up as she pulled down the kerchief that covered her nose and mouth, and her boots echoed as she strode across the hardbrick. She squinted her way to the bar, straining against the flash blindness that blocked her ability to see faces. Hushed whispers replaced the silence.

As she set her robotic left arm on the bar, her eyes finally adjusted and she could see the bartender staring at it. He shook his head and looked away quickly. He stuttered as he said, "How can I help you?"

"I'll take a Spring Root Ale." She handed over the credits.

Zana turned around and leaned against the bar, scanning the dark tavern. He wasn't there.

The bartender set the drink next to her right elbow and Zana turned around. It wouldn't do to crush the glass with her robotic grip, so she pulled it across the surface with her right hand.

She laid her left arm on the bar again and opened the panel on the wrist. She pressed a few buttons and a hologram popped up in the center of her hand. The murmuring at the bar grew in intensity and the bartender's eyes widened.

"You seen this guy around?" she asked him.

The bartender hesitated and tore his eyes away from the hologram. He shook his head and tried to go back to wiping the bar.

"You're lying," she said, making her robotic hand into a fist. The hologram popped like a bubble.

The man swallowed hard, blood draining from his face. "I...I...He was in here yesterday, but he left."

"And?"

"And he said something about going west, I think…"

"You think?" Zana narrowed her eyes.

"I know he said west. He definitely said west."

Zana nodded and picked up her mug, carved from a clumpy beetle forearm, turning around again so that she faced the room. A sigh of relief came from behind.

"So what did you do?" A little tow-haired boy looked up at Zana, his big blue eyes wide with wonder and sticky fingers reaching toward the robotic appendage.

Zana looked around and couldn't tell who the kid belonged to. He looked about four Foundings old and she couldn't see anyone who looked as though they missed him. She set down her ale and kneeled, unbuttoning and pushing her duster back.

She pulled her robotic arm closer to him and set it on her cybernetic knee. "Beetle attack, kid. I've never been a slave."

His eyes grew wider, "You mean you survived?"

She nodded, and answered, "But my arm and leg didn't."

"How did you afford the 'borg parts? They're really 'spensive…" His voice trailed off.

"My secret, kid. You wanna look closer?"

"Wow!" He reached out and touched the silver titanium that covered her left cheek. She leaned in for his touch and her black braid fell forward. He asked, "Here, too?"

"That's where one sprayed me with acid."

"It's true? They can spray acid?"

"Only the female cannonbeetle, and only during breeding season."

He grabbed a hold of the black braid and tugged it with a giggle. Zana smiled wider, tempted to pick the kid up and hug him.

"KRISTOF!" A woman squealed as she walked out of the kitchen. A plate slipped off her tray and fell to the floor.

The little boy winced and jumped back from Zana, putting his hands behind his back. The woman set her tray on an empty table and marched over. He started pouting before she even got there.

"What did I tell you about bothering customers?" The woman's voice shook.

Zana stood up and leaned against the bar again. The waitress looked at Zana with eyes full of fear and apologized. Zana gave a head tilt and took another sip of her ale.

The woman rushed away, dragging the boy by the elbow. "I didn't do nothing. She wasn't bothered, I swear!" The boy whined.

She said something under her breath that couldn't be heard. The boy's response made it obvious enough. "Un-uh! It was a beetle attack! Her face was sprayed with acid."

The woman looked back quickly and said in a harsh whisper that Zana didn't miss this time, "Beetles don't shoot acid—that's just a myth."

Zana smiled and headed for the tavern door, her boots resounding on the floor bricks where silence otherwise reigned. Everyone's eyes followed her once more. No matter to her. She raised the red kerchief over her mouth and nose once more to keep the ash out. Zana pushed the door open and pulled her duster in tighter to face the ashy eastern wind. At least it would be to her back as she made her way west out of this village near the east end of the Five Rims and into the mountains.

30. BLINK
KAT HECKENBACH

Robynn walked behind Denton and Strand, her arms crossed and shoulders hunched, peeking between their heads. If she wasn't so tall for her age, she'd be terrified of the two older boys. But she passed herself off as older so they wouldn't bully her like the other kids. Instead, they took her in, treating her almost like an equal. Almost.

She glanced around, nervous. They shouldn't be in this corridor— urchins didn't even belong on this level, where the rich lived and didn't want to be reminded of the poor and homeless. If anyone saw them they'd probably be accused, and convicted, of stealing—even without evidence.

She should just turn around, slip back to the lift and go down to their own level. *Who cares what they have to show me...it can't be that big a deal...*

Denton and Strand stopped suddenly, and Robynn nearly slammed into Denton's back.

"There he is." Denton cocked his head slightly to the left where a man walked toward them. Robynn sucked in a breath and pushed against the wall behind the boys.

"You really think he's a 'droid—not a guy franked into a cyborg? An actual 'droid?" Strand whispered, face turned so Robynn saw his profile. His eyes were wide.

Denton nodded. "Gotta be."

Robynn bit down on her lip. The man was getting close now—why weren't they leaving? Her stomach twisted as she willed herself to meld into the metal wall.

And then she noticed…the man wasn't even looking at them. He was only a couple of yards away. He should've been glaring at them, calling to have them hauled off. But he just stared forward, until he stepped up next to them.

The man turned slowly—stiffly—toward them. Robynn ducked her head behind the boys like a turtle pulling into its shell.

"Are you lost?" the man asked. There was something odd about his voice…

Robynn sucked on her lip. Could it be? Was Denton right?

"No, sir," Denton said. "We're just heading back to our rooms."

The man's head tilted to the side, and then he gave a courteous nod. "Well, then, get going." He stared as if waiting for them to move. Robynn noticed he didn't blink.

Denton and Strand looked at each other, their faces straining as if holding back laughter, and then they moved forward, exposing Robynn.

She froze. The boys kept walking farther away, but she couldn't make her feet move, or make her gaze break from the man's face.

He leaned in, hands on his knees, and whispered. "Don't worry, I won't report you. Get back to your level, though, before someone else sees you." His lips curled into a friendly smile. "Oh, and I'd make some new friends. Those boys aren't too bright. They wouldn't know a 'droid if it hit them in the face."

"So you're not?" The words slipped out before Robynn could stop them, and she bit her lip again.

"Of course not. I heard them whispering halfway down the corridor…and I'm just having a little fun with it." His eyes narrowed, and he patted her shoulder. "You believe me, right? Ever heard of a 'droid with a sense of humor? It's not exactly something you can install." He winked and straightened up.

Robynn relaxed, and nodded at the man. Then she headed down the corridor toward the lift. She stopped and hit the button. The doors to the lift opened, but Robynn didn't step inside. She gazed down the corridor where the man had been standing...where he'd spoken to her, and smiled, and winked...

...but not once had he blinked.

31.   DUE WAGES
   TRAVIS PERRY

Ernsto sat in the darkened room with the angel, counting his stacks of platinum coins. The pay was good, there was no denying that. And it wasn't as if the work was hard.

She watched him from the tank, her dark eyes glinting with reflected light from her own white bioluminescent body. The tentacles attached to the back of her head hung down almost like hair and her ray-like fins were spread wide, like wings, making her look especially angelic.

"But you're not an angel really," muttered Ernsto. "You're just a big fish, a smart one." He didn't feel fully convinced. He fingered a platinum coin, feeling the cold hard weight of it.

Why? floated into the back of his mind. The more time he spent with the angel, the more he could swear he didn't just know her feelings—he could hear her thoughts. He glanced up at her but didn't offer any answer to her question.

The door slid open, revealing Wizard Hobson, smiling as broadly as ever. "There you are! You certainly do like spending time here, don't you, my boy?" The man deliberately ignored the angel recoiling away from the surface of the glass, balling up at the back of the tank.

Eyes fixed on the wizard, he answered, "I like the dark. The quiet is good, too. You got experiments to run?"

"Not at the moment. I just have another job for you, Ernesto Manas." The wizard mispronounced his name in a way that for some reason made him smile.

He had more platinum and more luxury than he'd ever had in his life. But at that instant he decided he'd had enough; the time had come to go back to smuggling. He rose to his feet, a forceful "No" at the back of his throat.

But when Hobson's eyes met his own, he found his willpower ebbing away. The wizard started speaking and he couldn't even remember anymore what he had wanted.

Whatever the old man said, he had to do it.

32. THE WAITING GAME
PAULINE CREEDEN

Wind blew wisps of hair into her face as Zana Black set the rifle on the back of her cybernetic hand. She couldn't cup the barrel like she used to because fine motor control still eluded her. Through the scope her target came into range, but she couldn't gain a clear shot. The waiting game ensued.

Zana's breath filtered through her kerchief in visible clouds. Human prey never relied on scent for warning of a predator, so being upwind of the man she hunted made no difference. Zana continued to watch for the right moment.

"Dead or alive," but preferably dead was how the circuit peacekeepers wanted the men she hunted. These small-time criminals didn't compare to the one that she had hunted for five Foundings. The man who'd stolen her arm, leg, and soul still roamed free and she'd travel to the depths of Eclectia or the heights of Avenir for him. She snickered at the thought that he'd make it that far.

A warm body came and lay next to hers, trying to conserve his warmth as well as aid in keeping her own. She pulled her face from the scope and looked down at her right hip to find liquid brown eyes staring back at her. The sand-and-black shepherd laid his ears back in submission when he saw her acknowledge him, and his long tail swept the ash-covered hill.

With a smile she accepted his presence and looked back through the scope. A clear shot presented itself and she pulled the trigger.

"Piper, wait up!"

The voice echoed off the metal walls of the corridor behind her, distorted by the faint mechanical hum that filled this level. Piper stopped walking and turned around. Nik was jogging toward her, face solemn.

Piper spun on her heel and continued walking away from him. Why had she bothered stopping? *Jerk.*

"Piper, please! I'm sorry!"

Yeah, right. Her eyes burned suddenly, and she strained, willing tears not to form.

In moments she felt the heat of his presence behind her, matching her pace. His words came nearly breathless. "Please stop. I didn't mean it."

Piper inhaled, clenching her fists at her side. "Too little, too late, Nik."

"I was just teasing. I didn't know it meant so much to you. It's just a rodent."

Piper slammed to a stop and rounded to face Nik. "Not 'it', you heartless slug! He! And he is my best friend!" Her heart pounded, sending her pulse thrumming in her ear. Tears pushed past her lids against her will, but she ignored them.

Nik's brows knitted together and he lifted his arms as if wanting to reach out to her. But he pulled them back and crossed them in front of his chest. "I'm sorry. Really, I am. I came to help you find him."

Piper searched his eyes and found genuine concern. She closed her eyes and nodded. Then warmth infused her as she felt his arms wrap around her shoulders. She sank into him, resting her head against his chest. "Thank you."

He rubbed her back and she pulled away from him. He smiled down at her, his hair slipping out from behind his ear and hanging in front of one eye like a black curtain.

Piper took Nik's hand and led him down the corridor. Tara had said she'd seen something small and brown skitter across the floor in an area just around the corner only twenty minutes ago. They reached the juncture and Piper let go of Nik's hand. She dropped to her hands and knees. A shuffling thunk told her Nik had joined her.

They crawled around, peeking into any gaps in the metal walls, snaking around support beams.

"Here, Piper…" Nik's whispered voice was filled with excitement.

Piper snapped her head to the side and saw Nik kneeling in front of a gap between wall panels, arms stretched out to his sides. She scooted over to him and peeked over his shoulder.

"Freedom! There you are!" She pushed past Nik and scooped the brown, furry bundle into her palms. No more than six inches from nose to the base of his tail, Freedom perched on his back legs, whiskers twitching. His long, slender tail wrapped around her fingers.

Piper touched her nose to the tiny pink one.

Nik chuckled. "You know, he's actually kinda cute."

Piper turned to him and smiled. "He's the best."

Nik bit his lip as his eyes shadowed. "He's from the planet, isn't he?"

Piper swallowed and looked away. Was she ready to tell him everything? Indecision roiled inside her as Nik moved closer.

"We've been together for seven months, Piper. I've never asked you about your past."

She forced out, "I know."

He waited in silence. She felt his gaze, imagined him staring at her profile. She closed her eyes.

"He's from the planet, yes. So am I. My mom died when I was young. My dad was a bug hunter. He was killed. I was alone…starving. Pretty soon the traffickers had their eye on me. I couldn't bear the thought of ending up someone's…" Her voice cracked, but she steeled herself and continued. "I stowed away on a cargo shuttle from the planet to Avenir."

Nik's hand touched her shoulder…the gentlest touch she'd ever felt besides Freedom's nuzzling. She realized tears were streaming down her cheeks. They dripped off her chin and landed on her open hands, on Freedom.

"Was he your pet while you lived down there?"

She shook her head. "I found him at the loading dock. I was sneaking around, trying to figure out how to get into the shuttle. I'd set my pack down—my last piece of lavabread was in the pocket. Freedom snatched it and ran off with it. I chased him." Piper smiled at the memory and stroked Freedom's fur. She raised her eyes to meet Nik's gaze. "He led me to the rear hatch, and then straight to the perfect hiding place."

Nik stared, amazement shimmering in his blue eyes. "So that's why his name's Freedom? Because—" He stopped, as if the next word had caught in his throat, and then looked down at the brown rodent in Piper's hands and smiled.

34. ERNSTO'S DELIVERY
TRAVIS PERRY

The job the old man gave him to do was ridiculously simple. Pick up some container of special material, no questions asked. Show the forged papers on the way out of the mail hub and as needed on the way back, delivering the package straight to the angel's chamber.

It was so simple and trivial Ernsto could barely believe he'd been assigned to the task. Hobson might as well have sent one of the cyborgs for something like this. But a lot of the work he'd done for Wizard Hobson in his weeks on Avenir belonged to that category. Trivial, but well-paid. *As if he wants me around, even though he's got nothin' for me to do*…which made absolutely no sense.

The job went off without a hitch, as expected, except after he rode the stainless steel cargo lift up to the executive level. The Avenir governor's staterooms lay off to the left and other ministers appointed by the Peace Council had quarters to the right (Hobson served as Minster of Ethics, of all things). Ernsto showed his papers to the enforcer at the elevator and carried the box made out of processed bugshell toward Hobson's. Before he'd gotten more than ten paces from the checkpoint, he heard the elevator open again and a young voice behind him.

"You there, do I know you?"

He turned around with deliberate slowness. Behind him stood a fresh-faced enforcer with a crisp new uniform, with the silver emblem on the right side indicating Governor's Service. His name tag had the letters "R O M E R O."

"Don't think so," answered Ernsto slowly. Moving slow was always a good way to face a lawman for the first time. It tended to put 'em at ease…

"Your face looks familiar," said the enforcer.

"I get a lot of that. I resemble Stensin, governor before last."

The enforcer squinted at him, visibly wondering if that were the reason. "Your papers, please."

43

He showed the forms and studied the face of the enforcer examining them. This one showed no signs of bullying—a true believer in the occupation of law enforcement. Would almost be a shame to kill him.

"Everything seems correct. Please pardon my interruption, Mr. Jons."

"No trouble at all, officer," he answered.

Within moments he'd passed by Nasir and Rolf at the door, who still resented the way the old man treated him better than them. Once past the entry the sense of terror and distress stabbed at him, like knives in his eyes. The angel's distress pierced him. He barely realized that his pace picked up—he nearly ran into the angel's chamber.

Hobson, assisted by a pair of cyborgs, used multiple manipulator arms within the pressurized tank to press the angel down to the tank floor, while ratcheting down straps of some kind tight into her flesh.

"Ernsto, dear boy!" The wizard's smile spread his mouth wide, but his eyes were dead and lifeless. "Bring the package here, my lad."

Ernsto found himself stepping forward.

35. REALITY KILLS
PAULINE CREEDEN

"Cotton," Dr. Lee called the shepherd over from Zana's side as she approached his house. The dog loped toward the tall, thin, old man as he kneeled. He rubbed the dog on the head and looked up at her asking, "How has he been? Any coughing?"

Zana shook her head and pulled down her kerchief as she smiled, "Nope. Not a one."

Dr. Lee's family worked toward producing mammals that could withstand Eclectia's harsh climate. The typical lifespan of dogs had been two Foundings, but through selective breeding the Lees developed a shepherd hardy enough to live as many as five. The Lees gave Cotton to Zana at her visit last Founding. Now two Foundings old, Cotton was the first of the Lee Shepherds to live outside of their breeding facility.

Dr. Lee stood, his soft blue eyes fixing on Zana's as he said, "How much abuse have your cybernetic parts been put through this year?" Dr. Lee tended to use the words "year" and "Founding" interchangeably.

Zana shrugged and followed the old man past the security wall to the

44

house for her each-Founding check-up and adjustments with Cotton trotting in the lead. Mrs. Lee met them at the door with a smile, wiping her hands on an apron. The Lee house felt like home to Zana, and it gave her a heartwarming feeling. Mrs. Lee held out her arms for a hug and Zana slipped into them feeling a little awkward as she stood almost six inches taller than the round-faced woman.

"So what have you been up to this Founding? Meet any husband prospects?" Mrs. Lee asked, just like a mother with a spinster daughter.

Zana furrowed her brow and clenched her jaw. Even if a man could look past her robotic half, she just couldn't see herself in the domestic capacity. For now her focus remained on catching the man who haunted her every nightmare. She pulled away from the cheerful woman's grip and shook her head.

"Well, there's a nice young man who just moved into town…"

"Lucinda, leave Zana alone. She'll fix herself up with a man when she's ready." Dr. Lee's sympathetic blue eyes apologized for his wife.

"Besides," Zana said as she kneeled down and hugged the shepherd, "Who needs a man when I've got Cotton to keep me company?"

Lucinda Lee shook her head but left the subject alone, "Well dear, your room's been made ready for you. I'm sure you'll want a hot bath before dinner." The Lees piped in water from Adagio Bay and owned their own desalinization plant, so they could afford the luxury of a bath. "I made bugloaf for dinner along with Summer Mint Cookies for later."

Zana's smile returned. She could smell the mint cookies as she entered the door. The smell of home. Zana wondered what applications Dr. Lee might have to add to her cybernetic parts this Founding, and how long they would take. Zana and Cotton remained the most public of Dr. Lee's experiments.

After her bath, Zana stood almost naked in front of the full-length mirror while her long wavy dark hair dripped down her back. Her robotic arm and leg were light and as feminine as they could be, but still overpowered her human half. When she stuck her tongue over to her left cheek, she could taste the flexible titanium that covered the holes she felt in her skin.

Her own green eyes stared back at her and she shook her head as she remembered princess wishes and happily-ever-after daydreams. Reality killed them all. She sat on the bed and wrangled her wet hair into a braid.

When she came into the dining area, Zana sat next to the air purifier that pulled in the warmth of home and spit out the "fresh" air that smelled faintly of ozone. Cotton settled on top of her bare feet as she sat in the upright wrought-iron chair. Smiling, Lucinda came in and set the bugloaf on the table.

"Be a dear and get Rob for me?"

Zana pushed the chair back and stood. She started to feel like a teenager again. Cotton looked up at her with red-rimmed eyes, but got up to follow regardless of his fatigue.

When she came to the door that separated the main house from the doctor's lab, Zana knocked and then opened the door before a response issued.

She peeked her head in and smiled as she saw the welding sparks fly into the air. She called out to Dr. Lee, "Dinner's ready!"

The doctor pulled up his face mask and looked at Zana with a grin that she knew well. He pointed down at the large robotic wheeled contraption he'd been welding. "Know what this is?"

Zana shook her head and made a mock frown. "Nope."

"It's your new ride."

36. MISSED LIFT
KAT HECKENBACH

The lift doors shut with a quiet hiss as Robynn watched the man—'droid?—disappear around a corner at the other end of the corridor. She shook her head and jabbed the touch panel again, angry that she'd gotten so distracted and now had to wait on another lift when someone could come by at any moment and throw a fit about her being where she didn't belong.

Angrier that Denton and Strand had abandoned her...

Angriest because she knew she didn't dare say a word to them about it. She needed their protection. They were the toughest urchins she knew, besides Ave. But Ave couldn't be around all the time to stop them—or anyone else—from picking on Robynn. *Better to befriend the bullies than be bullied by them.* It was a matter of survival.

Tears burned her eyes and she chewed at her lip. It wasn't her fault she had no home, no parents. So why did she have to be treated like a stray dog?

The metal wall in front of her hummed, and a *ping* sounded with each change of number above the door. The lift was close. Robynn shifted her weight nervously from one leg to the other. *Hurry up, hurry up...*

And then movement caught in the corner of her eye. She snapped her head to the side, expecting to see a grown-up, someone ready to scream at her *(filthy little urchin!)*, and threaten to call Level Security. But it was a boy, crossing past the end of the corridor.

She stepped away from the lift doors just as they opened and jogged along the edge of the wall. When she reached the end, she peeked around the corner.

He snuck along, glancing side to side, like he was playing "secret agent." His clothes were clean, his hair trimmed, and he'd gained a few pounds, but Robynn still recognized him.

Gavin.

What was he doing here? Ave had told Robynn...well, something. It was always something. Excuses for why Gavin never seemed to be around.

Robynn skulked along the adjacent corridor, following as Gavin rounded the next corner. He stopped in front of a door and she ducked behind a support column, pressing her cheek against the cold metal.

The door opened, and Gavin stepped through. A man's hushed voice said, "You weren't followed?"

"No, sir."

"You're sure? There were some kids poking around earlier."

"No, sir."

A grunt, and then the man leaned his head and shoulders out the door, facing away from Robynn. She held her breath as he turned in her direction. It took everything she had not to gasp. It was him—the 'droid!

37.   EXPERIMENT
TRAVIS PERRY

In the chamber with the pressurized angel tank, Ernsto shuffled toward Wizard Hobson against his will. The feeling was not so much his legs disobeying his orders as whatever it is in him that controlled his legs no longer seemed to be a part of him.

Hobson's eyes were green-blue, he realized as he drew close enough to peer into them. And then in a blur he threw his hands against the wizard's throat.

Hobson gagged and his eyes bulged in surprise, but an instant later Ernsto found the control of his fingers no longer belonged to him. His arms dropped to the side—limp, like they were dead.

The wizard coughed and rubbed his throat. He laughed hard, as if it all were a joke, but an angry glint lit his eyes. "You have very quick hands, my boy. And a quick, violent will. I was not able to detect your intent before you struck. If I had, you never would have moved a muscle."

As if to prove the wizard's point, his thought to bash the old man's nose with his forehead left him feeling numb in his neck and back. He couldn't make any movement at all.

"How?" he uttered. He'd intended to say more, but the paralysis that gripped his body hindered his mouth.

"How do I control you? Simple, my dear friend. Chemical compounds, mind-enhancing compounds which I've discovered from my studies of the angel cerebral cortex. This one isn't my first...not even my first live one, but the other live one I captured, one I took myself when I was a much younger man, I moved into a pen under the sea, isolated, but still connected to the ocean. He called for help—mentally of course—after two days the facility was assaulted by hundreds from his tribe. I barely escaped with my life. But even more importantly than my personal survival, I retained the knowledge I had gleaned, knowledge I've been adding to and using for decades now. All wizards use knowledge derived from angels, but I assure you, with all due modesty, I am the greatest of them all."

"What...?" rasped Ernsto.

"What do I intend to do with you? Or the angel? Or both? I'm not quite sure what you mean. You see, I should be able to know, since I can enter your mind. But I don't fully—which simply is further proof that there is more work to do, more discoveries to be made. In spite of all I have learned from the tools provided by the angel brain, in spite of all the corners of the human mind I've learned to tap into, I still struggle to do what they do with ease—communicate complete thought to thought. I wondered for a time if perhaps the human brain were simply incompatible with such a form of communication. But you, my boy, you give me hope!"

"Why?"

"Why, because *you* communicate with the angel. Or better said, she communicates with you. That's why you enjoy being with her, even though you do not admit to yourself that's how you feel. It's because she touches your mind. I think," Hobson chuckled, "she's trying to heal your 'sickness' of violence...how quaint!"

"Now?"

"Ah, now. Now I get to experiment with the link that has sprung up between the two of you. That's why I haven't simply shut your mind down, by the way, or reoriented your will. I need to test you in a more natural state." Hobson turned to the cyborgs, "Strap him to the table."

Flat on the table, the two cyborgs finished with Hobson's command, Ernsto felt his body return to his control. Not that it helped—the straps were tight and strong.

The wizard had opened the box. It contained some sort of advanced drill, with a very fine bit surrounded by thin clear tubes. The bit whirred in the air as the professor pressed a button. "For brain tissue samples," he explained unbidden. "First you, then the angel."

No, no! he heard her mind say from inside the pressurized tank.

As the wizard moved the drill closer to the base of his skull, Ernsto said through gritted teeth, "If you do this, you'd better kill me. Elsewise, as soon as you let me go, you're a dead man."

"Oh, I imagine this experiment will last weeks. You and the angel don't die until after that. But I promise to wipe your memory of this moment. Tomorrow, you won't even know any of this ever happened. You'll think it's just another well-paid day on the job. I've already done it to you twice."

Great, he thought. He set in himself a determination to remember every detail.

I'll help you, said the angel into his mind.

"I saw your father." Dr. Lee's voice rose just above a whisper, his back turned to her as he examined her blood in the microscope.

Zana bolted upright and nearly jumped from the examination table. But she lost her balance and fell hard on her right elbow. The bone rang like a tuning fork. "What?"

"Your blood work looks good." Dr. Lee turned around, his blue eyes round and grey-brown brows furrowed above. "Zana, you shouldn't move suddenly; I took two pints of your blood. If your blood weren't so rare, I wouldn't need to take as much each visit. If you get injured again…"

"No," Zana's said with as much ferocity as she could muster in a prone position. She pointed a metal finger at the doctor and continued, "That's not what you said."

Dr. Lee dropped his arms to his sides and met her eyes. His brows raised in a plea for forgiveness. He shrugged as he said, "I saw him a month ago at the general store in Currituck." Dr. Lee's gaze explored the wall, ceiling, and finally settled on the window. "The man looked old, haggard, and tired. He wore circuit preacher robes. Whether it's a disguise or not, I don't know."

Her heart raced in her chest. Zana's voice shook as she spoke through clenched teeth. "I've been here for three days, and now you tell me?"

"You're going to need to rest a day or two from the blood loss before you go."

"You did that on purpose."

Dr. Lee nodded, refusing to meet her icy stare. "It was a month ago, he could be anywhere now."

Zana folded her arms across her chest, feeling the cold titanium of her left arm through the gauzy fabric of her shirt. She stared at the ceiling and said in a soft voice, "I will find him. And when I do, he's dead."

Tomika sat on the couch, knees bent, calves tucked under her. She leaned back and released a sigh as she stared at the object in her palm.

Despite numerous scratches, the metal spearhead glinted in the overhead light. Its edges were chipped and worn, but the tip was honed to a point that had nearly gouged Tomika's hand as she'd pulled the spearhead from the chunk of beetle meat she'd brought home from the market. Unusual to find a spearhead in a piece of meat, but not unheard of. Sometimes a hunter would break a spear and fail to recover the head and the meat would be sold that way.

Most of the scratches on the metal were merely evidence of use. All but the name etched in the center of one side.

Mary.

A common name. Too common to mean anything. Except the way it was written… in all capitals, with the "A" made from one fluid stroke so that it looked almost like a star. The same way Mary's husband Jax wrote the "A" in his own name.

Tomika had seen it enough times on Jax's artwork—carvings done on polished squares of beetle shell—to know it couldn't be someone else's writing.

This changes everything.

Jax was supposed to be dead. So how was there a spearhead with his wife's name on it sitting in her hand?

A spearhead…

Beeping snapped Tomika out of her thoughts. She lifted her head and looked at the vidscreen on the far wall. The name "X. Chambers" flashed in the corner of the screen. Tomika tapped her finger against her leg. If she didn't answer, Xavia would just keep calling. She leaned forward and dropped the spearhead into the basket sitting on the coffee table so it wouldn't be visible to the camera, then sat back up.

"Answer," she said.

Xavia's image appeared on the vidscreen. "Tomi, why haven't you called? I thought we were meeting for lunch today." She sat cross-legged in a hoverchair, a gold anklet flashing reflected light as she tapped her foot against nothing.

Right. Lunch. She'd forgotten. "Sorry, Xav, can't make it today. I'm not feeling well."

Xavia leaned forward. "You do look rather puny. Was it the meat you bought? It was bad, wasn't it? I tried to tell you…the stuff they sell down on that level is poor quality. The higher the level, the higher the quality—you should know that by now. It's why we pay what we do for these apartments. Next time—"

"Listen, Xav, I've got to go. I'll call you later. Maybe we'll do lunch tomorrow. Say hi to the girls for me. End connection."

The vidscreen shut off just as Xavia's mouth opened. Tomika raked her fingers through her hair, and pulled the long, black tresses forward over her left shoulder. She smiled as she thought of Xavia's words. *Yep, Xav, the meat was bad…*

A spearhead.

Jax was alive, and bug hunting. Which meant his death had been faked. It was the only explanation. Why hadn't she seen it before? Jax was the first to be arrested, and then every last "business partner" of his gets busted. He must have made a deal. A deal that meant banishment from the station to the planet below—leaving Mary with three kids to care for, and another on the way, all thinking he was dead. Tomika didn't know how the girl had handled it.

Or…did Mary know?

Tomika jumped up from the couch and plucked the spearhead out of the basket. She grabbed a towel from the kitchen, carefully wrapped the spearhead, and slipped it into her bag.

Tomika's footsteps echoed off the metal walls of the curved corridor. The electric hum of Avenir's core didn't travel to Tomika's upper level, but she could detect it faintly here on Mary's. She stopped and placed her thumb on the scanner by Mary's door. Her heart pounded, and she fidgeted with the silver ring on her right hand while she waited for Mary to answer.

The door slid open. Mary stood in the entryway, a sleeping newborn in her arms.

"Tomika, wow. When the vidscreen showed it was you at the door…"

"I know—it's been a while. I'm sorry. I should have called first."

Tomika shifted her weight. What was she doing? She couldn't have had worse timing. "I'll come back later…"

"No, it's fine. Come on in. Jacey will be sleeping for a while." Mary stepped back to make room for Tomika to enter. Tomika followed her inside, the door sliding shut behind them. They took seats in hoverchairs facing each other. Mary began to rock hers.

Tomika smiled. "Jacey…what a pretty name."

Mary lowered her gaze to the sleeping infant and ran her fingertips over the peach fuzz on the top of Jacey's head. "I named her after Jax, of course. It's not fair that he never got to know about her."

"You didn't tell him?"

Mary looked up, tears welling in the corners of her eyes. "I was planning to…the night he…" She closed her eyes for a moment and breathed deeply. "He was supposed to be coming home that night, to await trial."

Tomika stared at Mary. The unfinished sentence…*the night he*…echoed in her mind. Would that last word have been "died"—or something else? Disappeared. Left. Did Mary know the truth? Was she simply upset that Jax was sent away before she had a chance to tell him, or did she really believe him to be dead?

Tomika struggled for a way to find out. It had been a few months since she'd last seen Mary, their friendship decaying in the wake of all Mary was going through. Tomika's own life had gone on as usual, and the rift that formed between them seemed impossible to repair. Her mind refocused on the spearhead in her bag.

This changes everything.

Mary wiped her eyes and pulled Jacey close, kissing the tiny forehead. "She looks just like him."

"I bet that would make him happy to hear," Tomika said.

"It would." Mary laughed. "He always griped that none of our kids looked like his side of the family—as if my genes had somehow taken over. Well, he finally got his way."

They talked about everything, including Jax, but the conversation never took a turn toward anything Tomika could use. Still, their hoverchairs eased closer as they continued to talk, and the rift in their friendship seemed to shrink as well. Soon, Tomika's chair was touching Mary's, and she stared down into Jacey's face.

"You want to hold her?"

Tomika looked up and smiled at Mary. "Yeah…actually, I do."

Mary shifted her chair around to face Tomika and eased Jacey into Tomika's arms. The baby's head lay in the crook of Tomika's elbow. So small, so soft. Innocent.

Jax had not been innocent, but apparently he'd done the right thing in the end. Tomika wondered how Mary felt, either way. If Mary knew Jax was still alive, did it make her angry that he'd given up his family?

Tomika mustered her resolve. She needed to find out…but how? She looked at Mary, who'd leaned back in her chair and crossed her legs. Mary's eyes fought to stay open.

"Mary, why don't you go take a nap? I'll sit here with Jacey."

Mary glanced down at her watch. "Well, there's still some time before the kids get home from school. Wake me in fifteen minutes?"

Tomika nodded. Mary slipped out the hoverchair and smiled down at Jacey before disappearing into the bedroom. As soon as the door slid shut behind Mary, Tomika stood. Jacey nestled securely in her arms, Tomika walked through the living area and scanned for anything lying around that might clue her in to what Mary knew.

The apartment was neat, with just enough mess to show that kids made their home here. A stray toy lay on the floor, and the outer wall was smudged with little fingerprints. Tomika stepped in front of the wide porthole on the far wall of the main living area. Beyond the lower habitation ring, stars twinkled through the misty glow of red light that reflected from Eclectia, although the planet itself wasn't visible from this side of the station.

Tomika turned and gazed around the room once more, eyeing open surfaces. She told herself she would not snoop…not really…no opening drawers, no peeking behind cabinet doors…

She walked toward a desk that hugged the wall next to Mary's bedroom door. Sleek squares were stacked on top—but as Tomika reached the desk she saw that they were carvings made not by Jax, but Mary's children. She let out a sigh and leaned against the wall. Jacey wiggled in her arms, smacked her tiny lips, but didn't wake.

A muffled noise carried through the wall. Tomika pressed her ear against the hard, polymer structure and listened.

Sobbing.

She bit her lip and closed her eyes. Tears burned behind her lids. She eased one hand out from under Jacey, shifting the baby's weight so she stayed secure, and reached up to wipe the tears away. Her elbow bumped something sticking out from the wall, and Mary's sobs came louder and more clearly. Tomika opened her eyes, stifling a gasp, and looked at the button she'd hit with her elbow. Of course, the intercom.

She reached out to turn it off, but her hand stopped mid-way when she heard Mary say Jax's name. It came out muffled, but this time as if her face were pushed into her pillow.

"Why, Jax? Why did you have to leave us?"

Tomika held her breath, hand still poised in mid-air.

"I miss you, Jax…I miss you so much…."

Tomika swallowed and then snapped the intercom off. Jacey began to squirm in her arms, and Tomika turned and walked back to the hoverchair, where she sat and rocked until Jacey settled down.

Moments later, Mary's bedroom door slid open. Her eyes were red, but tearless. She smiled weakly. "Is she still sleeping?"

Tomika nodded. "Yeah, but only just. I think she wants her momma."

Mary smiled genuinely this time and walked over to Tomika. She eased the baby from Tomika's arms. "Ah…not momma she wants. More like a new diaper. Wait here while I change her?"

Tomika shook her head as she stood. "No, I should be going. Xav is pretty peeved at me for skipping out on lunch today. Maybe I can catch the girls before they leave the club."

"Well…" Mary shifted Jacey to one arm, then reached out and touched Tomika's shoulder. "I'm so glad you came by. Next time, don't take so long."

Tomika wrapped her arms around Mary and the baby. "You bet." She let go and backed up. "Now go clean up that little peanut. I'll let myself out."

Mary bobbed her head in a slight nod. "Thanks." She turned and walked toward the children's room. The sound of Mary's footsteps told Tomika she was far from the open door. Tomika crept into Mary's bedroom, where she pulled out the spearhead and unwrapped it from the towel.

She set the spearhead on Mary's nightstand.

"He misses you, too, Mary."

With that, she left Mary's and headed back to her life. But today had changed everything.

TOMIKA'S QUARTERS

AVENIR ECLECTIA
SPLASHDOWN
MICHAEL L. ROGERS

40. MEMORIES
TRAVIS PERRY

Ernsto Mons awoke in the cube of a bedroom the wizard had assigned to him. His head ached.

He sat up on the edge of his bed, mouth foul and parched, pain throbbing through his skull with every beat of his heart. A flash of something passed through his mind, like the fleeting memory of a dream.

For some reason he did not understand, Ernsto felt he *needed* to remember the dream. He strained to bring it back. Success seemed his for a moment, but then melted away.

He arose, drank water from a nearby steel bottle, and shuffled out into the hallway. Without thinking about why, his feet propelled him into the room containing the angel's holding tank.

Wide-eyed, the alien stared back at him, the normally-bright bioluminescence from her body now dim. He stared into her eyes as if there were something important there, some answer to a question he didn't even know how to formulate. After what seemed a long while he realized, somehow, that she couldn't remember it either.

An undefined sense of dread floated into him, a feeling that he was in danger and should flee for his life. *This is comin' from the angel*, he understood.

But Ernsto had no intention of running away. He knew, somehow, there was an enemy to fight and a way to fight him, if only he could come up with a plan. He also understood that whatever planning he did, it would have to be cold-bloodedly emotionless. Having any emotion at all would only put him in danger...

41. UNDERTOW (FLASHBACK)
PAULINE CREEDEN

Zana struggled to reach the surface. The memories enveloped and dragged her to the depths of despair. She wanted—needed to wake up.

Acid filled the air and rushed toward her face, and Zana squeezed her eyes shut against the pain. White spots danced behind her lids. She heard nothing but high-pitched ringing as she turned her head. The screaming came from her throat. Her face burned as though on fire.

Not again.

The ground slammed against her shoulder as she landed on her right side, but the pain focused on her left side instead. Her body turned from the momentum to her back and the pain renewed, dizziness threatened to pull her into unconsciousness. She struggled; knowing that if she passed out, her brother would be in danger. Clenching her jaw she forced her eyes open.

Don't.

A red dust cloud surrounded Zana, but the sun still sifted through. She squinted, the white dots fluttering like annoying flies. Her mouth was closed, but she tasted dust and her left cheek moved in and out each time she took a ragged breath.

She tried to pull her left hand up to touch her cheek, but nothing happened. Her arm didn't follow her mind's command. *Is it broken?* She thought through the pain, unsure and unable to locate her arm. The ringing subsided so that she could hear the giant cannonbeetle's legs thumping the ground in a scurrying motion as it retreated. She wondered at how it didn't finish her.

Fear seized her. Where was her little brother?

Don't look.

"Zane?" She cried, afraid that if she moved she'd pass out. Zana's voice cracked lower than she intended and sounded foreign to her. It was deep, groggy, and echoed funny. Her tongue felt dry, swollen, and strange in her mouth.

"Zane?" She called louder, but the force of the word caused the white spots to crowd her vision and increase tenfold. Blackness seeped in to the corners of her sight, tunneling her vision. She tried to get up, but her left arm did nothing and her right arm had no strength. Tears-filled her eyes as she stared at the red sky.

Please don't.

Dizziness seized her. The world seemed to spin. Zana closed her eyes again and turned her head. The movement caused pain to shoot through her body and the blackness closed in. When she opened her eyes, half her vision had gone dark. She fought it again. When the spots retreated, her brother's face appeared.

"Zane! Thank God, I thought…" She stopped as a black fly landed on his open eye.

42.   THE SPIDER IN THE CHAPARRAL
KAYE JEFFREYS

Traces of web hung from a branch of one of the trees. Reece stopped his one-rider at a safe distance and searched the small island of grey-green trees in the sea of yellow-grey scrub grass. *Rose won't be happy that a spider has moved into one of her nature projects.* He'd come back later with others from the mining camp to flush it out. No one takes on a spider alone.

A cry drifted on the wind from the other side of the chaparral.

Reece unholstered his rifle and made a wide circle around the growth of Rose's trees, searching it and the rippling grass. There was movement in the shadows of the low hanging branches. Spindly legs of a large spider pulled a rope of a web into the chaparral.

Thirty feet away someone fought, unseen, except for the violent shaking of grass around her.

Weren't lassoing spiders extinct? Yet one methodically hauled in its prey from the cover of the trees.

Reece climbed off his one-rider, counting on the hope that the spider could only lasso one prey at a time. He propped his rifle against his vehicle and located the scythegun under the seat. He pulled it out and fumbled at the switches. He fought to hold the cumbersome thing steady in his trembling fingers.

Slow down and do this right. He forced a steady aim.

The spider hesitated, recalculating.

Reece fired. The scythegun cracked.

A shriek ripped the air.

Then all noise and movement in the chaparral stopped except for the leaves manipulated by the wind.

Reece aimed again at the motionless spider, and waited. He listened with ears deafened by the gun's crack and spider's shriek. The wind shifted and increased though it sounded muffled in comparison to the pounding of his heart.

Collapsed in the beaten down grasses, the nomad didn't stir except for her exhausted breathing.

Reece took a step back and searched the horizon for other nomads. There were none. Very strange. He had to decide if he should help her and break one of their laws or walk away and avoid trouble. So far he knew that you don't touch them, you don't talk to them, and you aren't ever supposed to look at their females. He searched the horizon again expecting to see riders pour over the hills any second. Only wind disturbed the grass.

The webbing wrapped around the girl's ankle had rubbed it raw and bleeding. He could not walk away when a Higher Law compelled him to help.

Never looking directly at her, Reece used an old rag to protect his hand as he grasped the sticky web. He sawed through it with his knife a full two feet away from her foot. Then he stepped back.

She crawled then rose to her feet and limped away through the waves of grasses. Picking up speed to a shaky run, she disappeared over a hill, never looking back.

"You're welcome." Wind whipped his words away to parts unknown.

What did he expect? A handshake, a thank you, eye contact?

Reece climbed onto his one-rider and started it up. He had to tell the others that lassoing spiders were not as extinct as they thought.

43. NAMING
KAT HECKENBACH

Gavin lifted his head, blinking. His eyes ached from straining over the microscope. Dr. Spiner had shown him how to work all the buttons and dials, how to focus and find the tiniest of particles. It had been fun at first, but today's work was boring and Gavin couldn't stop his mind from wandering.

"Dr. Spiner?"

The wizard-scientist's eyes were all that moved. And at that they only peeked out from under his shaggy bangs for a moment.

"I know it's late, and you're tired, son. It won't be much longer though." His hands shuffled nimbly among the various instruments in front of him.

"I just had a question, sir."

"Hm?"

"What's your first name?" Gavin hoped he hadn't crossed a line by asking. It had only been a few months since he started his apprenticeship with Dr. Spiner, and the scientist had never treated Gavin like the child he was. Other than calling him son—which put a lump in Gavin's throat each time he thought about it, even though he knew it was just a nickname.

Dr. Spiner raised his whole head this time. "It's Spiner, of course."

Gavin felt his forehead scrunch. "But...but you're Doctor Spiner. I thought..."

The scientist shifted on his stool. "What kind of first name is Doctor?" He smiled, but it was a smile that didn't travel to his eyes.

The smile dropped and he sighed. "My first name is Spiner, Gavin. I abandoned my last name years ago. I suppose it's still in my records, but no one knows it, not here. I'm just Spiner...or Doctor Spiner. And no one, until you, has asked me about it."

Gavin's skin flushed hot. "I'm sorry, sir. I didn't mean to..." He reached for the microscope again, but before he could put his eye against the lens Dr. Spiner was standing beside him. Gavin slowly looked up and met his dark eyes.

"I don't mind, Gavin. I come from a family I'm not very proud of, that's all." The scientist lifted his hand and stroked a stray hair from Gavin's face. "You don't have a last name either, do you?"

"Just what the other kids call me. "

"And that would be?"

Gavin swallowed, throat burning. "Talker."

This time the scientist's smile lit up his whole face. "Seems we both need one then." He turned, grabbed his stool and pulled it over. When he was seated, he leaned his elbow on the tabletop, work seemingly forgotten. "What shall our new last name be, son?"

44. INVENTORY
TRAVIS PERRY

Rolf and Nasir smiled at him as if they shared a secret he didn't know. Ernsto did not, could not, let himself get annoyed by them.

Days ago he'd figured out that those two doorknobs were not the source of his problem. They were not the ones causing the blanks in his memory. They were not the cause of the angel's terror.

Hobson was the enemy, of course. The wizard's friendly confidence gave him away.

Ernsto strolled by the door guards and waved, letting a friendly slowness pass over his face. The guards had both been raised on Avenir...they were predisposed to think someone from "down under" was a simpleton, an ignorant rustic. He let them think that—it served his purpose.

He supposed the insight into these men had come to him from the angel. He found in himself, more and more, that he longed for the information and understanding she gave him.

He entered his cubicle of a bedroom. On his person at all times he carried the only key to a lockbox. The box contained a curved tool and a signal jammer. The signal jammer he turned on, in case there were bugs or unknown video dots in the room; he placed the tool between tight fitting wall panels and cranked to the left. A portion of the aluminum wall sagged forward. Inside the wall he eyed over his collected inventory. He added to it his latest two acquisitions. A pair of flash-bang stun grenades found their places among homemade explosives, a plasma blaster, tranquilizer gun, projectile pistol, and three razor-sharp knives.

Ernsto sealed the panel and suppressed his emotion of triumph. *Soon, old man. Soon 'nough you'll know exactly how I'm feelin'.*

45. UNFORGIVEN
PAULINE CREEDEN

Dr. Rob Lee set down his Colander Mint tea and regarded his charge. Zana had bags under her eyes. "Nightmares?" he asked.

She grumbled and grabbed a cup for her own tea.

The gentle hum of the air purifier filled the space of silence between them. Zana threw herself unceremoniously into a chair, the metal of her left leg scraping the iron on the side of the cushion with a squeak. Rob pulled the tea to his lips, blowing the foam before taking a sip. Cotton flopped down on the floor beside her, ever the canine shadow.

Because of the wind outside, the kitchen glowed orange as the low sun filtered through the volcanic dust. Even in the colored light, Zana looked pale. Her dark hair produced an unnatural contrast in her ghostly skin. Because she'd been in the mountains for the last few months, she'd dealt with the worst of Eclectia's winter cycles. There wasn't a chance she'd let any of her skin be exposed up there. Rob set his cup into its saucer gently and made his left hand into a fist a few times, trying to loosen his tight joints. "We should talk."

Zana's emerald eyes glowered with malice. "You want to talk now? Why not two days ago?"

"Look, I'm sorry about that. We needed to get your check-up and repairs done before you ran off chasing that man. It's grasping for wind."

"Who are you to decide that?" She slammed her cup on the table, and it sloshed tea on her hand. "That man left Zane and me for dead. We were too young to be beetle hunting to begin with. Once I found out what kind of monster my father was, I've made it my life's work to bring him down and every criminal like him."

"Zana, you can't let this continue. Can't you see that it's eating you up inside? Don't you see what you're becoming?"

"I am becoming what my father made me." She held up her cybernetic arm, the metal palm outstretched toward Rob. "Does this look like the kind of hand that could hold a baby? Do you expect me to get married and live happily ever after? Mrs. Lee is dreaming."

"What will you do once you find him?"

"I'll kill him."

"Then what?"

Zana stopped, her eyes widened as if slapped in the face. For a moment, Rob saw the innocence and vulnerability he'd seen in her when he'd first found her. Her lower lip trembled. "I haven't..."

"You haven't thought that far." He gently finished for her and flexed his hand again. "Zana, there is more to life than revenge. You're a smart girl, compassionate, and talented in so many ways. I could really use your help here. You're good with machines, and my dexterity isn't quite what it used to be."

Her forehead wrinkled as she studied the contents of her cup. She shook her head slightly then nodded. "Maybe you're right." She shrugged and looked up, her eyes pleading. "But I'm closer than I've ever been."

"It was a month ago, Zana." He softened. "Your father could have gotten to Avenir in that time, or Quatermain. He could be anywhere. You are no closer, I promise."

The bags under her eyes made her defeat palatable. She lowered her head and finished the dregs of her cup. "I'm so tired, Dr. Lee."

"Why don't you go back to bed, then?"

She nodded and stood, the wrought iron chair scraping the floor bricks. Cotton followed her as she left the room and headed for the hall.

"You look tired, dear." Lucinda breezed past Zana in the hallway with her singsong voice. "Maybe you should head back for bed."

Zana mumbled a response and scratched Cotton between the ears before continuing down the hall.

Lucinda's long dress hem swept the floor as she busied herself in the kitchen. Its spotted white pattern glowed in the orange light. Rob smiled at the familiar dance she made from cupboard to cupboard preparing the breakfast. Her steps brought her to the table.

"That girl really ought to take better care of herself," Lucinda began as she collected Zana's cup. "If she would just give the guy a chance, I just know that young man who moved into town would…"

"Lucinda, please." Rob held up his hand. "Not now."

"Fine, but—" The door slammed in the wind and made her jump.

"No, she didn't." Rob pushed his chair back, incredulous. He rushed to the window, and pulled back the gauzy curtain. In the cloud of red dust, the shadows of a long coat and a dog moved southeast on the road toward the suns. Rob shook his head and felt a sting in his chest. "She did."

46. BYBLOS
WALT STAPLES

The man in the brown habit wore the battered face of a former boxer. As he shuffled, long experience caused him not to notice the tremor running through the walls and floor of the abandoned mine shaft. Sheba was just being Sheba.

The Abbot halted his silent progress down the hall of the scriptorium. He eased open the Judas slot on the door marked "Ignatius" so as not to disturb those on the door's other side. From within came a newly cracked voice, "…In the beginning was the Word, and the Word was with God, and the Word was God. He was in the…" The tall, stooped man slid the slot closed.

He continued to the next cell. Its name was "Jerusalem." This time, he heard, "…and the word was God. He was with God in the beginning. Though Him all things…" He smiled and went on to "Douay."

He listened and began to frown as he heard, "…The same was in God—" A much older voice cut the younger off, "No." It continued more gently, "No, Bede, it goes this way; now listen carefully. 'The same was in the beginning with God. All things were made by Him, and without Him was made nothing that was made.' There, you see?"

The Abbot's forehead cleared as the first voice said, "Sorry, Brother Eustis," and began again, "The same was in the beginning…"

He thought about Brother Eustis as he walked toward "James." The old friar had earned a proper retirement years ago, but continued to teach the young Douay Bibles. The Abbot shook his head and smiled, old men and old hunting dogs.

As if conjured by the thought, Fezik, the oldest ratting dog, trotted by. He wagged at the human and went about his business. He and the chief cat seemed to have a competition as to who could bring Brother Trout, the abbey cook, the most rats.

At "James," the ancient heard, "…All things were made by Him, and without Him was not anything made that was made. In Him was life, and the life was the light of men. And the light shineth in…"

He went on greatly cheered. The new crop of Bibles were coming along well. Even young Bede showed promise. By Advent, all six of the present class would be ready to go out to their respective churches. The Abbey of Francis might produce priests, but they were crippled without his Bibles. Too many illiterates lived in the poor corners of Eclectia and the space surrounding Avenir. Now Avenir's nanofactories had built up enough to produce books and recorded Scriptures again, but these were only for the very rich. The church leveraged the one resource it had in abundance—people—to provide for the needs of the poor to hear the Word of God…he caught himself. No! In that direction lay Pride. He whispered an Act of Contrition.

He turned his thoughts back to their original path. Yes, he thought, six new Bibles by Advent. His face broke into a toothless grin of pure happiness. His expression sobered somewhat as he was reminded of the problem of Brother Eustis. Which of the older Douays should he pick to replace the old friar when the sad time came? He padded on through the halls of the Abbey of Jerome.

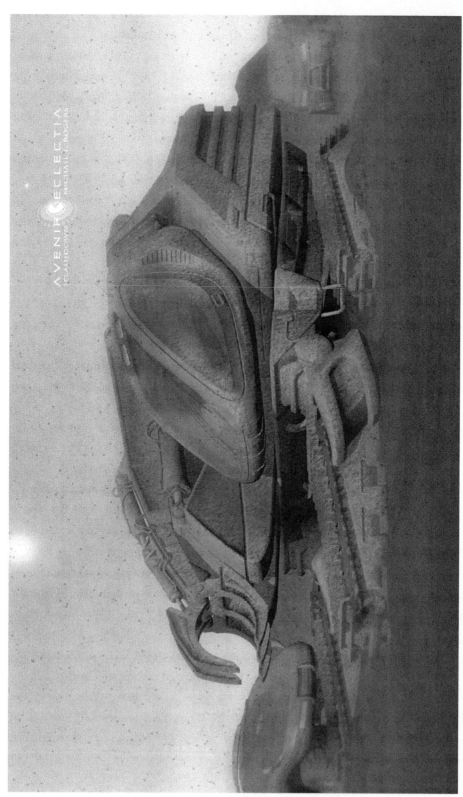

Reece scratched at the porous rock with his pickax near the top of Red Rim. He took a deep breath through his gas mask then let the air wheeze out through the valves. In the distance Black Rim smoked and rumbled sending vibrations through the entire mountain. Blue Rim spewed molten rock in a plume of red-orange toward the heavens. Reece chipped at the rim stone again. He hated sweating in the oppressive heat just to be skunked. The Lady in Red was being stingy with her jewels.

Brett had to be doing better. He always did better. Older brother, more experienced, more patient with the tedious work of seek and find. He had a way with the Lady. She saved her best diamonds for him.

Reece glanced over at his brother.

Brett knelt on one knee and grasped his mask.

"Brett?" Reece called through the comlink.

His brother didn't answer.

Beyond Brett, Dad stood up and surveyed the work area. Venting volcanic gases warped the view and caused static in the link. "Everyone in." Stisttt, "We have a malfunction." Dad sold most of what they mined to the Avenir Diamond Company, trading for gear they needed to survive at the company's mobile outposts. He treated his family like a work crew and directed them as such.

Reece attached his pick to his belt and climbed over the jagged rocks toward his brother. Dad came from the other direction.

Brett slumped as they approached. Dad and Reece hoisted his arms over their shoulders and carried Brett away from the rim. They crunched brittle rock and stirred ash as they selected stable footing away from the noxious gases.

"We have to get him off this mountain, fast," Dad said calmly to the entire team. And then, "Rose, you'll get to the multirider before the rest of us. Fire her up. We gotta get to First Aid," stistt, "maybe have to transport to Last Stop."

Reece adjusted his hold on Brett. "What about the offering?"

"We will bring it back later." Dad's breath labored through his mask.

"Should I break off and take it to them alone?"

"Absolutely not. Brett's health is number one priority. We will deal with the offering when we know he is safe."

Or dead, the thought popped into Reece's mind as the floor of his stomach dropped away. He pushed the thought away and continued distracting himself with, "Will the Nomads accept it later?"

"We will deal with that when the time comes. Keep focused on getting Brett to safety."

48.   A PERSONAL WAR, PART 1
TRAVIS PERRY

Rolf reached inside his jacket for his weapon, too late. Ernsto shot the needle gun into his neck, through the carotid. Nasir, much faster than Ersnto suspected, drew his plasma blaster and fired.

Ernsto had already leapt forward into the doorway at the front of Wizard Hobson's quarters when the hot plasma passed his back. Without looking, he squeezed off five needle shots behind him as he charged toward his room.

Plasma bolts hurled past him and a searing burn engulfed his left shoulder. Normally he would have picked a spot with good cover and held his ground. But he couldn't, not with Hobson somewhere nearby.

Run, had said the angel into his mind, *run*, she said, revealing Rolf and Nasir's thinking—this time, they intended to kill him as he walked past, his living usefulness finished, as was hers. But he'd never been the type to run—and there was no way he'd let Hobson have the angel.

He charged past the pressurized aquarium that held her on the way towards his room and its hidden weapons. The angel's eyes were wide and frightened, her ray-like wings tapped the glass in her distress. *No, no, don't kill*, her mind told him.

"Sorry babe," he shot back as he exited her chamber.

"Ernsto!" The voice belonged to Hobson. Something informed him if he looked back he'd lose his will to fight. Whether it was the angel that told him this or his own mind, he never knew.

He sprinted into his small room and slid shut the door by pressing the yellow button on the right side of the frame. He held his thumb to the pad for his print to lock it. Next he flipped the knife hidden in his right sleeve into his hand and stabbed the control panel, penetrating its thin aluminum face three times, hoping the door servo would never operate again.

His key for the lockbox he jammed into the slot and threw open the box. Within seconds he used the tool to open his hidden panel in the wall, the hiding place for his weapons.

His eyes searched and saw…nothing. He reached his left hand into the gap and felt nothing.

A slow chuckle came in through the room intercom. "Ernsto, my lad, did you really think you could hide a weapons cache from me? In my own private section of Avenir?"

Ernsto didn't answer. His stomach balled into a knot.

"Now be a good lad and fix whatever you've done to the door and come on out. We need to sit down and discuss this rationally, man to man."

I'd rather die first, he thought, eyeing his sleeve knife and hoping this time the wizard knew exactly what was on his mind.

49. SHADOW
KAT HECKENBACH

Robynn's legs cramped from kneeling behind the support column. And leaning against the cold metal wall was making her back ache. Why hadn't Gavin come out of that man's room yet?

And he was a man, Robynn had decided. He had to be. The no-blinking thing was creepy, but his eyes were far too human. Even the cybernetic eyes she'd seen before lacked the spark of life she'd seen in his. And who would build a droid with such shaggy hair?

The door swooshed open and Robynn flinched, her heart suddenly fluttering like a hummingbird's. She peeked around the column. Gavin leaned through the doorway and peered down the corridor. Then he stepped through; the door swooshed closed behind him.

Robynn stood and stepped out into view, arms crossed, as Gavin crept past. "What were you doing in there?" she whispered through clenched teeth. She smiled as Gavin jumped.

His eyes narrowed, distorting his little boy features. "None of your business, Robynn Shadow."

The words hit Robynn like a brick. Gavin had never used that name for her. The other kids called her that, of course. *"Robynn Shadow in the shadows...hiding, hiding...in the shadows..."* Because she didn't like being the center of attention—as if there was something wrong with that! She wasn't *hiding*. And she didn't care what they thought anyway.

But Gavin...

Anger surged. Hurt anger that clawed its way out as tears burned her eyes. "Fine, *Gavin Talker*, do what you like!" She spun and stomped down the corridor.

"Robynn, wait!" His footsteps pounded behind her.

She could have easily outrun him, even out-walked, with her long legs and his short ones. But she didn't speed up, and in moments he was next to her.

He tugged her arm. "I'm sorry. Please, Robynn."

She stopped and looked down at him. His eyes were wide.

"I can't tell you what I was doing here. No one can find out. Only Ave knows...and if she trusts me, then you should, too." He squeezed her arm tighter. "And I'm sorry I called you that. I know you hate Shadow as much as I hated Talker."

"Hat*ed*? What, you like it now?"

He smiled then, his wide eyes lighting up and his cheeks pushing out. "Course not! The kids'll probably still call me that, but it's not my name anymore, not for real."

Robynn scrunched her mouth to one side. "So let's hear it," she said. "What's your 'real' name?"

His eyes shifted down. "Okay, it wasn't my idea...I know it sounds kinda strange...but it's a real Earth name." He looked up again. "Collodi."

Robynn tilted her head, tightening her brow. "You mean like Carlo Collodi? The guy that wrote *Pinocchio*?"

"Pinocchio?"

"It's an ancient story. About a man who doesn't realize he wants a son, but he makes this puppet that becomes a real boy—because they love each other so much."

Gavin stared at her, wide-eyed again, lip quivering.

Robynn knelt down. "Are you okay?" she asked as she wiped a tear from his cheek.

He nodded and smiled. "Very."

Eyeing his knife, Ernsto Mons' first thought was to slit his wrists in defiance, choosing his own time of death rather than letting Hobson pick it for him. But then a memory drifted back into his mind, a memory he somehow felt the angel had helped bring back to him.

The wall wasn't my only hiding place. He glanced at his mattress. The bed in his nearly bare room had been an acceleration couch once on Avenir during the long-ago voyage from Earth. Some of the couch's panels and braces had been stripped away since then, but it retained the same basic frame. The original mattress, on the other hand, had long since decayed and had been replaced by a hand-crafted type from the surface of Eclectia. This new mattress showed no signs of having been disturbed...except along one edge, near the head of the bed, where the hand stitching looked subtly different from the rest.

Ernsto knifed it open there and tore mattress fabric with his hands. Inside, his hands found three capped titanium pipes with fuses, filled with what he recalled having stuffed inside—an ancient recipe for homemade explosive, ammonium nitrate saturated with liquid hydrocarbon.

What he didn't have was the flame to ignite the fuse. After seconds of thought that seemed to stretch an eternity, he began to unscrew one of the caps on the threaded pipe. Once open, with his knife edge he pried a hole in the control panel to the door and bared an electrical source wire.

Suddenly, his ears heard a gas hiss into the room from a vent low along the door and his vision blurred. He held his breath, while with as much care as he could muster he scooped a dollop of wet gray pipe filling out from the open tube with his knife, grounded the blade on the edge of the panel, and moved the hot wire close to the knife blade and the small portion of explosive on top of it, which without the power of a blasting cap, should burn rather than blow up. *At least I hope so.*

The wire sparked but the current bit him, forcing his muscles to contract. His arm jerked away, flicking the flaming yellow onto the mattress, which immediately leapt up and burned bright, so much so that the whole room might burst into flame. *That works,* thought Ernsto, still shock-dazed.

He seized another pipe bomb, lit its fuse in the mattress flame, rolled it to the bottom of the door, and dove behind the bed—tipping it over as a shield behind his back, jamming his fingers in his ears. The clap of the explosion he barely heard because the overpressure knocked him unconscious.

He regained consciousness, confused, breathing something that made him cough, his ears ringing so loud he could hear nothing else. The mattress, riddled with gaping holes, didn't burn very bright, suggesting he'd only been out for an instant. The door bent outward at the bottom, about fifty centimeters worth, but the inside of the room clearly had taken the worst of it—its metallic walls were gouged and pitted with shrapnel in the pattern of a misshapen cone. And Ernsto felt the warmth of what must be blood flowing down his back.

His eye caught hold of the third pipe bomb. Its fuse had caught fire— with him still trapped inside the room.

51. DANGEROUS JOBS
KAYE JEFFREYS

"Are you hungry?" Dad stood in the door of Brett's sleep cubicle. "Gordy made chicory millet soup, good for lung health."

Brett propped himself up. "It smells good. Bless Gordy."

"You can eat a little?" Dad handed Brett the metal bowl.

The soup still steamed in the warm bowl. "Food is starting to sound good."

"You gave us all a scare." Dad sat down next to Brett's bed.

The savory broth and wild vegetables tasted good and went down smooth.

Dad stroked his chin. "Kellie doesn't look like she's taking it well. She looks worse than you do."

"She told me she's not burying another husband. I'm not allowed to die before her." Brett saluted like he was an enforcer.

Dad saluted back, showing his white teeth in a mirthful smile. "Like we have that much control."

"I told her that I'd be ready to go up to the Rims soon."

"The Clinic lady said it would take time."

"Don't listen to Lessie. She's from undersea and doesn't know how things work up here." Brett shook his head as he remembered the scolding he got from Lessie in the circuit office.

Dad leaned forward. "This time I'm listening."

"But Madame Bleu was showing off for us. Did you see the fountain she shot up?" Brett spread his fingers and reached for the roof of his sleeper. "She was telling us to come visit her next, that we wouldn't be sorry if we did."

"We aren't cleared to go back up yet." Dad crossed his arms and leaned back.

Brett suspended his spoon in front of his mouth. "That's right, the offering."

"Tomorrow, Reece and I will send up a flare and meet with them."

"What if they don't accept it?"

"Then we will go back to what our ancestors did."

"Hunt?" Brett's stomach became queasy. "Isn't that dangerous?"

"Playing Rim Roulette isn't dangerous?"

"It doesn't seem as dangerous as prospecting." Brett set the bowl of soup on the shelf next to his bed. He could no longer eat with the sour feeling in his gut. "Reece got in some good practice the other day with that spider."

Dad took a deep breath and covered his eyes as though he didn't want to see something. "Reece got lucky. He saw the spider first."

52.   A PERSONAL WAR, PART 3
TRAVIS PERRY

Ernsto grabbed the third pipe bomb, its fuse half burnt and still burning. The contents of the first, the one he'd opened, had already caught fire, adding to the flames without exploding. He frantically searched for the knife to cut the fuse of the bomb in his hand, but his eyes did not pick it out among the flaming and shrapnel-pitted carnage of his cubical room.

A glance at the pipe showed the fuse down to only two centimeters. He jammed the end of the pipe between his lips and bit off the fuse with his teeth. Its flaming end singed his tongue.

Spitting it out, he finally glimpsed the knife blade reflecting a yellow glint of fire and snatched it up, pocketing it. Glancing at the damaged metal mattress frame, one of the legs caught Ernsto's eye. The blast had nearly detached it from the bed.

He wrenched it free, put the pipe bomb under his arm, and charged the door with the bed leg held to his chest like a battering ram. He dove forward and smashed into the concave door curve left by the exploded bomb. The impact of the leg hurt his ribs and pectoral muscle more than the shrapnel wounds in his back had hurt. But the already-damaged metal at the bottom of door split open about ten centimeters.

His ears, still ringing, heard a faint shout from the other side. He spun back, lit the short-fused pipe bomb in the nearest piece of flaming mattress and threw it through the opening in the door. He flinched to the side but didn't have time to plug his eardrums before the blast. This time, at least, he did not black out.

He stood up, aware that fluid poured down his left earlobe, the side of his face that had been closest to the door. His lungs ached from the smoke but he'd responded without thinking why by taking shallow breaths and living without gulping air as long as he could.

The door had split open down the middle from about the height of his chin to the gash he already made near the floor. With the bed leg he pried the gap open and slipped out of his room. Right at the doorway were the fragmented pulpy remains of two cyborgs, who had a mostly intact metallic tank with them of some kind, of the gas they'd been pouring into his room, perhaps nitrous oxide. Apparently one of the cyborgs had shut it down before death, maybe because N2O is an oxidizer—not safe around flames.

Five meters away, Nasir lay on the couch of this common room that adjoined his sleeping area. His eyes were open and glazed over, a look of surprise permanently pasted onto his dead face. His chest and neck were punctured with shrapnel wounds.

Ernsto took the plasma pistol clutched in Nasir's still-warm right hand. Hobson, who would have been near his door at one point, was nowhere in sight now.

Deliberately projecting a bloodthirsty determination, he said out loud, "Stay away from the angel, old man. Or I *will* kill you."

Reece moved his goggles down from his forehead to cover his eyes and searched the horizon again. "The wind is picking up. Soon we won't be able to see. Do they know we are here?"

"Yes." Dad crouched down and rested his hand on the ground.

"What if they don't come?"

"We don't go back up to the Rims until we make the offering. Don't worry. They're here." Dad stood and brushed dust off his hands. "More than usual."

"Is it because we were late with the offering?"

"More likely because of the nomad you saved from the spider."

"What?"

"Come with me and keep your mouth shut."

Reece followed Dad down the hill to the meeting rock.

Several dozen mounted nomads crested the opposite hill and stopped.

A single beetle with two riders broke away from the rest and descended to meet them. They reached the rock first and dismounted.

Dad put up his hand in silent greeting. The rider, Senjab, did the same. His smaller passenger stood behind him to the side, her head bowed and face covered with a veil.

"Is all well?" Dad asked.

"All is not well." Senjab pointed at Reece. "Your son touched my daughter." He motioned back toward the girl behind him.

"Dad, I didn't—"

Dad put up his finger.

Reece shut his mouth, bit his lip, and breathed hard through his nose. Why did he stop to help a nomad?

"This is a serious charge." Dad spoke loud over the wind but remained calm.

"Sanja has become a shame to her people and must be cast from us."

Sanja, so that was her name, the little liar. She stood, head bowed and speechless. The wind whipped her garments about her.

"What can be done to resolve this?" Dad clasped his hands behind his back, stepped back with one foot, and turned so that he didn't face Senjab square on but at an angle.

"She must join your people through marriage to your son."

Reece's lip escaped his teeth. "Dad!"

Dad held up his finger again and gave Reece a sharp look.

Reece put his hands on his head and turned his back to them. Stupid Nomads and their stupid, stupid laws. He should have left her to be spider food. An immediate sinking feeling hit as his insides rejected the thought. He took a deep breath. He had done the right thing and could have done nothing else. He would rather face the consequences of doing a good deed than disappoint the One who loves all.

Dad said in his even tone, "Will you receive our gift and may we continue to mine Mt. Olympus?"

"Things between us will not change if you also take Sanja because your son has shamed her."

Reece turned back around and stared at Senjab. Were the streamed accusations really necessary?

Senjab ignored Reece's glare.

Dad nodded once. "We will take Sanja to live with us."

"Then it is done." Senjab gave a shallow bow.

Dad handed Senjab the pouch of cut diamonds.

Senjab mounted his bug and rode away, never looking back at the daughter he left behind like camp debris. Sanja gave no visible sign that she had been discarded by her father. She stood rigid against the wind, all expression hidden by her veil. Maybe her people falsely accused her like they did Reece.

"Sanja." Dad's voice was gentle towards the girl, even over the fierce wind. "Come with us." He turned and walked back to their multirider.

Reece walked alongside his father still needing to make his case, not just for himself, but for the thrown-away, little girl that followed them. "Dad, I didn't touch her. Nor did she touch me."

"We will discuss this later." Dad didn't scold, but his words were firm. "Right now we have to get out of this wind."

Each movement brought a spasm of pain to his back and his left ear felt like a hot poker had been shoved inside it. In the angel's chamber, Ernsto maneuvered the robotic cart carrying the portable pressure tank to the circular lock near the floor, below the transparent wall that physically separated him from the angel.

Two doors entered this room; the one behind him he felt confident was secure—shut tight, its locking mechanism damaged. His left hand held the plasma blaster, covering the door in front of him as his right hand worked the controls to the circular entrance into the angel's tank.

Waves of comfort and empathetic caring emitted from the angel, reminding him of his grandmother's touch when he'd been sick as a child, a warm soothing blanket and hot honey tea from her gentle hands, her voice telling him she loved him. The angel's care probed not only into the suffering of his body, but reached deep into hidden parts of himself, working to soothe the damage he'd done by destroying other men.

The light near the door flickered and he fired on the entryway, a plasma bolt peeling the blue paint on the metal sliding door. *Easy, easy,* said the warm embrace of the angel's mind.

He replied, "Babe, the lock's ready. You needa come out so I can transfer you to this tank, so I can take you back where you came from." His voice rasped in a whisper, but he knew she understood him. He hadn't actually needed words at all.

She came out and he physically pulled her from the lock and briefly her body was in his arms, wet and rubbery.

Now she suffered the pain of low pressure and his mind clumsily tried to comfort her with it's okay, it's okay. But then she was in the portable tank, the lid sealed shut, and the rising water pressure returning her to normal.

At that moment the door snapped open and two enforcers scrambled into the room, plasma pistols raised, shouting, "DROP YOUR WEAPON!"

He was ready to kill or die trying—the angel flooded his mind *please please please,* begging him to stop. His left arm twitched to raise his weapon but he found his hand had let go of it.

It dropped to the floor and his heart accepted what the angel wanted. He would allow himself to be captured.

Behind the first enforcers came two others, and then another two. The first pair threw him to the ground and handcuffed his wrists together. They hauled him to his feet and he saw there were now at least ten enforcers in the room and a plainclothes peacekeeper and some firecrew. Among them, in the safety of their numbers, stood Hobson, a triumphant smile on the wizard's face.

55.   ARREST
H. A. TITUS

Cara sat on a catwalk, the shadows obscuring her as she watched the smuggler unloading his ship. She'd noticed him last night, handing out bread to a few orphans in the marketplace. He looked nice, so she'd followed him so she could get a look at his ship. She wouldn't have dared with some of the smugglers, but this man she trusted as much as she could trust anyone.

His ship was a newer model, sleek and pristine. If she ever got her hands on a ship half as good as this one, she'd be happy.

It wasn't quite fair, she told herself. She liked flying. When she was five Foundings old, she'd snuck on board a trade ship for a round trip to Zirconia and back. But, being an orphan, she'd never be accepted in a flight school, even if she had enough money to pay for the classes.

Maybe this guy would give her lessons. He'd handed out food, hadn't he? That was more than any of the other smugglers, or even the honest merchants, would do. It was strange that he would care about the orphans, yet disregard the Peace Council's laws.

Footsteps echoed in the corridor. Cara stood up and leaned over the railing. Three enforcers strode down the row of docking bays toward the ship. She looked back at the stack of boxes. The smuggler had gone inside.

She bit her lip. Did she have time to warn him?

The smuggler ducked out of his ship just as the enforcers reached his stack of cargo. They stood facing each other for a moment. Cara could see the smuggler's face, his blue eyes calm, his muscles relaxed. Didn't he understand what the enforcers were there for?

One of the enforcers finally cleared his throat and spoke. "Pieter Kinsrol, you're under arrest."

Pieter. So that was his name. Cara expected him to make a run for it, or dart back inside his ship and try to escape. Instead, he nodded and spun around to receive his handcuffs.

Cara gently slapped herself. Had she just seen what she thought she'd seen? Who in their right mind would just let himself be arrested?

As the enforcers led Pieter away, Cara jogged along the catwalk to keep up. There had to be a way to help him. And by the Whale, she was going to find that way.

56. SANJA'S VEIL
KAYE JEFFREYS

Sanja had never been inside one of their metal machines before. The angular thing bounced across the rugged hills like a wounded beetle. The jerking made it hard for Sanja to pretend that she was an unfeeling stone. She had wanted to disappear like a vapor, but that was impossible. So she settled on becoming stone.

"Rose, pay attention to your driving," their father sat on the middle bench next to Sanja. "You are going to run us into a crevice. I'll have to repay the company if you destroy their vehicle."

"I'm too angry to drive." The daughter's boldness would be unacceptable among Sanja's people.

The father gripped the seat in front of him. "Reece, take over for her before she kills us."

The brother and sister traded places while the machine bucked and rolled on.

Rose glowered at Sanja as she dropped into the bench in front of her. "She lied about Reece so she could get out of arranged marriage." The daughter waved her hand in big movements at Sanja.

Sanja refused to feel indignant or angry. She was rock, a stone, unfeeling.

The father crossed his arms and looked down. "We don't know anything about anything yet."

"Dad, do I have to marry her?" Reece looked back at the father.

"No," their father said. "We are not bound by their laws. We follow our own."

"But what about Senjab?" Rose continued to stare back at Sanja as if she could see through Sanja's veil and break through the rock defenses.

"All I promised him was that she could come live with us." Their father looked at Sanja. "And I will keep my promise. Sanja is welcome among us for as long as she needs."

The vehicle jerked sideways suddenly. It tipped and hovered at an angle in the wind a few moments as though deciding if it would fall on its side. Then it landed hard, right side up.

Father, son, and daughter looked at one another. Then Rose spoke. "See. It's not just me. The wind is too much."

"Reece, batten down. This should blow over soon."

Reece moved his hand over the machine's devices. Small explosions sounded at the four corners around them.

The wind rocked the vehicle.

After a short silence the father said. "Rose, you will have to share your cubicle with Sanja."

"I will not! She might kill me in my sleep!"

"Rose!"

"I'll let her sleep in mine." Reece stood up and walked back to sit next to Rose. "I'll take the central area like I did when that Bible stayed with us. Zaibry can go stay with Brett and help with the kids."

"Thank you, Reece. Is this okay with you, Rose?"

"Whatever." Rose flopped backward in her seat so that Sanja couldn't see her anymore. It was a relief to be away from those seething eyes.

"Is this okay with you, Sanja?"

Sanja could not believe the father asked her. Nor could she guess why it mattered to him what she thought.

Unmovable stone slowly gave way. Sanja nodded once.

57. ESCAPE, PART 2
TRAVIS PERRY

"Thank you, gentlemen," said Hobson. "If the firecrew could proceed on to deal with the blaze my internal sensors say is raging in one of my rooms, I'd be most grateful. But as for this man, this Ernsto Mons, please allow me to deal with him myself."

The firefighters moved toward the second door but the enforcers stood in place, looking confused, as if there was something not quite right with what Hobson had said. After a long moment, one said "Sure" and the lone peacekeeper in the room said, "Sounds reasonable" and then suddenly all of them murmured a chorus of agreement.

All of them except one. "No," said a young dark-haired man in the uniform of the governor's personal security detachment. "That's not normal police procedure. This man needs to be arrested and processed for trial." Ernsto recognized the young man as Officer Romero, whom he'd met once by chance. For some reason, more than half of the enforcers in the room wore the uniform of the governor's security detail—apparently they'd been nearby.

Hobson smiled at Romero and gazed directly into his eyes. "Young man, I realize you work directly for the governor and I can't tell you how much I appreciate your help with my personal crisis here. But I am a high government minister myself and can be completely trusted in this matter. The man is my employee; please allow me to deal with him."

"No, sir," said Romero. And then a battle erupted of a sort Ernsto had never seen before. Hobson's eyes blazed and his voice rang out words. They were not foreign or magical words like in fairy tales; Hobson told Romero in a torrent of words why he should relent, why he should do as he was told, why he was duty-bound to obey, but the rhythm of his speech was hypnotic and Ernsto found he could not retain in his mind anything the wizard was chanting. Romero balled his hands into fists and stared right back at the wizard. In a low voice the enforcer muttered words Ernsto could not hear, but they reminded him nonetheless of the prayers his grandmother used to make.

He felt the angel reaching out in this fight too, somehow knowing she comforted and helped Romero. The words from Hobson hammered on with power and Ernsto felt as if he were no longer himself. His whole being, everything about him, turned numb and he dully watched, barely perceiving, as the invisible battle before him raged. It stretched on timeless, perhaps minutes, perhaps hours.

In an instant it was over. Hobson stopped speaking. Sweat poured from the wizard's brow and he huffed with effort. His eyes lowered to the ground.

Romero turned to Ernsto. "Let's go. Take the tank. I'm bringing you into custody."

The other members of the governor's detachment followed Romero and all of them exited Hobson's quarters as a group. Walking out the door, Ernsto felt an astonished sense of relief. He was still alive, even though probably going to prison. Still alive, but better yet, free from Hobson...

58.   SEED SCATTERERS
KAYE JEFFREYS

Sanja pressed her face against Rose's back and clung to her for survival's sake. These crazy miners drove their little machines too fast over the hills, hitting every bump they could find. Sanja only raised her head up to look as Rose slowed down and stopped at a tiny grove of teneeshee trees set in a rift in the slope.

Sanja had become very good at jumping off the back of these riding machines. She pulled off the hard, clumsy hat they made her wear and readjusted her goggles while Rose turned off the noisy rider. Then only the sound of wind filled their ears.

It must have been a new grove since the tallest tree stood three feet. Teneeshee trees can get a full 8 feet high at maturity. The tiger grass around the trees had not spread very far into the crannies of the lava field.

"Looking good." Rose had her hands on her hips and nodded with approval.

"You planted this one?"

"Yes, the trees and the grass. There is enough shelter here now. We can plant a couple capariousтрees, laidir gourds, and some thorny fan. Let's get the seeds." Rose turned to the riding machine.

Sanja moved forward and helped her unstrap the pack.

"You know," Rose said, "I'm glad you came to live with us. Ever since Brett's accident, neither Reece nor Zaibry have been able to help me with this and it's more fun with company."

Sanja almost smiled. But then stopped herself. The feeling of her own safety and acceptance brought guilt when she remembered her family and the danger that hung over them. Sanja stole a look over the lava field wishing she were a tiny bug that could fly away to them, if only for a moment, to see if they were well.

"Come on daydreamer." Rose's teasing broke into her thoughts. "You can stare off into space once we scatter seeds and collect tiger grass."

"You can't eat tiger grass or make baskets or garments out of it. It is worthless."

"True, but we want the seeds because it grows anywhere."

"So does lava brush. And you don't have to do anything to help it grow."

"Aye, but the lava brush doesn't prepare the ground for other plants nearly as well as tiger grass."

"Why do we go to all this trouble? Won't these things happen on their own?"

"Sometimes they will. But it doesn't hurt to help it along. We all use these plants. And the Hermits say that the Founders used to do this sort of thing all the time, trying to make Eclectia a better place to live."

Sanja never understood when they brought up the Founders. Her people rarely spoke of them. If they did, it was usually in the form of a curse. "But you don't know if this mountain will cover itself with more flowing rock and kill everything."

"We don't know whether she will or she won't. Either way, it doesn't matter. You keep on casting your bread on the water and scattering seeds because you never know what the future holds. And the seeds we scatter today may save our necks tomorrow."

59. ESCAPE, PART 3
TRAVIS PERRY

In the early morning hours, the holding cell's lights dim, Ernsto awoke from his thinly padded steel bed to the sound of the cell door opening. He sat up, clutching his single blanket for warmth.

Officer Romero stood on the other side of the open door, an unknown peacekeeper beside him. "Come on," said the young officer. "We're getting you out of here."

"What…why?"

"I believe Hobson means to kill you. And the angel as well. I don't think we can keep you safe here, or anywhere else I know of. He's too well connected and too…powerful."

As Ernsto stood up and dropped the blanket, he felt the crude bandages on his back sticking to the bright yellow jumpsuit he'd been forced to wear. "I don't suppose you brought a change of clothes for me?"

"Yes, but not here. We need to move, no talking."

The two men escorted him out of the Avenir upper brig. For some unknown reason, no other officers were in sight. Through a back corridor they escorted him to a loading dock. A familiar black pressure tank on a robotic wheeled cart waited there. *Ah, angel babe, so glad to see you,* said his mind. A familiar rush of warmth answered him back.

"On the other side of the airlock is a shuttle, with clothing and some equipment inside," Romero said. "You do mean to return the angel to the sea, right?"

"More than anything."

"Then take her and go."

"Er…as much as it's not like me to question good news, won' this get you in trouble?"

"Possibly. But who knows that the infamous smuggler Ernsto Mons didn't force his way out? Not that I would ever lie about that. Or anything else. But I hope people draw their own conclusions. I don't suppose you'd be willing to come back here for trial, after you set the angel free, risk to your life or not?"

"I don' suppose you'd believe me if I said I would?"

"I don't believe so," replied the enforcer with a grin. "Well, don't think this means I won't put your face on every enforcer bulletin I can. You'll be more famous than ever after this—which will make it very tough to sneak anything past anyone ever again. I'd give up smuggling if I were you."

Before he could answer, the unnamed peacekeeper inserted himself into the conversation. "If it wasn't for the angel, I wouldn't do anything for you. If I see you on Avenir again, I'll shoot you on sight. Understand?" The tall, gray-haired man scrunched his eyebrows together as he spoke, making his menace clear.

"Understood," he said mildly, some part of his mind surprised that he'd let anyone threaten him without any desire to threaten in return.

Officer Romero shook his hand before he departed, but the peacekeeper kept glaring at him and warned, "Hobson is still after you. If you don't keep a low profile, he'll have you dead within the week."

"Understood," he replied again, this time in a whisper.

Within minutes he had changed, astonished to find his coin bag inside his pants pocket. He then powered up the small shuttle, getting ready for the quick flight to Eclectia, the angel in her portable tank behind him.

60.   ANCHOR TO THE WORLD
H. A. TITUS

Pieter Kinsrol sat on the catwalk, looking wistfully down at his ship, the Anchor. He'd always liked that word. Something firm and strong, to hold you fast. The ship was his anchor, holding him fast—otherwise, he might have set himself adrift a long time ago.

The sound of feet pinging along the catwalk made Pieter raise his head. A girl in a tattered jumpsuit came to his side, sat down, and started swinging her legs.

"Hello," she said. "Why aren't you in your ship?"

"Two Foundings of probation. They haven't installed the electronic sensors yet."

"I was wondering what sentence you got. They wouldn't let me into the courtroom to hear. Not even to testify. Guess no one likes hearing the truth from an orphan."

He remembered seeing this girl as he handed out food.

"So why'd you do it?" She turned her face up toward him.

"Do what?"

"Smuggle. You're rich, so why did you have to smuggle to feed us?"

Pieter chuckled wryly. "How did you know I was rich?"

"You look it."

Pieter sighed and rubbed his face in his hands. "I started smuggling 'cause I was bored. Better than getting addicted to drugs for a rush. In the marketplace one day, I saw an orphan beaten because he tried to steal food. I felt ashamed, because I had enough money to feed all of you, and I was keeping it to myself."

"Well, thanks." The girl stuck out her hand. "I'm Cara."

"Pieter."

Cara's heels made thudding noises against the catwalk. "Y'know, if you still want to help the orphans, you could make 'em a school, where they

85

could learn jobs so they wouldn't have to steal no more."

Pieter looked down at her and saw a familiar light shining in her eyes. He remembered seeing that own light in his reflection's eyes, as he stood at the window above the docking bay as a young boy, watching the ships.

"Well, the only thing I'm good at is piloting ships. Maybe I could teach that to the orphans. Why don't you come tomorrow, and we'll talk about it some more?"

Cara's eyes sparkled as she nodded and rose to her feet.

As he watched her dance away, Pieter felt a warmth of satisfaction in his chest. Maybe he had more than just the Anchor to hold him here now.

61.   EVOLUTION
JEFF CARTER

Dr. Kwame Singh basked in the shimmering blue light and felt the pulse of ocean currents against his skin. Even though he was thirty kilometers beneath the surface of Sheba, he felt as though he were in the oceans of Eclectia. The miners had used the blue mineral pectolite to gild the walls of their cathedral with every color of the sea. The rhythm of the waves came from a circle of drummers beating a slow and somber cadence. Since a lifetime of inhaling grit had rendered them unable to sing in loud voices, they offered up prayers with drums made from the shells of giant sea snails.

He thought of his frustrating time in dank Port Xenia. The study of Theological Drift had come to a halt around the same time as the Avenir. His parents and grandparents had made their contributions, charting the fracture, conglomeration, and slow alteration of Ancient Earth religions. The long journey across the void had opened space for a spiritual Cambrian explosion. Kwame intended to capture it by pioneering a new field called Evolutionary Theology.

The colonists of Port Xenia were wistful about the so-called 'angels' they rarely glimpsed through the portholes, but there was nothing ecstatic or transcendent in their middling culture. The first true believers he met were the miners on their pilgrimage from Sheba. Their hair was unkempt and their skin was like leather, but their eyes were tranquil and electric. These men and women had contact with the 'angels' more frequently and intensely than Dr. Singh had ever observed.

86

He had followed the miners back to Sheba and discovered the cathedral that they had built by hand. A bright light carved across the ceiling, interrupting his reverie. Supervisor Braun was stomping towards him, his helmet light glaring. "Third shift is starting. Break it up."

As the miners shuffled out they genuflected to the statues of patron saints that had been streamlined with fins and curving fluke tails. The supervisor looked at his chronometer and scowled. "Isn't there an abbey topside for this? If they don't spend less time banging drums and more time working, the technology we depend upon will fail."

Dr. Singh smiled with dawning understanding. "They risk freezing vacuum and hellish inferno every day to feed their families. Do you really think it is just technology they depend on?"

62. BEGINNING OF A DREAM (FLASHBACK)
H. A. TITUS

Nine-Founding-old Pieter Kinsrol flinched as the sharp, tinkling crash indicated that yet another bottle had been thrown against the wall.

"I said to get me some of the *old stuff*. I'm not drinking this garbage."

Pieter crept to the door of his closet-sized room—a luxury even for the rich on Avenir—and closed it softly. He could still hear his father railing against the servant, the politicians, the peacekeepers, and anyone else who had offended him lately, but at least it was muffled.

Pieter sat on his bed and pushed the metal window blind to the side. Having a window was, again, a product of his father's wealth. He smiled and pushed his fist against the glass, then splayed his fingers so his entire hand pressed against the cool, smooth surface.

To him, this was how space would feel. Smooth, cool.

Quiet.

Pieter stared down at Eclectia. How would it feel to traverse that rough, red surface?

A transport ship came into view. The metal hulk swung around, surprisingly graceful despite its bulky lines and behemoth size, and bright blue blazed from the thrusters on the back.

Pieter grinned. Forget traveling on the surface. Someday, he'd *fly*.

63.   DESCENT
TRAVIS PERRY

The shuttle separated from Avenir, Ernsto's steady hand guiding the controls. As the vessel pushed away from the station, the commo panel lit red.

"Government shuttle two alpha, this is Avenir Control, please respond."

Ernsto grimaced before replying. He didn't know much about spaceship protocols at this level. All his previous experience with Avenir Control had been to the lower cargo levels. "Control, this is two alpha, go ahead."

"We have no scheduled flight itinerary for your vessel. Please dock at sector four bravo of the station ring until control receives your plan."

"Sure, sector four bravo. Headed that way."

He eased the vessel outward to the habitation ring. He actually had no idea where 4B might be relative to where he was, but he had no intention of docking anyway.

"Your current location is sector two," volunteered control.

Ernsto steered the shuttle to follow the ring clockwise. Soon he passed some one hundred meters over a giant number 3 painted on the gray metal ring encircling the metallic dark shape of Avenir. *So four should be next; bravo will be in the middle of the outer edge of the ring.*

At 200 kph he hit sector four in less than 30 seconds. He maneuvered the shuttle to the edge of the ring and plunged downward. The alpha docking port at the top of the ring held a cutter with enforcer stripes. The vessel broke free from dock as he passed by and fixed a laser on his ship, a missile-guiding type, flickering spotty red at the rear of his cockpit window.

"Dock now or we will fire!" blared his radio. Ernsto accelerated hard, throwing as much rocket exhaust backward as possible.

Pressed hard into his seat at the four gee acceleration, his back screamed in agony. "Return to dock now or we will fire!" shouted his com system. He shut it off and plunged downward toward the gray skies of Eclectia below.

His anti-collision radar picked up no fewer than four vessels in pursuit, far more than would be expected from a missing flight plan. It seemed Hobson had found him already…

89

64. A VERY IMPORTANT QUESTION
HOLLY HEISEY

Three fingers tap on five in mnemonic blue light of the fazing screen. Tap tap tap. Once five, now three; Kerin Rhi left the ground, the water, and the world and its dangers for higher sights. He is smart, so he is here. Here is a ten by ten meter cabin on Avenir, walls slightly wedged, where he sits on his white couch and watches the peacekeepers like a god. And this disturbs him.

Kerin has decided to ask an angel what angels undersea think of the Peace Council. He has decided this is smart, but to be safe, he has of course triple locked and bypassed the security protocols of even his Council line. Maybe he is a god and doesn't know it; but it would not be good for others to think he thinks of that at all.

The screen fazes on an orange-red infrared signature, a blob among blue-green swirls from the waters below. He doesn't know if a god-link can be made this far, but it is near Approaching, and he must try. He sits forward on his couch and squints at the screen. He is not a wizard. None in his family were wizards, how can he possibly presume to talk to an angel?

How can you presume not to?

He jumps so high he almost hits his head on the bulkhead rail and floats carefully down in this less than normal gravity.

How can he presume not to? "How can I presume not to what?"

To talk to me, stupid.

Kerin blinks at the screen, wets his lips and says feebly, "Stupid?" Stupid is one thing he knows he is not. Of course, this is not an angel; it must then be a demon. Which is almost as good. He sits forward again.

"Are we gods? Are Peace Council members gods? It often feels like so, yea, it does."

The demon snorts and the blob of red ripples in the water. *Gods. What is a god? What makes a god a god but the people who worship it? Are you worshipped?*

Kerin thinks about this, his thoughts waving with the slow churning on the screen. "I am...perhaps."

Perhaps. You mean you do not know?

"I..." He thinks some more. "The peacekeepers look up to me, and I look down on them."

Well?

"But I don't know if they worship me."

So ask them.

"What?"

Ask. Them. It can't be so hard, especially if you are a god. And if you are, they'll want to know.

Kerin blinks. He hasn't thought of this. It is so simple, of course. He opens his mouth...then closes it again. He leans forward to divulge his great secret. "I can't speak to them. I am a member of the Peace Council; they can't know who I am."

Secrets are good. Secrets are somewhat godlike.

Kerin sits back, satisfied.

Ten decks below him on the station, the wizard Encimanion Coriander Peronnel wonders at the spike of neural activity between Avenir and a plot on Eclectia he's long suspected to be haunted by demons. His hands track the signal in a rush—to Room Eight in Ward Two of the Rich Men's Happy Bin. He sighs and makes a mark in his log beside "Kerin Rhi, marginally psychotic"—fifth time this month. He'll speak to Kerin later, but now, as the signal's already gone, he sends his scanners onward.

65. BURIED TREASURE
H. A. TITUS

Cara rattled the lid on a metal storage container. "Pieter, this one's stuck!"

She heard his footsteps clanging overhead, then Pieter jumped down into the cargo hold, forgoing the ladder, and hunched to avoid banging his head. He wedged his fingers under the lip of the container and pulled hard. After a few jerks, the lid popped open.

Cara peered inside. The container was a jumble of clothes and cables.

"Why are we cleaning again?" she asked, lifting a stained shirt out of the mess with a pinkie finger.

Pieter shrugged, took the shirt, and tossed it on the ever-growing pile of garbage. "The *Anchor* is due for a clean. It's not like we'll be going anywhere soon."

Cara nodded. Once the sensors were installed, Pieter would be allowed to fly as long as he stayed away from hotspots frequented by smugglers. It was just the installation that was taking so long. She reached into the box, jerked out a tangle of cables, and tossed them to the side. Pieter turned to sorting them as Cara dug into the box. More clothes, more wires, more clothes—

"By all the stars in the sky!" she said, pulling out yet another wad of clothing. "How many clothes do you need in space?"

"Oh, half of those were disguises that I never needed." Pieter grinned sheepishly. "I have a weakness for disguises."

"I guess so." Cara looked into the box to see how much more she had to go, and drew a sharp breath. A book sat at the bottom of the container. A print book. An old print book, by the look of it.

She carefully fit her hands around it and drew it out. The soft suede cover was spiderwebbed with tiny cracks. The book was sturdier than she first thought. The pages, though yellow and thin, were still attached to the binding.

"What's this?" she asked Pieter.

He glanced at it and shrugged. "An old family book my mom gave me. Said it was the only possession left from our ancestor on the generation ship. I've had it buried in my boxes of stuff for years. Never was one for books."

Hmm. Might be worth a look at. First time I've ever gotten the chance to read a print book. Cara put it to the side and continued sorting through the garbage. She'd read it tonight, if she got the chance.

66. GOODBYE
TRAVIS PERRY

The shuttle trailed black smoke as it dropped toward the ocean. Ernsto struggled with the controls to slow the landing. Behind them, somewhere, two other vessels were hunting for them in Eclectia's atmosphere.

He'd originally aimed for Zirconia but he realized it would be impossible to enter the city, not with enforcers chasing him. They'd surely radio ahead.

At an unknown location on the high sea, somewhere in the Zirconia region, the shuttle hit the water hard. It bobbed upward due to the air in the hull, but immediately afterward the fractured ship began to slowly sink.

Ernso unstrapped and seized the angel's pressure tank and shoved it toward the airlock, which he moved to release. Lock open, ocean water began pouring into the vehicle, hastening its doom. Ernsto quickly released pressure, unlatched the tank, and hauled the angel out. He shoved her into the water and plunged in after her. Seconds later on the surface, coughing cold green water, he scrambled upward, coming to his feet on top of the still-sinking shuttle.

Beneath a nearby wave he saw the angel's glowing white light. The low pressure at the ocean surface caused her pain, yet she looked past her own agony to project worry about what would happen to him.

"I'll make it, get out of here!" he shouted. There was no way for her to save him anyway—she needed to dive to the ocean depths; he could only survive on the surface.

Her mind projected understanding and regret. She dove deeper.

At that moment it struck Ernsto that he'd never loved anyone the way he'd loved her, not even his grandmother—certainly far more than any woman who'd ever shared his bed. Her mind had been so beautiful, so kind, so gentle and soothing. How would he survive without her? He fell to his knees, astonished that his heart was breaking, astonished that if he could have swum after her, he would have followed her to her underwater world and been her husband if she'd have him.

Her mind reached out to him in pity. He could feel her embarrassment at his gushing emotion. It never had been like that for her. She'd cared for him...but like a pet...

On his knees, the ocean rising, he buried his hand in his face and wept. He'd been like a pet, like a savage dog taken in by a gentle woman who believed a little loving kindness would calm its vicious ways. The love of his life, yet to her only a pet, an animal. This pain—he knew he'd never overcome it.

His peripheral vision caught a vapor trail of a shuttle overhead. It turned in a big arc across the ash-gray sky back his way, apparently having spotted him.

Ernsto Mons stood upright on the shuttle hull, water now lapping his ankles. He pulled the plasma pistol from his belt and aimed it at the incoming shuttle, his mood hardening.

"Come on," he rasped. "Come kill me."

67.   A CREATURE OF WORDS
JEFF CHAPMAN

A rocksnout slithered over the rocks on the eastern lip of the Zircon trench, a rift in the ocean floor that plunged for kilometers and yawned to a kilometer at its widest point as it zagged along the edge of the continental shelf. Four legs on the rocksnout's underside ended in four-fingered feet that gripped the rocks on which the female rested while she pumped water through her mouth and over her gills. Her mottled black and brown body tapered for two meters from a wide, flat snout, one meter across, to a forked tail only centimeters wide. Three dorsal fins rose from her back and a pair of pectoral fins jutted from her sides. Bony crenellations that mimicked lichen-encrusted stone covered the top of her snout and at its tip three luminescent tendrils wiggled with the current.

The eyes on either side of her snout took in the smallest specks of light and tiny holes arranged across the underside of her snout picked up the electrical impulses of beating hearts. She was ninety seasons old and ready to mate for the first time. She heard the low thrumming of a male somewhere in the deep ocean night. She picked out the subtle variations of tone and rhythm in his thrum, a rocksnout's version of speech. She responded. She called herself Thrawto.

With a swish of her tail, she glided over the ocean floor. It seemed odd to swim, to fly over unbroken fields of sediment. She spent most of her life crawling over rocks on the wall of the trench, searching for caves and crevices that afforded a lair to wait for prey to investigate the glowing tendrils at the tip of her snout. There was no room to swim in the caves and it was not wise to swim in the depths of the trench.

Thrawto swam for hours until hunger gnawed at her stomach. Something glowed on the horizon to her left, a gathering of the bright, winged ones, she assumed. Their accumulated light would blind her and she would not eat them. They passed their thoughts and meant no harm.

She sank to the bottom behind an outcropping of rock encrusted with the browns and greens of sea lichen, a favorite of the grazing fish on which rocksnouts thrived. Thrawto nestled in the silt to wait.

A heartbeat, large and strong with an unfamiliar rhythm, approached. Thrawto tensed, ready to attack or flee or hide. Tremors rippled through the silt. This creature crawled over the ocean floor, a lumbering target.

It emerged from behind the rocks in front of her. An odd creature, she thought. A pulsing stream of bubbles rose from its bulbous head. A single, glowing eye stabbed the night. A hump protruded from the creature's back and a limb emerged from each corner of its body. No wings, no webbing, no fins or tail. Thrawto readied to strike. She had eaten stranger animals in the trench.

The creature leaned toward her, peering at Thrawto's worm-like appendages with its single eye that emitted a shaft of blinding light. Her eyes squeezed shut on impulse. In perfect coordination, her legs pushed and her tail snapped. She shot forward, grabbing a lower appendage near the body, hoping to sever the limb and immobilize the creature before it fought or fled. Her jaws worked from side to side and her rows of serrated teeth cut like a double-edged saw. The flesh tasted strange and no sweet blood flooded her mouth. It grunted and thrashed and slapped her bony snout, but amid the screams, she heard sounds and rhythms repeated.

"Kazzeee. Kazzeee."

Words?

Thrawto relaxed her jaws and the creature fell away, flailing its arms, trying to swim most ineffectually. No blood fumed from the jagged wounds in its hide. How curious. A storm of silt enveloped the struggling animal and snuffed its light. Thrawto gave a kick with her tail and left the odd creature to its fate in the deep ocean night.

68. BREAD AND WATER
H. A. TITUS

Cara peered through the crack that led from her hidey-hole to the marketplace. Orphans, hunters, and merchants scurried around the large area, giving no sign that they'd seen her worm into the pile of broken beams.

Another night safe. She sighed, snuggled down in her pile of rags, and pulled her one whole blanket up to her hips. The space was just big enough for her bed and a wooden crate of belongings, but she preferred it over the shared rooms at the orphanage.

Cara reached into the crate and gingerly pulled out the book she'd found in the *Anchor*'s cargo hold. The leather cover crackled as she opened it to the first chapter.

Genesis.

She read through several books with odd sounding names like *Exodus* and a really boring section called *Numbers*. She skipped ahead and found *Judges*, a book with some weird stuff in it, like a guy getting a tent stake pounded through his head.

That's gross. As she paged toward the back of the book, she tried to remember when she'd learned to read. Most of the orphans couldn't read or struggled to sound out basic words.

She'd been able to read when she was five, she knew that. She remembered standing on the street corners and reading the marketplace signs for fun while she waited for her dad to come collect the money she'd gathered from pick-pocketing that day.

At least, he'd said he was her dad. Cara shivered and turned a chunk of pages. A line in red caught her eye and she paused to read it.

"Will you give me a drink?"

She backtracked. A teacher named Jesus was traveling through a place called Samaria when he met a woman by a well. As they talked together, Jesus told her about this water that could give her eternal life.

Now this was interesting. Lots of people wanted eternal life. She kept reading.

Several chapters later, she found a story where Jesus talked about being the 'bread of life'. How could bread and water give life? How could a man be bread?

With a buzz, the lights in the marketplace dimmed. She shut the book and looked out. The stalls were shuttered, the street deserted. *Must be midnight.*

Cara put the book in the crate and plopped her head on her pillow. Just as well. She needed to sleep on what she'd read tonight.

69. PATIENCE
TRAVIS PERRY

One advantage to getting older is patience comes easier. The thought seemed to come from nowhere, interrupting Elsa's rambling talk with God. "Now where were we, Lord..." but she fell silent when her eyes caught movement.

Beyond the pile of black volcanic rock that served as her hunting blind, she saw the movement in the lure she'd been waiting for. Back toward the cave. The mammothbug was about to come out.

Elsa glanced down at the wick of her bronze cannon. Its white tuft stood straight up, still in place, still dry.

Months ago her family had run out of the money required for the ammunition for their modern weapons. But she still knew how to mix black powder, keeping the cannon handed down through her grandfather's line the only viable hunting weapon the family had.

The bug pushed its massive hairy head out of the cave, its bulbous red compound eyes glimmering in light of the setting sun. It had pulled back its "trunk," the hairy bug-like lure it had laid out in front of its cave, which it would wiggle seductively to draw in lesser bugs, as preparation for its once-in-five-to-eight day walk outside to regurgitate the exoskeletons of its prey.

The head hesitated a moment at the entrance, as if it knew Elsa were there. She held her breath and waited, unmoving. Finally, after what seemed to be endless minutes of motionlessness, the creature the size of a small house pulled itself over volcanic rubble, rumbling out of its lair.

She gently lifted the heavy butt of the cannon, lining up the shot. The bug's death would bring food and clothing to her little ones. But with the cannon, she had only one chance.

At just the right moment, she flicked the lighter and touched it to the wick. Thunder roared in the narrow valley as the cannon threw Elsa back.

70.   CAFETERIA DUTY
HOLLY HEISEY

Hoepi ladled a slap of green algae slosh on another cracked tin tray and watched another miner's nose wrinkle in disgust. If the powers that be could afford to hold a hundred and twenty-nine miners in a station tethered to the coolest spot on one half of Sheba…well. They could afford to give those miners decent meals. And hire a cook, for once. She was stuck with cafeteria duty.

A rumble of voices at the door made her look up, not because they were loud or male but because she recognized the first and her hand faltered just a beat on the ladle.

"Hey!" One-armed Micki, her latest victim in the slop line, jumped back to avoid getting green slosh on his coveralls.

Hoepi turned back to the slop line and started to blush, then thought better of it. "You just watch yourself, Micki." Which made no sense, so she turned her back and stirred the steaming pot of proto-meatballs with a vigor.

"Hey."

She whirled. Tennant. She met his eyes for the briefest flicker.

"Hey, Hoepi."

He knew her name.

She shook her head. *Yeah, idiot, of course he knows your name. You only mine with him every second five-day.*

She brushed dark hair from her eyes. "Yeah, what do you want?"

Tennant held up his tray and gave her a weary, flashing grin. "Some puke-my-guts special with a side of almost-ham." He patted his flat stomach. "Worked hard today."

Hoepi flustered and dumped green slosh and proto-meatballs in a mess on his tray. He turned to the tables…then stopped.

"Hey Hoepi. Was gonna play handball later in the tank. Want to?"

She opened her mouth. He turned more fully, an impish smile on his cracked lips. "Say yes."

She nodded.

"Good enough!" He flopped down at a table and promptly fell into terse conversation with another knot of miners.

Hoepi stepped back from the slop line. A grin stretched her mouth from ear to ear.

"Hey, Hoepi!"

She turned to the next in line and scowled at him. "What?"

71.   COG
      H. A. TITUS

"Hey Cara, where ya been lately?"

Cara trotted faster. "Buzz off, Denton!"

A foot slid between her shins, nearly making her do a faceplant into the metal floor. Cara caught herself against the wall and spun to get her back to it.

Denton and Strand crowded in close, while Robynn hovered behind them. Cara crossed her arms over her chest and gave them her best glare.

"Been missin' ya around the market," Strand said. "Where ya been?"

"Busy," Cara said.

She noticed that several other orphans had stopped, listening to the conversation. A couple of them were old friends, but they didn't look too inclined to stand up against Strand and Denton.

"Busy doin' what? Someone said you made friends with a rich kid," Strand said.

Denton frowned. "You turnin' your back on us, Cara? For what, expensive toys and pretty things?"

Someone else snickered. "Little young to have a boyfriend, aren't you, Cara?"

"He's going to teach me how to fly!" she said.

They all stared at her. For a moment, Cara thought they believed her. Then Strand snorted and rolled his eyes.

"Yeah, right," Denton said.

"No one's going to trust an orphan with the controls of a ship," Strand said. "The best we can hope for is bug hunting when we get older."

"But logically, she could be telling the truth," a boy with welding goggles pushed into his mop of red hair said.

Denton glared at him. "No one asked for your logic, Cog."

"I guess you've cleaned the earwax out since we last talked, since you can obviously hear me this time," Cog said, a smile curling the left corner of his mouth.

Cara noticed that despite Denton's angry glare, he looked hesitant to even get close to Cog. Then she noticed Cog's right hand was metal. That explained it—Denton had probably tasted that metal hand once or twice before.

"Explain your logic, Cog," she challenged. "Why don't you think I'm lying?"

"Flying is so far above our status. Why would you use that for a lie if you wanted to be believed? It's like a boy with blocks claiming he's God just because he can build a tower and knock it down—outrageous. It's so outrageous that if you were lying, no one would believe you. So I think you're telling the truth."

Most of the kids had moved on by now with exaggerated sighs about the weird ways Cog's mind worked.

Denton still looked unconvinced. "I still think she's lying."

Cara shrugged. "You can think that all you want. I wasn't interested in your opinion anyway."

"Little—" Strand started.

Cog slipped in beside Cara and put his hand on her shoulder. "Since you're not interested, Denton, then why don't you move on?"

Strand and Denton both shot glares, but Robynn whispered in Denton's ear and he slowly turned away. Cara watched the threesome disappear into the marketplace, then she looked up at Cog.

He grinned. "You were telling the truth, right? So far my logic has been right, and I don't want Denton and Strand to hear you were lying after all."

She jutted her chin. "I don't lie."

"That I believe. So is there any way I can get in on these flight lessons?"

She paused. She liked working alone with Pieter—they were a good team. But Pieter *had* told her to keep an eye out for any other orphans who wanted to learn to fly. And if there were other orphans around, it would cut those stupid stories flying around about Pieter being her boyfriend.

Yuck.

Cara jabbed her thumb over her shoulder at the hangars. "Dock Seventy-three. Tomorrow morning at eight."

"Can I bring my sister, Clock?"

Cog and Clock. Cara had heard some weird names around Avenir, but these two probably took the cake. "Sure. Just be there at eight sharp."

Cog's grin curled around to the other side of his mouth. "Got it."

72. FORGIVENESS
TRAVIS PERRY

The fist-sized cannonball made a neat puncture in the seam that ran down the middle of the mammothbug's exoskeleton. Dazed by the blast of the cannon as she was, this was not the first thing Elsa noticed.

The first thing she realized was the bug charging her way, roaring in pain. It wasn't until long moments afterward that some detached and objective part of her brain realized the shot actually *had been* in the right place, it *should have* hit the bug's heart, killing it instantly…

Her mind pondered but her body scrambled up the rock face immediately behind her, knowing the bug would come straight after her and was a poor climber. She moved as fast as her elderly frame would bear, the bug roaring behind her—too close. The only thing that soothed the bitter certainty that she would die was the fact she had been certain of her own death before—and lived.

"Help, Lord!" her mouth said, it in turn operating independently of her slow-moving body and shot-critiquing mind. She found hand-and-toeholds and moved upward, not fast enough, she knew, as the bug's roar drew terrifyingly near.

But then from behind her came the muted crack of a scythegun followed an instant later by the roar of its projectile breaking the mammothbug's back. Elsa glanced down and saw the bug's last twitching movement before death. Its carcass was not even two meters from the rock face.

Behind the bug's body, she saw her savior, a grim-faced bearded man, in new-looking clothes, about a hundred meters away. "Thank you, young man!" she shouted and waved, feeling her face spread in a wide smile.

He approached without saying a word until he was close, holding his hunting spear in his left hand and the scythegun in his right. By then, Elsa had recovered her cannon and her skeleton saw. She would need to cut the carcass in pieces and carry it in bits to get it home. She'd be lucky to get it all back before the scavengers arrived, but once she returned with the first piece, the children would help with the rest. She began her work, starting to saw off the right front leg.

"What are you doing?" said the man, now only meters away, his firearm not quite pointed at her but not quite pointed away, either.

"Oh, taking home some of this kill for my little ones." Observing his scowling face, she added, "Since you were so kind as to help me, perhaps you would like to take half for yourself?"

Now the weapon pointed itself directly at her. "This is my kill. Move along outta here."

"Surely there is enough here for both…perhaps you would like to take three-fourths of the beast? I really need at least a small part for my family …you see, one of my sons abandoned us long ago and the others have died

101

in the hunting, the last leaving a very pregnant wife and five little ones behind." She smiled as sweetly as she knew how, trying her best to appeal to his sense of human decency.

"My kill, old woman," his voice growled, not sounding particularly human. "Shove along. NOW."

She moved, bitter tears streaming down her face. *Why, dear God,* she thought, *would you save me from a quick death only to let me die a slow one?*

She glanced back behind her and saw the man carving her bug into neat slices with a powered blade, paying no more attention to her at all. And it came to her in a flash of insight what she should do. There were a whole series of little ridges in this narrow valley—she should duck behind one, reload the cannon with the last of her powder and the last cannonball and kill the man stealing the food from the mouths of her little ones.

Behind a ridge no more than twenty meters from her intended prey, the powder and cannonball in place, heavy guilt flooded Elsa's soul. *This is wrong*, she acknowledged and knew with bitter resentment that no matter what it would cost her, her God demanded one thing from her: forgiveness.

Elsa wept bitterly.

73.   UNTIL AGAIN
KAYE JEFFREYS

"Jereth, wait!"

Only one voice on Avenir had the power to slow Jereth down…and that was it. Jereth stopped pushing through the crowd in the narrow corridor and turned.

A man in a flight suit cussed him. Jareth lifted his chin and stared him down. The crew member looked away and scooted around. Social status had its perks.

Jaren caught up with him. "Are you leaving without telling me?"

"If I told you, then I'd have to explain." Jereth looked up at the silvery lighting system rather than at Jaren. Regret hollowed his stomach.

"I know why. It's *him*. You had another fight."

"You heard us?"

"Not just me."

"So much for maintaining appearances." Jereth adjusted his pack's strap on his shoulder. "How did you know I was leaving?"

"I found the note that you scheduled for tomorrow. The 'take care of Neenah' note. Where are you going that you can't take your cat?"

Jereth deflected him. "Will you take care of her?"

"I will spoil her. Where are you going?" Jaren wasn't thrown off.

"Zirconia. I explained in the note." Jereth lied but gave Jaren the best believe-me look he could summon. After all, he *was* going there first.

"I come of age soon. You couldn't wait?"

"*He* would have expected it and stopped me. I can't risk that. These walls are closing in on me." Jereth scanned the bobbing heads of people rushing to and fro. A woman glared at him as she pressed by. This time Jereth smiled. They were in the way and he didn't care. He was over this place.

"Don't forget me." Jaren's words brought Jereth out of his small enjoyment.

"I could never forget you, brother."

"Half brother." Jaren hung his head.

Jereth rested his hand on Jaren's shoulder. "You are the only brother I have."

Jaren wouldn't look up. This was what Jereth was trying to avoid. An emotional separation.

Neither of them were good at it. He fought off a tear that pricked his right eye.

"Look at me." Jereth released Jaren's shoulder, brought his forearm in front of his chest, parallel to the floor, and fisted his hand.

Jaren reluctantly brought his arm up so that his fist touched Jereth's elbow and Jereth's fist touched Jaren's elbow, making the sign for the Farewell Promise.

They said in unison, "Until again."

74.   A MATTER OF HUNGER
GRACE BRIDGES

Smith loitered in a dim corner of the Level 18 marketplace in the central core of Avenir and chewed on his last lavabush seed. There'd be no more until another freighter docked—and then only if he was in the right place to catch any that dropped during transfer.

He peered along the row of meatmongers, noting which had shelled their wares already and which merely laid out the sections of beetle carapace with the meat still inside. He preferred the ready-to-cook variety, because it was quicker to "dispose of," and there would be no evidence except in their stomachs.

A rumble within reminded him to be quick about his task or he'd lose the opportunity. He gave the signal agreed for today—three sharp raps on the nearest support strut. At the metallic clangs, two dozen ragged children emerged from the shadows, roughly grouped in two gangs who proceeded to charge at each other with full-throated yelling and blood-curdling screams.

The merchants, fearing the worst, ducked for cover and ran into the outer passage. The crowd of shoppers rolled back in waves with cries and screams, one of whom came down often enough that he recognized her— Tomika. But she didn't scream like her friend.

Now ignoring the crowd, Smith darted along the tables as he unrolled his antigrav sack, a clever device that suppressed the artificial gravity field for its contents. Slab after slab of the best beetle steak slid into its dark maw.

He paused only once to look up at the staged fight—the kids actually enjoyed this, he could tell, and grinned at their exaggerated anger and fake punches.

Smith stuffed one more massive steak into the bag and pulled it along in the air behind him to a little-used service corridor. He tapped a strut to signal dispersal of the battle, then slipped inside a hatchway with the treasure clutched tight.

Tonight, the children would eat.

75. HOSPITALITY
TRAVIS PERRY

Elsa studied the grim face of her pastor, Elihu Simmons.

"Elsa," he said with the raspy wheeze of the early stages of ash lung, "You know I don't get paid hardly a thing by the congregation, that I hunt bugs to make my living, just like you."

She stood at the entryway to his cave. He leaned on the chiseled doorway as he spoke with her, looking down at the ground, his face tinged with red, framed by his ash-flecked beard and graying mane of hair. His gaunt wife in the room behind him cast uneasy glances her way.

"That's why I haven't asked you before now, Preacher. I know our church isn't rich—we're lucky to have a church at all in this place. The rich churches build their universities and cathedrals but don't do anything for us—"

"Give 'em credit," he interrupted, "They send travelling ministers on a regular circuit. And give out things. Like old clothes and such—"

"But you live with us. You're one of us and share our troubles. That's why I've always respected you, Preacher. That's why I've been a faithful member of your congregation. And never asked you for any help…until now." Tears clouded Elsa's eyes.

Simmons cleared his throat, still looking down. From somewhere behind his wife a baby began to wail. "Sarah," he said after turning his head back. "Please fetch all the bug legs we've got on the shelf. I can always go back out for more."

His wife's eyes showed the whites of her astonishment, but she arose without a word. In less than a minute she was at the doorway, handing them over to Elsa in a rough sack woven from the long fine bristles that line the legs of powder bugs. The sack held six scrawny legs.

"Thank you so much, Preacher. God bless you," sang Elsa.

Pastor Simmons's face flushed a deeper red. "I'm just sorry I couldn't give you more, Elsa. Very sorry. Would you like to come in for some tea?"

"No thank you. Have to get back to feed the grandkids! They haven't eaten in three days." On an impulse she kissed his cheek. The pastor's face somehow looked even redder, glowing like the ruddy sunshine during a dust storm. His wife first was astounded, but then she smiled—perhaps because she saw no threat in a woman more than twice her age.

Elsa turned away, striding back toward her home. She knew there wasn't much meat in these half-dozen gangly legs. But it was more than a day's worth, which was more than she had any right to expect. For the Lord had taught the disciples to pray, "Give us this day our *daily* bread."

Pieter leaned back in his bed and closed his eyes.

In a way, night was a relief. It meant Pieter could go back to his cubbyhole of a living space and disappear from the world for a while. Away from the prying eyes of the enforcers. Out of range of the stares from people in the docking bays who recognized his picture from the news reports.

It meant a break from Cara. He liked the girl, but sometimes her incessant questions grated on him. *You had so much money, why did you get bored? Do the rich people really have cyborgs to serve them? Do you know where Avenir came from?*

Lately, her questions had been taking a disturbingly spiritual turn. *Who was Jesus? Why do you think the book you gave me talks about 'living water'?* He didn't want the reminders of his mother.

But when he shoved away the cares of the day, *she* always took their place.

Chocolate-hazel eyes, silk-straight black hair pulled in an elegant knot at the nape of her neck. A fierce temper and even fiercer devotion. Jokes and small talk late into the night, a glass of wine while watching stars out the glass-fronted captain's deck.

Much worse than a few distrustful stares or never-ending chatter.

Her heart-shaped face was always in his mind, that playful fire dancing in her eyes. Even in the heat of battle, she had that spark, that vivacity, that filled his empty heart with hope and love.

She had been another mistake in the thousands that weighed on his chest. If he thought about her too long, his brain would start reciting his other mistakes.

It was like she was a piece of fruit in the bottom corner of a large orange pyramid, and if he took out his memories of her, the rest came tumbling down on top of him.

Pieter groaned and rolled onto his side, squeezing his eyes shut so tightly that his head started to pound. "Go away, Amaris. Please, please go away."

77. DODGER
FRED WARREN

Smith leaned against the corridor bulkhead and smiled as Kate ladled out stew to the queue of ragged children, each waiting patiently for their portion. It had been a good raid—enough meat, vegetables, and water to sustain his little army for a week, maybe two. Maybe they ought to try for blankets next time—heat to the lower levels of the Avenir station had been intermittent the past few days. They could stitch some of the material into fresh clothing.

"You're a fool, Smith."

He slid a hand toward the knife in his back pocket, then relaxed as the speaker emerged from the shadows. "Evenin', Wallace. Come for a bowl 'o beetle? Kate's in top form tonight, and it's as fresh as it comes."

"Already ate. Better'n this slop."

"I doubt that. State your business, or begone."

"Why're you still playing nursemaid to this pack of sewer rats when you could be second in my gang and live like a king?"

A toddler circumvented the line and went straight to Kate, bowl outstretched. She administered a mock scolding, then filled his bowl anyway.

Smith chuckled and pointed at the child. "I like them. Better than I like you."

"Whuzzat?" Wallace snatched at the pocket of Smith's coat before he could react, coming away with a tattered book which he held up for inspection in the dim corridor lightglobe.

"Give that back!"

Wallace grinned, revealing a row of discolored teeth, several missing. "As I live and breathe...Oliver Twist! I remember when the wizards came and passed these around. Waste of time. Hardly any of us could read."

"Enough could. Some of us still teach the young ones." Smith grabbed the book from Wallace and stuffed it back into his pocket.

"Rot and drivel, every word. But you believed it, didn't you?"

Smith didn't reply. He returned his attention to the children.

Wallace's eyes lit up. "Aha, you *still* do! *That's* why you won't join up with me. You fancy yourself the Artful Dodger, watching over your band of adorable urchins. Do you line them up in the marketplace when the

107

Welfare Society matrons come 'round? Little tin cups and thumbs in their mouths, hoping some rich, barren hag makes an Oliver out of one of them?"

"Shut up, Wallace."

"Now me, I always admired Bill Sikes. He was a man's man, owed nothing to nobody." He looked Kate up and down, running his tongue over blistered lips. "Saw something he wanted, he took it."

"Sikes found himself dangling from the end of a rope." Smith took a step to the left, putting himself between Wallace and Kate. "You keep mixing it up with the peacekeepers, they'll Frank you. You'll spend the rest of your life with a head full of chips and wires, scrubbing toilets for those barren hags you despise."

"You think they don't do the same to the little cherubs they adopt? Rich folk want their pets obedient and housebroken."

Smith seized Wallace by the collar and flung him down the corridor. "Get out of here. Don't show your face on this level again, unless you want it rearranged."

"Last chance, Smith. Drop the apron, and be your own man. I won't ask again."

"You have my answer."

Wallace straightened his jacket, locked eyes with Smith for a moment, and spit on the deck as he stalked away.

The children fed, Kate left the kettle to stand beside Smith as he watched Wallace vanish into the gloom. She slipped an arm around his waist. "Friend of yours?"

Smith shook his head. "No. Not anymore."

78.   JUST REMEMBER (FLASHBACK)
   KAYE JEFFREYS

Jereth crept around the corner, resting his little hand on the wall. Mommy sat on her bed in the dark with her face in her hands. Her shoulders shook. Jereth had never seen her cry before. She often stared off into space. But the child had never seen silent sobs make her whole body shudder.

He could take it no longer. "Mommy, don't cry."

She turned. "Jereth, what are you doing here?"

"Sergie brought me home early." He looked to the floor, ashamed.

"Come here." She reached with both arms. Jereth ran to her. She lifted him up and set him on her lap. Mommy always smelled sweet like the desserts Sergie made.

"Why are you crying?"

She smiled at him. A tear pressed from her eye and she wiped it away. "Sometimes I get sad."

"Why, Mommy?" He brushed a strand of her hair away from her eyes, like she did to him when he cried.

After looking at him with eyes that said, 'I love you so much,' she said with her mouth, "Jereth, I will tell you if you promise never to tell your father. He would be angry if he knew I told you."

Fear pulled on Jereth's stomach. He knew his father's anger and whispered, "I won't tell."

Now Mommy stroked his hair. "I miss my home."

"We *are* home."

"This is my home now, here with you. I lived somewhere else before."

"Where?" Jereth snuggled into her shoulder.

"I'm from the High Country of Eclectia."

He twisted a bead on her long necklace between his finger and thumb. "What is Ecle...tia?"

"You will learn about it in school. But if something happens to me, I want you to know about our family in the High Country."

"What is going to happen to you?" Jereth sat up. Fear tugged again.

"Nothing," Mommy's smile soothed him. "I just want you to know about our family so that if you ever want to leave this place, you can go find them."

"They are my family too?"

"Of course they are."

"How will I find them?" Jereth yawned, rested against her shoulder and twirled the bead some more.

Mommy rubbed his back. "Look for them among the Miners of the Five Rims. Can you say that? Miners of the Five Rims?"

Jereth shook his head and pressed his face into her blouse, ready for his nap.

Mommy whispered in his ear, "Then, just remember."

109

79. DILIGENCE
TRAVIS PERRY

The four grandchildren lay next to one another on the fiber mat on the cave floor, wrapped around by two thin blankets. While they slept sound after their first meal in days, bug leg soup, Elsa reevaluated her life. She couldn't hunt forever; there was no doubt about that.

She seemed immune to ash lung; she thanked God for that, unlike her son and daughter-in-law, both now dead. But her strength had faded from what it used to be and she wasn't getting any younger.

Hunting had changed, too. Once mainly the livelihood of families determined to strike it out on their own and be independent in this harsh land, it had become a commercial enterprise. Hunting bugs, taking parts back to the new Palmer camp by Adagio with all its tents for paid shipment to Zirconia or up to Avenir, was a business that paid poorly, poor enough that usually only desperate souls turned from whatever they had done before to hunt bugs here. They mostly hunted with spears, because killing in silence allowed them to take in more beasts in the long run than did firearms, which brought in more money. But it used to be, hunting never paid at all. It used to be that nobody came here from elsewhere. Back then, none of the hunters had fancy backup weapons like those scytheguns…

Hunting had changed, continually filled by a fresh pool of hungry young men. An old woman just could not compete.

Tears streamed down her face when Elsa understood what that meant. She would have to abandon the cave, an ancient lava tube into which her great-grandfather had hewn out a door by hand. The family would have to move into the tents of the new camp, with all its danger, or the town, with all its crime and debauchery. *Lord, lord, oh lord, please give me the strength.*

In the morning she hauled up a fresh bucket of water from the well carved out by decades of work by her grandfather. A hot spring filled the well, so the bucket steamed in the cool morning air.

The youngest child, Misha, age five, was already awake and beaming at her with joy. "Dear child," she said, kissing the curly locks of his head.

She woke the other three, having them wash their faces and hands in the warm, mineral-bitter water. They ate the breakfast she'd warmed of leg soup. By then the bucket water had cooled enough for drinking, and all of them took long draughts.

They loaded up all their kitchenware—the pot, two knives and a ladle, and bugshell plates and bowls. Elsa added the household goods, the one precious family Bible, passed down from generation to generation, the blankets, the mat, and the cannon, along with a single old spear. The children carried each one a portion of the goods, but Elsa reserved the heaviest thing, the cannon, for herself.

After the long walk of nearly a whole day from Tube Hill, tears rimmed her eyes to see the beaten-up tents of Palmer camp outside of Adagio, their new home.

She sold most of their goods, especially all the metal. She found work cleaning the tavern floor, in exchange for paltry broken pieces of bugshell and food, even though her people had always frowned on all forms of liquor and any association with it.

She labored late into the night, exhausting herself in the twilight hours, forming shells' bits into little bowls and plates and smaller items. She exchanged her few goods for bigger pieces, enough to eat off of, and with discipline and diligence, there was enough left over to sell to the Palmer Trading Company about once every other week, many dozens of hours of toil for a few small copper coins.

She saved her coppers and her one silver piece, struggled to trust the Lord to not worry about camp robbers and what the hunter men might try to do to her one granddaughter, and prayed and prayed and prayed for her grandchildren every waking moment and sometimes in her dreams. The grandchildren helped her in her labors, even though none of them knew why she was working so hard to save coin.

Insight, from the Lord no doubt, had told her that she would not live long enough to see the grandchildren reach adulthood. She had to provide for them past her own life, even if the life she gave them would be strange, dangerous even.

All the copper she saved, all the continual ache and pain of her endless handiwork, all served one purpose: to pay the passage to send her grandchildren to the orphanage in Zirconia.

Hazy whiteness blurred with colors as they moved in and out of his line of sight. The sound filtered to his ears, sounding similar to the time that Denton had shoved his face into a vat of brine for salted bug meat.

The one thing that he could clearly feel was the pain—the throbbing ache in his right wrist, and—not really pain for his left hand. More like a cramped, prickly feeling. Like someone had been clutching his hand tightly for hours.

One word, a familiar word, floated by, and he grasped at it, rolled it around in his head like a bearing, until he understood it.

"Cog?"

He forced his eyes to focus. They felt bruised and ready to fall out of his face.

His sister's blue eyes came together, clear in the blur. "Hey, sleepy-head!"

A second face joined his sister's, a woman in white with a funny-looking cap on her head. "Stay calm, Clock. Your brother just went through a lot of trauma—you shouldn't excite him."

"Trauma?" Cog muttered, trying to sit up. His right wrist felt weird. He was putting all of his weight on the wrist, not the palm of his hand. Why? Was his hand asleep and bending under the wrist weird?

He looked at the empty space where his right hand should be. A splotchy red and white bandage wound around the stump of his wrist.

His heart lurched. "Clock?"

"It's all right, it's all right," the nurse whispered hurriedly. "You just had an accident."

Accident. His memories came flooding back. It hadn't been an accident. Money had run out. He hadn't been able to find work for two weeks. He'd been stealing food for Clock and a meat vendor had come after him with a knife.

The nurse's lips drew together. "Such a shame," she murmured under her breath. "Such a waste." She turned away. "I suppose I should contact the orphanage about you two. Goodness knows that you'll need someone to take care of you now."

Clock's blue eyes flared. "Don't you worry about us. Cog's got a mind of metal and gears. Right now I bet they're spinning so fast that there's smoke just about ready to come out his ears. So don't you worry about us—Cog can take care of us. Right, Cog?"

Maybe so. Maybe not. But he wasn't about to go to an orphanage, not after the horror stories he'd heard from runaways.

Cog grinned at his sister. He had to be confident, for her sake, even though his own insides felt like gelled bug's blood. "Sure, sis. Sure."

81.   ROSE
FRED WARREN

I would show Rose Maylie in all the bloom and grace of early womanhood, shedding on her secluded path in life soft and gentle light, that fell on all who trod it with her, and shone into their hearts.

Smith's palm light flickered, and he knocked the device against his knee to restore its pale glow.

The energy cell was failing. He'd need to steal another tomorrow, but it would last long enough for him to finish. He flipped the final page in his tattered copy of *Oliver Twist*.

Kate brushed away a few bits of litter, sat down beside him on the floor of the corridor, and leaned back against the wall, wrapping her skirts around her legs, her breath fogging in the chill air. "Moppets are tucked away for the evening, and the guard's posted."

"Thanks, love."

She peered over his shoulder. "Thinking on Ave again?"

"How did you know?"

"When she's on your mind, you read that last chapter over and over again. Surely you've memorized it by now?"

"I want to remember her as she was. Kind, sweet, and sensible—if I'm the Artful Dodger, she was Rose Maylie."

"And yet you parted ways. You've never told me why."

"She fell ill. Fever, pain, delirium. After she recovered, she began going off by herself, down to the deepest levels of the station. She told me she'd had a vision—there were angels on Eclectia, and they'd chosen her for a great mission. She needed to stay as close to the planet as possible so she could hear their instructions."

"Is that all? Hardly the most eccentric behavior we've ever encountered."

"She became obsessed. Before, it was just me, her, and the other orphans, living one day at a time, getting by. I hoped…I even dared to plan for the future. Our future, together. After the fever, she started talking like a revolutionary, saying things needed to change, humming that idealistic old colonial hymn everywhere she went. We argued. She took half the children to wherever she goes to commune with the angels."

"I caught a glimpse of her a few turns in-station from the passenger terminal last week, sending her moppets to beg, same as us." Kate shrugged. "If she's planning a revolution, I think she'll need larger soldiers."

Smith sighed and slid the book back into his pocket. "The children still worship her, even the ones who stayed with me. I'm afraid one day she'll lead them all on some foolish crusade to right all the wrongs of Avenir, protected only by *their* pure hearts and *her* angels. She'll get them all killed or turned into little wind-up dolls for the aristocrats, just like Wallace said."

Kate surveyed the filthy, corroded corridor. "She's a mite older than you—perhaps the weight of responsibility weighs heavier on her shoulders. Can't say I disagree about things needing to change around here."

Smith shook his head. "The only way to save them is to help them survive to adulthood and steer clear of the gangs. They may have to work the mines or hunt beetles, but they'll be able to make their own choices and fend for themselves. In the meantime, a few…the smart ones, the pretty ones, the lucky ones…might become Olivers and find themselves a *real* life where they'll never be cold and hungry again."

"Fewer ladies or gentlemen of means venture down here each Founding. I think we frightened off a couple of likely marks during our last raid. Poor timing, that."

A soft whistle echoed down the corridor, followed by two more, louder each time. Smith stood up and dusted himself off. "Poor timing all 'round. Blasted enforcers picked a fine night for a random patrol. Wake the babes, Kate. Two levels down, four corridors outward ought to be enough."

She scurried away as Smith began to gather their few possessions. *And what of us, Ave?* he wondered. *What will our fate be?*

No matter how many times he read the ending, the Dodger landed in prison. Alone.

"Jereth, what are you doing here?" Kinsee stood at her door, motherly as always.

"You said to drop by whenever I'm nearby."

"I certainly did. Come in, come in." Kinsee stepped back.

Jereth walked in, set his pack on the couch, and surveyed her friendly entertaining room. Some of the best times he'd ever had were spent here with his school mate, Lessie, and her parents, Kinsee and Mitchel.

"You can stay in Lessie's room until she returns. Sit down." Kinsee sat down herself and motioned for Jereth to do the same. "What brings you under the sea?"

"Lessie finally got to me with all her talk about aid work landside. I want to join her team up there."

"Aid work? You, Jereth?"

"Yes, me. Don't act so surprised." He leaned back into the comfy sofa.

"You know that her fiancé is with her?"

"Carter? I introduced Lessie to Carter. He has nothing to worry about from me."

"It won't keep him from worrying." Kinsee shook her head then put her hand on her cheek. "Aid work? You, Jereth?"

"Aren't I allowed a social conscience?"

"You will hate it up there. It's nothing like the contained systems of Avenir and Zirconia."

"Are you trying to talk me out of helping the less fortunate? I'm serious about this, Kinsee. I've raised my own support." He patted his pack.

"I'm trying to help you understand the hazards of going landside for someone like you."

Jereth feigned mild offense. "Someone like me. You mean spoiled?"

"Vulnerable." There was nothing but concern in her voice. No judgement, no condemnation.

"The Landsiders aren't vulnerable?"

"They have built up some natural tolerances that you simply don't have."

"What about the children?" Kinsee had a soft spot. If he brought up children maybe that would make her believe him. "What tolerance do their

116

little ones have?"

"But you doing aid work?"

"Stop saying that. You are starting to hurt my feelings. Yes, Kinsee, I want to do aid work."

He hated lying to her as much as he did his brother. But he hoped it would get him to a place where he would never have to lie again.

83. SCHOOL BEGINS
H. A. TITUS

"C'mon, Cog, I said eight sharp! Where are you?"

Cara muttered the phrase for what seemed the thousandth time. Pieter turned away from tinkering with the navigation console.

"Maybe he decided not to come."

"He has to come. How will anyone take us seriously if the only one you ever teach is me?"

"Then you'll be the only orphan to ever fly a ship, and everyone else will wish they'd taken advantage of it while they could." Why was she making this into such a big deal? Pieter turned back to the console before he could snap at her.

He'd woken up in a grim mood, thanks to his continuing dreams about Amaris. He had no idea why her memory continued to dog him, and it was enough to make him dread sleeping.

"Oh, there they are!" Cara darted out onto the dock.

Pieter stood and looked out a porthole to assess his two new students. Cara was shaking the hand of a girl perhaps two Foundings younger than her. The girl had kinky-curly blond hair and seemed just as chattery as Cara, though she used big gestures on top of it.

A boy several Foundings older than Cara hung back behind the two girls, fiddling with the welding goggles pushed back in his shock of red hair.

With a shock, Pieter realized the boy's other hand, hanging down at his side, was metal. How had an orphan come by an expensive prosthetic like that? Of course, it wasn't covered with synthetic skin, but Pieter doubted anyone other than the richest aristocrat could afford skin grown in Avenir's nano-factories. His own father certainly hadn't been able to afford the skin for his prosthetic.

What were the odds that there were now two non-cyborgs in his life that had metal prosthetic limbs?

The trio came up the gangway, and Pieter stepped away from the porthole. The blond girl's gasp was loud and amazed as she entered the Anchor.

"We get to learn to fly this?" she squealed.

"Eventually," Pieter said.

The girl yelped and jumped, spinning in mid-air to face him. Her face was bright red.

"Pieter." Cara stepped up. "This is Clock." She nodded to the girl. "And her brother, Cog."

Pieter tried to keep from staring at Cog's metal hand. "Welcome aboard the Anchor."

"She's a pretty little ship," Cog offered.

Pieter smiled. "Thanks."

"So, what do we get to do today?" Cara asked.

Her impatience made Pieter shake his head. "What positions would you eventually want?"

Clock cocked her head to one side.

He explained. "I can teach you a lot about piloting and maintenance, enough to get into a ship's position, but I don't know enough about navigation to get you on a ship—you'll have to start as a different position and find someone who is willing to mentor you."

"What about gunner?" Cara asked.

"I could teach you that, if you really want to know. It's fairly basic."

"Well, I know what I want," Cog said. "Anything you can teach me."

Pieter raised his eyebrows.

"Maintenance sounds the best choice for me, but the more I know about the ship, the easier I can fix it. Not to mention that it makes me more valuable as a crew member."

"Maintenance," Pieter said dubiously. Hardly the most glamorous choice, one he'd expected.

"It'd be perfect for him," Clock piped up. "He already knows a lot of the basics and has taught me. He even built his hand."

"Cloooock!" Cog moaned, his face turning a shade that clashed with his hair.

He'd built the metal hand? Pieter rubbed his jaw. That meant Cog knew a lot more than the 'basics', whatever his sister claimed. He could very well have a genius on his hands. The thought made him wince.

Before he could say anything, Cara said, "Cog makes sense. Maybe you should teach everything to all of us, Pieter."

Clock nodded, her curls bouncing every which-way around her head.

Pieter stared at the three. What had he gotten himself into? These kids were asking for knowledge that had taken him several years to acquire. Were they up for that? He knew orphans. They were usually content to slide by on the smallest amount of effort. That's why so many of them stuck to the streets, ignoring the orphanages' offers of education and jobs.

But Cara had already stuck with him for several weeks. And Cog—that metal hand didn't speak of someone who was content with sloppy work. If Clock was anything like her brother...

"It could take a long time to learn all of that," Pieter told them. "Several years at the least, if you work hard and are diligent about coming every day."

All three kids bobbed their heads.

"Okay then." Pieter gave them a small grin. Maybe everything would work out. "Then let Avenir's first Orphans' School of Flying begin!"

The kids surprised him by giving loud cheers and jumping up and down, their fists pumping.

Pieter watched them celebrate and felt his grin stretching wider. For the first time since he'd met her, he had a feeling he was doing something that Amaris would approve of.

84.   LIARS AND THIEVES
KAYE JEFFREYS

Jaren reclined on his bed. Neenah batted at Jaren's toe with her paw then stretched herself out with a long yawn and let her head flop over the side of the bed. Jaren looked back at the forms on his note screen. There was so much to fill out before becoming a full citizen of Avenir.

Neenah jerked into a crouched position and stared toward Jaren's bedroom door. She bolted from the bed to hide under the desk.

Father was home.

Jaren concentrated back on his forms.

The door to their appartment opened. An unfamiliar growling sound entered with Father's heavy footsteps.

"Jaren, we need to talk."

This could not be good.

Father set a cage on the carpet in the front room. A small dog chewed on the bars from the inside as it growled.

Jaren's stomach hollowed out. "What's the dog for?"

Father had that smirk on his face. "This is Boris the Cyber-Mutt. Isn't that a funny name?"

Jaren didn't feel the humor. "Why is he here?"

"He's programmed to hunt down pests, especially unwanted cats."

"Neenah is not a pest. She's Jereth's cat." A shiver ran through Jaren.

"Jereth stole money from me and you won't tell me where he's gone. I will not pay to feed the cat of a thief, first born or not. And I certainly won't support a worthless cat when my younger son betrays me to protect a thief." Father bent over and put his hand on the latch of the cage.

Jaren made a bold face but could find nothing inside to back it up. "I told you, I don't know where he went."

"You are lying." Father opened the cage. Boris shot out like a missle toward Jaren's room. A blur of brown and white, barking wildly.

"Stop! I'll show you his note." Jaren tapped his note screen to bring up Jereth's letter.

Neenah howled and then shrieked.

Jaren shoved the note in front of Father's face. "He went to Zirconia, see? Call off your mutt."

Father pushed a button on the side of the cage.

The barking and screeching silenced.

Jaren bolted to his room.

Boris trotted past him with blood on his mouth and scratches on his face.

Little drops of blood stained the carpet by the desk. Jaren kneeled on the floor and reached under the desk for Neenah. A lump hardened in his stomach.

She hissed and scratched him. "I'm so sorry, Neenah." Jaren leaned back and pulled a blanket off his bed. He used it to shield himself against her claws as he fished her out. He gently wrapped the blanket around her as she fought against him. "Let me help you." He gathered her up and raced through the front room.

"This could have been avoided if you had told me the truth." Father stood with his arms crossed and victory in his eyes. "You know I hate liars and thieves."

Jaren stopped at the door. He turned. "You hate liars and thieves? Then you should hate yourself." He looked down at Neenah. Her struggling weakened. "I hate murderers."

85. ARISTOCRAT
FRED WARREN

"What were they thinking?"

John swirled his vodka, sending the ice cubes tinkling softly inside the glass, as he gazed at Eclectia. It was a putrescent tumor of a world, spattered in ochre and rusty orange. Even the ocean was a murky green-gray, mostly shrouded in clouds of volcanic ash. It looked more like a drainage pond than a living sea.

"Sir?"

"The Founders. Whatever possessed them to plant a colony here? It's the most unwelcoming place imaginable."

John's pale, expressionless valet methodically laid three tunics on the bed for his master's consideration. "It is the only habitable planet within several hundred light years," he said, without looking up from his task.

John chuckled and leaned against the window. Scooping out most of the domestic servants' gray matter and replacing it with something more...practical...did wonders for their efficiency, but little for their conversational skills. "It was a rhetorical question. Still, I would have risked traveling onward. After taking one look at this blighted rock, I would have put everyone back into hypersleep and set sail for the next available star."

"That would have added nearly five hundred years to the voyage. Most of the colonists would not have survived."

He stabbed a finger at Eclectia. "You call that living? Raking globs of metal from volcanic fissures? Chasing meat-beetles across the desert until your lungs ossify from breathing ash?"

The valet straightened the third tunic, inspected his work for a moment, and nodded. "There are the undersea cities."

"Even better. Life in an aquarium, praying the next earthquake doesn't shatter your little goldfish bowl. No, this isn't a colony. It's a joke. A monumental, insane, moronic joke bequeathed to us by an ancient troupe of comedians who couldn't comprehend how pathetically un-funny it was."

"Will you be wearing the black tunic this evening, sir?"

John walked over to the bed, lifted a sleeve on one garment, brushed the lapel on another with his fingertips, and sighed. "No, the blue tonight, I think…with the diamond studs. Something to put me in a festive mood. It's supposed to be a party, after all."

He returned his attention to the window, and the planet beyond. He sipped his drink. There was nothing but to make the best of it, he supposed. The Founders hadn't left them any other option. Things could be worse. John Milton thought ruefully of his namesake, who in this time and place might have chosen his words differently.

Better to rule from heaven than serve in hell.

86. MEETING AT MADDIE'S
KAYE JEFFREYS

Gritty wind is hard to breathe, even through a face mask. And boots are heavy to walk in. In fact, you don't really walk in them. It is more of a trudge. Jereth trudged down clearance between buildings that passed for a street in Adagio. Once past most of the permanent structures, he arrived at the pub, just outside the tents of the Palmer hunting camp. He pushed against the heavy door and went in.

"Shut the door," some lady called from behind the counter. That must be Maddie.

Jereth did as she said then moved the goggles from his eyes to his forehead and removed the mask from his nose and mouth.

A man at one of the tables stared at him. Jereth turned away and found his own table. The man was familiar but Jereth didn't take a second look.

The man got up, threw a coin onto the counter and left.

Jereth didn't sit for long. The door opened again and two people walked in. Lessie spotted him immediately, "Jereth!" she ran to him and gave him one of her famous bug hugs.

Her eyes were red and her face smudged, just like everyone he'd seen landside. "I can't believe you are here. I'm so glad to see you."

Jereth smiled. "It's good to see you." Then he turned to Carter and extended his hand, "And you too."

"Jereth." Carter shook his hand but kept a guarded expression.

Lessie put her hands on her hips. "You better have a good reason for abandoning the cat I gave you."

"Neenah? She likes my brother way better than me." Jereth pulled out a chair for Lessie.

Lessie sat. "Yeah, right. Jereth, you look great."

"I wish I could say the same about you." Jereth motioned for Carter to sit by Lessie.

"After a while you'll look like us. Are you ready to get grit in your eyes and nose?"

"I already have it in my teeth." He wasn't kidding.

Lessie laughed. "That will teach you to keep your mouth shut when you breathe."

Then it hit him. He remembered who the man was.

"What is it?" Lessie put her hand on Jereth's arm.

"Nothing." Jereth glanced at the table where Jax sat moments ago.

"Liar. You look like you've seen a ghost."

"Maybe I did. Some guy I know from Avenir was in here."

"So?"

"So, he's supposed to be dead."

Lessie shrugged. "Probably just someone down here who looks like him."

"Probably." Jereth grimaced. Too bad he wasn't smart enough to fake his own death. Then he wouldn't be looking over his shoulder for his father's thugs.

Mayor Edard Jonzn genuinely loved Adagio. Which didn't mean he was above laying aside a bit of money for himself from time to time.

The disaster-relief committee meeting was to take place in only two hours and the watergate engines that sealed off the port were down, damaged and left closed after the tsunami from the last fiveday. This was bad, because the Zirconia representative normally rode in on his personal submarine only an hour before the meeting. And Mayor Jonzn desperately wanted him to make it for this particular disaster committee reunion.

Just over a Founding ago the fresh-faced "Lieutenant" in his quasi-military uniform, a legacy from the days Zirconia was military-run, had entered his office after a committee meeting, asking if he had any bugizzard cigars. The very question marked him as an outsider—very few people on Adagio had ever even heard of tobacco, let alone smoked it. For an Adagio native, a "bugizzard cigar" was simply a "cigar."

He'd invited the clean-shaven kid over to his hand-crafted steel desk with a warm smile, looked him over, and handed him a cigar. The lieutenant had lit it with practiced ease and taken an appreciative puff. This made the young man seem different, as if he were the kind of person who kept up an appearance of propriety in public, but who secretly would have made an excellent customer back in the days Jonzn was Adagio's number one bar-and-brothel owner. The "Lieutenant"—really a sort of deputy mayor—had laughed nervously after that and then made an unusual statement:

"I have something heavy in my pocket. I don't want to bring it back to Zirconia with me." He pulled out of the front right pocket of his pressed aqua blue trousers a small handful of coins. Gold coins. Lieutenant Macbane's face flushed red. Obviously this had been his first bribe.

"For…for you, sir," he stammered as he placed them on the mayor's desk, seeming uncertain of what to do next.

Mayor Jonzn, on the other hand, had not been a virgin in the arena of "under the table" payments. "Of course, son," he'd said. "You can rest 'em right there. I'll give 'em a good 'ome, room and board, so to speak." He grinned and the Lieutenant giggled nervously.

When nothing else came, he'd prompted, "Was there anything you might want in exchange for me giving said wayward coinage comfortable lodging for the night?"

The young man had seemed to come to himself after that, drawing his stance up taller. "Just remember that Zirconia is your true friend. Adagio's interests are our interests. We expect...uh, I mean, hope for...your support should we ever find ourselves in disagreement with... other interests." By that he'd clearly meant the "governor" from Avenir.

The mayor needed no convincing for that. He hated that butt-licking skyscrubber anyway. So it had been a win-win situation. Free money for doing what he would have done in any case.

But now, with the watergates down, he'd miss this month's payment. With his daughter hounding him about buying her a new nanoweave dress imported from Avenir for her birthday, he needed every glimmer of extra coin he could get his hands on.

He stood in his office, built of ashbrick with flexible mortar and painted white with sea-conch paste. He disliked the smell, but he'd long ago covered it with the odor of burning cigars. The black phone receiver in his hand had been hand-carved from a bug's leg. Sweating nervously and smoking, he shouted into it. "I don't care what you do, I want a gate open. You have one half-hour!"

"Sir, I've got a broken servo on the west gate and on the east, the main rail is bent. I could rig the backup motor on the east side to pull open the west, but there'd be no way to close it again in an emergency— "

He cut off his chief engineer, "Sounds good, make it happen. Now!"

"But, sir— "

"You're a clever man, you'll have this solved by the end of the day."

"Maybe...but what if there's a tsunami between now and then?"

"Shut your face-hole and do as you're told," snapped the mayor. He sucked hard on his cigar, his right hand trembling.

88. WORSE THAN ASH LUNG
KAYE JEFFREYS

Jereth scraped corrosion off the terminals on Lessie's scope with a wire brush. Wind blasted the windows of the circuit office with a constant shower of ash and grit particles. The glass rattled but held against the onslaught.

Lessie sat down at the table across from him in the service room. "Why are you here?"

Jereth glanced up then focused again on cleaning the innards of her scope. Lessie wore that serious look of hers. He was in for it. She wouldn't let go of the issue until her questions were answered.

"Stop ignoring me, Jereth Davis. Why are you here?"

"To help the less fortunate." He blew dust from the prongs and examined them closely.

"Don't lie to me. Your heart is not in this."

"Why are you here?" Jereth scrubbed at the last few deposits of corrosion and blew again.

"Don't change the subject."

He put a new power pack in Lessie's scope and replaced the cover. "Why do you think I'm here?"

Lessie leaned back in her chair. "The Tyrant?"

"Avenir is not big enough for both him and me." Jereth set Lessie's scope down and slid it across the table to her.

She picked it up and looked at it without seeing it. "So why landside? Why not undersea?"

"He has too many connections undersea." Jereth tapped his leg with the wire brush.

"You'd risk Ash Lung and a whole lot of other things rather than deal with your father and his connections?"

Jereth set the wire brush on the table and clasped his hands on his lap to keep from fidgeting. "There is no dealing with my father. Not directly. Not through any of his connections. He's not like your parents."

"I know."

Jereth shook his head. "No, Lessie, you don't know. Because if you knew, if you really understood, you wouldn't ask how dealing with him could be worse than Ash Lung."

"Let's review. Little ones, what's your job?"

Three hands shot up. "Begging!"

"But we have to be polite," said Jeremy.

Molly nodded. "No grabbing or screaming."

"Tears and sniffles are okay," Pip chimed in.

Smith clapped his hands. "Excellent. Stay where you can see Kate, and do not leave the marketplace with any of the marks, even if they promise to take you home and adopt you. If they tell you that, bring them to me, and say I'm your guardian, understand?"

"Yes, Smith."

"That's my clever poppets. Now, Charlie and Cecile. Your turn."

Charlie shoved his hands in his pockets, looking bored with the whole affair. "I take the near side and Cecile takes the far side. We stroll around and stay casual. Look for the big'uns."

Cecile fiddled with a lock of blonde hair and recited her part: "When we find a mark, we lift one thing and take a roundabout path to drop it in Kate's bag." She scowled at Charlie. "One thing. Last time, you got greedy and nearly got us all caught by the enforcers."

"Did not!"

"Did so!"

Smith waved them down. "All right, that's enough, you two. Charlie, she's right. The marks are smarter these days, and some of them are just waiting for us to dip a finger in their pocket. Make sure they're distracted, then in, out, and away. As for you, Cecile, I need you to concentrate. Sometimes it seems like you're really shopping, not just pretending to."

The hair-twisting accelerated. "I'm sorry. There are so many interesting things. It's hard not to look. I'll try."

"Good girl. Kate will be at the center with the drop bag, playing crier for the fishmonger. As for me, I'll be working the margins, the standoffish folk who can't decide if they're too good to mix with us rabble. If there's any trouble…"

Five voices replied in chorus. "Bolt for the safe spot!"

"That's right. Everyone's on their own then. No heroes. If Kate and I can help, we will, but I want the rest of you to scuttle out of there like prime racing beetles and never look back."

Kate plucked at his elbow. "It's time, love."

"Very well. Let's keep our wits about us. Be light-fingered and pitiful. Tonight, we feast!"

~~~

Smith would have preferred a larger raiding party, but there'd been more enforcer presence of late, and one of the beetle-meat vendors had missed the carcass they nicked last time. Some of the merchants, like the fishmonger, were friends and allies, but a few wouldn't hesitate to turn Smith and his entire brood over to the authorities if there was any profit at all in it.

"Salt-Cod-Ohhh! Fifty the kilo!" Kate's voice trilled over the market's hubbub, bringing a smile to Smith's lips. He could think of only one sound he liked better. Best not to dwell on that. He tugged on his cap and scanned the crowd. No enforcers on patrol today, thank heaven. The little ones, with tearstained faces and outstretched hands, intercepted customers who'd just made purchases and were struggling with the change.

Meanwhile, Charlie and Cecile were threading their way among the shoppers crowding the aisles between stalls. Charlie paused to pull something from the pocket of a corpulent man who was arguing with a cloth merchant. Smith was relieved to see he didn't double-dip but moved smartly along. Only a practiced eye would have noticed anything amiss. Cecile was focusing on the womenfolk, tapping a succession of purses and waist packs, twirling along like a ballerina. She had promise, that one.

Suppose I'd best earn my keep, or I'll never hear the end of it. Smith sidled up to a well-dressed gentleman who was perusing a counter stacked with colorful insect shells. "Fine selection here, Guv'nor. Needin' something special for the lady of the house?"

The man didn't even look at him. "Yes, confound it. My Joanna is simply mad about these shells. It's the latest fad. Her friends use them to serve party favors and appetizers. Rather disgusting, to my way of thinking, but she won't be denied."

"They do add a spot of color." Smith leaned over to whisper in the man's ear, simultaneously reaching for his back pocket and the wallet bulging there. "But if you're looking for the best price, you ought to speak

129

with Miz Whitman, four stalls down."

"Indeed? Why, thank you. I'll do that."

"Happy to be of service. Enjoy your..." Smith frowned. Something had caught his sleeve. From the corner of his eye, he could see a thin, pale man standing behind his mark. The fingers that were holding onto his shirt shifted to grasp his forearm. The grip was strong. Inhumanly strong.

Gritty ash. The twit had a Frank watching his back.

The cyborg tapped the gentleman's shoulder. "Master, this man tried to steal your wallet. I've sent a message to the enforcers. Shall I restrain him until they arrive?"

"My wallet?" The man fumbled at his back pocket, then turned to glare at Smith. "Thief!" He backhanded him across the face, drawing blood. "Stinking low-deck trash! Hold him tight, Sixty-Three."

Smith tried to bolt, but the Frank wouldn't budge. It was like being handcuffed to a post. He hoped Kate was sending the children out of the market. She wasn't shouting out her advertisement for fresh fish any more. No one else in the crowd seemed to have taken notice, but he knew the enforcers would arrive in moments, and his heart sank as he writhed in the cyborg's steely grip.

Then he heard something strange—and familiar. The market's babble stilled. Every eye sought the ethereal music, children's voices wafting through the air, raised in song.

A pilgrim race, we wandered long
Through endless night and barren space
'Til whale's eye and angel's song
Revealed you here, our resting place

Arise, Avenir Eclectia
Stand firm, Avenir Eclectia
Be strong, Avenir Eclectia
Live on, Avenir Eclectia

There, at the entrance to the marketplace, stood Ave, surrounded by a ragged choir of orphans, their faces tilted upward, eyes closed, countenances radiant.

They sang the anthem over and over again, as the crowd listened in reverent silence. A woman standing near Smith wept, her hands pressed to her face. Even the Frank was transfixed. His grip on Smith's arm slowly relaxed, then released altogether. Smith leaped to one side, shedding his coat as the cyborg snatched at it, too late.

As he sprinted for the exit, Smith took one final, backward glance at Ave.

Their eyes met, and she smiled.

90. YOUR MOTHER'S PEOPLE (FLASHBACK) KAYE JEFFREYS

With graduation from tertiary school in a week it was hard for Jereth to take this last Seacology field trip seriously. It was hard to take anything serious that wacky Professor Bonswarzick taught either in the classroom or here on the observation decks of Zirconia. Others hung on his every word. His eyewitness stories concerning angels had half the class mesmerized including Lessie who scanned the sea held back by glass as though an angel would appear any minute. Of course, Lessie also had an eyewitness account concerning an angel.

All Jereth ever saw was oppressive amounts of water that filtered and colored the sunlight, causing dull and splotchy patterns on everyone. Oh, and the occasional floaty thing that meandered in the sea without enthusiasm.

Jereth whispered in Lessie's ear, "Kind of romantic, huh?" At least he hoped she thought so. All he felt was boredom and was looking for a diversion.

Lessie leaned into Jereth's whisper, a smile pulled at her lips.

"Let's go find a quiet corner somewhere and you can tell me about your angel sighting again." He pulled her away from the center of the room and she came willingly, even as she kept searching the sea.

In the corner Jereth put his arms around her and pressed his cheek against hers. It was all right that she searched over his shoulder for angels. She snuggled more when she thought of them.

"So tell me again what that angel said to you," he whispered in her ear.

Lessie whispered back. "She told me go landside and help the less fortunate."

"She said all that?"

"Not in those words. Not in any words. It just felt like she said something like that. She thought it to me."

"Fascinating." He pulled her tighter.

"There she is." Lessie broke free and rushed back to the middle of the observation area amidst the other spectators who gasped and spoke in hushed tones to each other.

Jereth stood alone in the corner glaring at the thing that hung suspended in the water out beyond the glass. He missed Lessie's warmth already. Why did it show up now?

It looked like it smiled at him. Then he felt it enter inside his thoughts. *Your mother's people.*

Jereth could not breathe. A weight on his chest kept him from getting air. He had to get away from it. So he turned and left.

In the rest area, Jereth supported his weight with one hand on the sink and rubbed water on his face with the other. He could not shut out the alien voice in his head.

Your mother's people.

What about them? he thought back at it.

Release Lessie and go find them.

Why would I look for filthy grit breathers on a God-forsaken vol…?

God-forsaken?

Then Jereth understood. It was never his place to decide who or what God had forsaken. But he asked-thought again. *Why should I look for them?*

If you don't you will turn into your father.

Jereth covered his eyes and nose with one hand while he continued to support his weight with the other on the sink. His mouth turned dry as it silently formed the words, "I don't want to be weak."

If you find your mother's people, you will also find strength.

Jereth's resistance drained away with the cold water down the sink.

The feeling of the angel's presence backed away. The weight on Jereth's chest lifted. He took in a deep breath. And then another.

A custodian walked in, "There's a young lady out here worried about you."

132

Jereth stood up straight. "Yeah." He wiped his hands on his clothes and checked to see if all the pain of his life had leaked out down his front. It hadn't. At least the angel had left him a little dignity. "I'll take my girlfriend to a nice place to eat, then take her home."

"Good, treat your lady right."

Jereth managed a meager smile. "I will."

91. DISASTER VISITATION
TRAVIS PERRY

Lieutenant MacBane showed up for the meeting just in time, ushered quickly into the building adjoining the mayor's, taking his seat among the half-dozen key players at the conference table. He was too late in fact to hand off his "package" to Mayor Jonzn prior to the disaster-relief committee meeting. This put the mayor in a rather foul mood.

After what "up abovers" in Avenir, in space, and on Sheba and Quatermain called "The War" (because it had been their only one), which the landsiders and undersea dwellers called "The Great War" (because there had been others on Eclectia), the Peace Council had been established to provide for a common legal system, with common police and military service, throughout all the diverse settlements in the system. Since Avenir had won the war with the help of the spacers, naturally the Peace Council met there and represented Avenir and spacer interests more than any of the people dwelling "down under." All combined undersea colonies had exactly one representative on the council, the same number all landside colonies had. One.

The Peace Council directly controlled peacekeepers and through them, the enforcers. They also appointed governors to each significant individual location, in all regions: on the ground, underwater, and in space. The governors employed "ministers" to assist them. But these appointees did not replace native local governments and institutions where they had already existed...

"Our first item for the agenda should be the Avenir Gratitude School. Avenir has paid over two hundred thousand credits to establish this groundbreaking institution, yet all we've got for our troubles is a floor, four walls with doorways and windows, and a ceiling. We've gone through three contractors, and costs keep overrunning—"

"Hey, first off, this is bidness for the education committee, which meets next fiveday," snarled Jonzn. "Second, maybe if you paid in real coin like everyone else uses, you'd get better results than you do with your useless Avenir credits!"

The governor's eyes opened wide. "Useless! My dear mayor, any of the over two hundred and thirty merchants and vendors on Avenir will fully redeem all payments made in credits, plus your local money market allows transfer to your backward hard currency, if your contractors insist—"

"At a substantial loss!"

"This is by no means *our* fault, Mayor. If the Avenir Investment Ministry's help is of no interest to you, AIM can just as well send monies to other backward areas. Such as the Zirconia orphanage, for example—"

"Not that Avenir has an orphan problem," said MacBane, rolling his eyes, chewing an unlit cigar.

The governor didn't even glance at the official from Zirconia—his eyes remained fixed firmly on Jonzn's. "Are you saying I should recommend to the Peace Council that AIM withdraw its assistance?" The governor leaned back in his aluminum frame padded chair that he'd brought with him to the meeting. Apparently the wrought iron chairs around the mayor's polished brass conference table weren't good enough for him...

Jonzn hastily changed his sneer into the best smile he could manage. Avenir credits were unfair—they benefitted the up-above economy at the expense of everyone else—and they didn't amount to all that much real money. But they were a lot better than nothing and his people needed everything he could get for them. "Look, I'm sorry, Gov'ner. Had a bad mornin'. Didn't get my lava tea this day. Of course we both want and need your help down 'ere." In the back of his mind Jonzn was wondering if he could start a rumor that would work its way up to the council and get this skyscrubber of a governor fired.

"In my opinion—" said MacBane. He didn't finish, because at that moment the tsunami warning siren sounded over the city of Adagio, the signal to close the watergates, the only things protecting the city from certain destruction.

Jonzn squeezed his round belly out from underneath the table and ran for the door to his office. There, panting from the short sprint, he picked up his landline phone and dialed the main engineer house at the gates.

Sweat drenched his head for reasons that had little to do with running.

"Tell me you got the gates fixed!"

"No, sir! The west gate is still open and won't close. I repeat, the west gate is still open!"

92.   GHOST
FRED WARREN

The room buzzed with conversation, punctuated by the occasional titter or guffaw. Glasses clinked, and a Bach sonata lilted overhead.

It was oh, so pedestrian.

John Milton hated parties. Hours of making polite conversation with people he didn't particularly like, listening to timeworn music, imbibing watered-down drinks, and nibbling reprocessed hors d'oeuvres.

He tried not to think about what might have been reprocessed to create the pretentious snacks as he scanned the crowd. Most of these drones were irrelevant—mid-level administrators, Spacer Guild functionaries, a few merchants and peacekeeper staff officers. Of more interest was the handful of Peace Council members sprinkled about the room. John's import-export business was comfortably profitable, but a few insincere compliments and discreet bribes were necessary to prevent government inspectors from looking too closely at his books.

Time to turn on the charm. He drained his cocktail and set the empty glass on the bookshelf he'd been leaning against. After straightening his blue satin tunic and twisting one of its diamond studs into proper alignment with the others, he set sail for Councilor Mkembe, who was dithering over a tray of canapés.

A flash of red caught the corner of his eye, and as he turned toward it in reflex, he hesitated. A willowy blonde woman in a low-cut crimson gown smiled at him from a corner of the room. Her eyes beckoned in counterpoise to the ironic tilt of her lips. He didn't recognize her, but John smiled in return. How could he refuse such a cultivated invitation? Perhaps the evening wouldn't be a total bore after all.

He altered his course, knocking one of the cyborg servants off-balance and sending a plate of finger sandwiches clattering to the floor. No one, including John, paid it any mind. The servant bent down and silently

135

collected the spilled food as John swerved around and through the loose circles of chattering partygoers.

The woman's smile widened, and it was dazzling. Her eyes were cerulean blue, her skin smooth and perfect. There might be three comparable beauties on all of Avenir. How could he not have noticed her before? John shouldered his final obstacle, a corpulent bureaucrat, out of the way and reached toward her.

She vanished.

93. LOOSE END
KAYE JEFFREYS

The bustle of the circuit office in Spring Plant Valley had died down for the night. Jereth sat in the darkened office alone. The closer they got to Last Stop the less ready he was to face whatever he found there. Soon it would be time to jump. He hoped there was a place to land.

The light flicked on. Carter stood in the door. An expression of confused disdain played his face. "Why are you sitting in the dark?"

"Just thinking."

"Are you packed for tomorrow?"

Jereth nodded.

"Then go to bed."

"We need to talk."

"About what."

"I think Lessie is onto me."

"Lessie? Onto you?" Disdain won out over confusion. "We are all onto you. We all know that you are using us to burn your old man and prove to him that he can't control you."

Jereth resisted the urge to defend himself. It would just prolong Carter's tirade. Better to let him run out of fuel.

"You are a user and you will never be anything else. Why Lessie and Kinsee put up with you, I'll never understand." Carter dropped into a chair by the door. Fortunately, Carter ran out of fuel quickly.

"Now that you've had your say, listen to me."

Carter put up his hands like he didn't care.

"I don't want Lessie to worry."

"Worry about what?"

"If I were to disappear suddenly, it would upset her. But I don't want to warn her before I go because she'll question me to death. You know Lessie."

"Disappear? What are you talking about?"

"I have a connection to make."

"What connection? There is nothing out here but tumble brush and spring weed. Are you coming down with High Country Hysteria?"

"Just promise me, Carter. If I make that connection, you make sure Lessie knows that I'm okay?"

Carter threw up his hands again and looked away.

"If I make that connection, I'll be gone. I'll leave you alone with Lessie once and for all. Promise me you'll talk to her."

Carter shook his head slowly like he didn't understand.

"Talk to her!"

"Okay! I'll talk to her."

Jereth sat back in his chair. Carter was a man of his word even if he gave it begrudgingly. The last loose end was tied up. Still, it didn't steady the uneasiness in Jereth's gut as he prepared to turn away from everything and everyone he had ever known.

94.   DISASTER AVERSION
TRAVIS PERRY

Adagio Mayor Edard Jonzn's mind raced for a solution. A tsunami coming in, the west water gate damaged and open—open at his command, no less. The tidal wave would push into the harbor and sweep east across it—he saw it in his mind's eye—to the lower land on that side…where his office stood…which held the conference room where the Avenir governor and the Zirconia deputy mayor, "Lieutenant" MacBane, ostensibly still waited.

Jonzn barked some quick orders over the phone to his engineer and sprinted out of his ashbrick office, through the white-conch painted doorway into the next building over, which held the conference room. At the polished bronze table sat the Avenir governor in his own chair, resplendent in his fancy nanoweave suit, his eyes wide in shock, his face drained white, along with two of his so-called Ministers.

"Where's MacBane?" shouted Jonzn.

"I…I don't know," said the governor. "He left."

Jonzn charged back out of the room, out of the building, his heavy belly jiggling in his too-tight gray suit made of Zirconia cotton. Down the hill toward the nearest sea dock he ran.

MacBane stood outside his personal submarine, in the act of stepping into it, its motors already powered up, as Jonzn shouted down, "Wait! I need your help!"

The Zirconian official paused, clearly considering pushing off without Jonzn. Instead, he answered, "Hurry up! The bay is already receding."

Jonzn saw it too…water pulling back, out of the bay…only to come back not long from now with a vengeance. He hit the end of the dock and literally jumped into the sub, landing on his hands and knees and scrambling back up to the nearest seat.

"Seal the hatch!" shouted the pilot from the single seat right behind the two round windows on the left and the right sides of the nose of the sub. "Shove off—I'll get it!" snapped back MacBane and the pilot did as he was told, the boat flying forward on the surface of the bay, twin propellers thrusting it ahead in a roar of biomass diesel. Water sloshed ankle-deep into the vessel before the Lieutenant sealed the door, which swung down from an overhead hinge.

Jonzn had always called himself an agnostic, but was seriously reconsidering the value of prayer…*Dear God, dear God, dear God…let there be enough water to make it to the gate!*

The submarine drove forward on the surface, headed for the west gate. Jonzn explained his plan in brief words.

MacBane tapped his lips with the end of the bugizzard cigar he'd been chewing. "It might work. There's a hook near the tail for the chain. But if there's not enough water at the gate…" his voice trailed off.

The chief engineer and five of his men were fixing the heavy steel chain to two rings on the inside edge of the western watergate—only the inside of the gate had the walkway where they could access it—just as the submarine pulled up alongside, careful not to get too close to the shore on the left side. MacBane broke the seal of the door and swung it up enough for Jonzn to shout instructions, new water sloshing in. The bay had receded but there remained for the moment enough water by the gate for the submarine to function. The engineer crew hooked the chain to rear of the sub and without further command the pilot pushed his throttle lever ahead as the lieutenant resealed the door. Once the chain pulled taut, confirmed by shouting and waving engineers, the pilot pushed the lever as far down as it would go and the engines roared like thunder.

The watergate, designed to roll on a track with relative ease, began to move...just a bit. The submarine jerked and shuddered as its propellers bit into the still-receding water...and the gate moved more, more quickly now. It needed to make it just over four hundred meters.

"Dear God, dear God, dear God," chanted Jonzn, his hands pressed to either side of his stubble-whiskered plump face, rocking back and forth in the passenger seat to the right of MacBane. A round portal window on his side of the sub faced away from the action of the moving gate, but gave him full view of Adagio and its harbor...which was mostly dry land by now...fishing vessels stranded on a downward-pointing curve.

Now the gate must be moving quickly, for the submarine started accelerating and the chain hadn't broken or come loose. Jonzn's prayers ceased and a smile tugged at the corner of his lips, in spite of his still-pounding heart.

Then the submarine hit land with a horrible scraping and ground to a halt. The gate, however, contained considerably more inertia than the submarine. It kept plowing ahead, its end now visible in the pilot's portside window as Jonzn looked forward.

The chain, which had gone loose as the massive gate caught up to the ten meter submarine that had pulled it, went taut again as the huge wall of the water gate passed it, rolling smoothly on its track. The chain twisted the sub around violently, now pointing tail first, and the rolling gate jerked the vessel along behind and began dragging it through the mud and rocks that once had been deep underwater in Adagio harbor.

As the submarine jerked and scraped with the horrible scream of tortured steel, Edard Jonzn instantly rediscovered the value of prayer. As he bounced, the submarine scraped, as he prayed and cursed, some part of him still looked out his portal window, which now faced the gate. The gate was beginning to slow, it was slowing, the dragged submarine acting as its brake...it would not make the last hundred meters or so to closure with the east gate...it would not make it...*dear God, dear God.*

And Jonzn then noticed some sort of structure on the floor of the harbor not far from the gate. A stone archway…as if some ancient civilization had built something in the bay, now revealed by the emptied water. But Jonzn knew that wasn't the case, there had been no ancient civilization…or he thought he knew.

Looking through his portal window, the only one looking out that side of the sub, Jonzn saw stepping through the doorway a man with golden hair and a golden sword in his hands. In a single effortless motion he slashed the chain dragging the submarine and stepped back into the arch. Then both the man, and it, vanished from view. Jonzn's mind assumed the sub had moved somehow so the arch was no longer in view. But later he realized that wasn't what happened at all.

The gate kept rolling, slowly rolling, to closure, meeting the east gate at the center of the harbor.

The gate had closed just before the tsunami hit, saving Adagio. And not too hard, either, since Jonzn realized that in his original plan, the submarine would have been trying to slow the gate as it hurled shut and probably would not have been able to undo built up inertia in time—dragging the submarine for over one hundred meters had barely managed to slow it just enough. If things had worked the way he'd planned them, he would have smashed the ends of the gates to smithereens, the west gate rolling closed far too fast, which would have been its own disaster, destroying the center where the gates met…like how the Zirconian submarine had been destroyed. He owed Zirconia, more than ever, for the use of that vessel— that was for sure. He tried to put out of his mind the other help that had come literally from the middle of nowhere.

He and his chief engineer stood over a rough metal table in the engineering gatehouse, examining the ends of a sliced chain. The man turned to him, "Boss, what I can't figure is how you would have done it. Maybe with explosives or something you could, not that you had any on you that I know of—but it wouldn't turn out like this at all." The separated pieces of chain were perfectly smooth, mirrored metal, as if cut with a high-powered laser.

Jonzn took three quick drags on his cigar and laughed. "Now, now, you can't 'spect me to give up all my secrets, Fred. Maybe I cut that chain out there and maybe I didn't. I didn't get in the position I'm in by tellin' everything I know."

With a grin he added, "Which won't keep me from taking all the credit, of course." He winked at the engineer, puffing cigar smoke.

95.   DREAMER
FRED WARREN

John Milton left the party via the door nearest the spot the beautiful woman in the red dress had occupied before she vanished. He didn't believe in ghosts. If he wasn't hallucinating from fatigue, this was probably the handiwork of some joker in Network Control peeved that his new electronic toy wasn't in last week's shipment from Adagio.

Joker or not, the man knew his business. John had seen holograms before, but never one so perfect, so lifelike as this one.

He turned a corner, muttering to himself, and was nearly to the end of the dimly-lit corridor before he realized it was a cul-de-sac. He whirled about to retrace his steps, and pulled up short.

She was there. Close enough to touch.

The woman tilted her head, an amused smile playing across her lips. "Hello again, John. I'm so glad you decided to pursue me. I was hoping we might talk awhile, in private."

"Who are you?"

"Someone with an interest in this colony…and in you."

"If this is somebody's idea of a prank, I'm not finding it at all amusing."

"It isn't a prank. I simply want to ask you a question. A serious question."

He folded his arms across his chest. "I'm listening."

"Who controls Avenir Eclectia? Where does the true power reside?"

This was the question? A half-educated child could answer it. "The Peace Council, of course. They govern the colony, enforce law via the peacekeepers, adjudicate disputes, regulate trade…"

She frowned. "Come now, you have more insight than that. Let me put it another way. Why are you living in luxury on Avenir rather than scrabbling after insect carcasses in the ash, on Eclectia?"

"Trade. I broker the exchange of raw materials from Eclectia, mostly through the Palmer Trading Company, for processed goods from Avenir's nanofactories—and I'm very good at what I do."

"It seems terribly inefficient. Why aren't there any nanofactories closer to the source of the raw materials?"

His irritation was mounting. He'd had this conversation a million times with all manner of politicians, petty bureaucrats, and spacers. "Well, the factories require a zero-gee environment for maximum throughput, but I suppose the real reason is that we can't replicate them. The technology is held by the First Families...but they're all Dreamers."

"Yes, we are."

Her words were like an icy rivulet of water down his spine. John edged backward, away from the woman, until he bumped into the featureless metal wall at the end of the corridor. If the stories were true, there was a person directing this image, but its true form was a bloated, deformed travesty of humanity, or a disembodied brain, or an amorphous *thing* floating in a nutrient vat, somewhere in a dark, armored recess of the station. "You're lying. The Dreamers are wired into a virtual fantasy world. They've abandoned all human contact."

She smiled and slowly closed the distance between them as John flattened himself against the wall and turned his face away. "Oh, not *all* human contact. It's a useful bit of propaganda, and not entirely false, though we're much more intimately involved in the affairs of this colony than anyone, including the Peace Council, could imagine."

The image flickered as she bent forward to whisper into his ear, and he squeezed his eyes shut as his hands clawed against unyielding metal. "We represent an unbroken line from the original command crew of the Avenir, and we still take our responsibilities *very* seriously. One of those responsibilities is stewardship of the nanofactories. They are the true heart of Avenir Eclectia. Without them, the colony dies. No machines, no weapons, no replacement parts, no medicine. The hunters can't hunt, the miners can't mine, the undersea cities and the station fall into disrepair, and plague ravages the population."

He could feel her breath, warm and feathery on his cheek, and a wisp of spicy perfume hung in the air. *No. That's impossible.* He forced himself to open his eyes. She stood five feet away now, her blue eyes drilling into him. Measuring him. He swallowed hard and forced out the words: "What do you want with me?"

142

"We've been watching you for some time, John Milton. You are intelligent, energetic, and ambitious. Most of all, you are one of only a few people on this station who understand that our colony is doomed unless the status quo is changed. You have a vision for its future, a vision that we, with slight variations, share."

She blinked out of existence for a moment, then reappeared at the corridor intersection. The calculating expression was gone. Her eyes were moist. Pleading.

I'm dying, John, and I have no heir. I'm inviting you to take my place. Join us. Become a Dreamer.

96. SMOKE EATER: HERO
WALT STAPLES

"Fresh Fish, door!" the squad leader bawled.

Tyler Takku, Fire Team 6's "Fresh Fish," was an ugly little man—though his mother didn't think so. He was short and squat, as were the others of the fire team. It was a must as they hauled heavy equipment into Avenir's tight spaces and survivors or bodies out.

The atmosphere feeding from his "bunker gear" or fire armor's life support system tasted faintly of smoke and burning volatiles; something he'd ceased to notice while in training. It was only at times like this, when he should be concentrating, that the sensation snuck into his awareness. No matter how often the filters were changed out or the bunker gear was cleaned, the bouquet remained. He shook his head, clearing the cobwebs.

The shop's door was the normal atmosphere-tight kind found on the other businesses on the mall. The large temper-plast windows attempted to not remind patrons that hard vacuum waited its chance outside.

He ran through the Snuffy's Alphabet—C-A-E-S: Contain the fire-cut Air circulation-cut Electrical current-Search for victims—in his head as he helped place the temporary airlock over the door. Behind the windows the shop looked frightening close to flashover. He bulled his way into the lock ahead of the other firefighters. It was this aggressiveness to get to the fire that caused the Snuffys to refer to each other as "Idjits"—they ran toward danger rather than away.

"Fresh Fish in the lead," sounded in his earphones from both the

143

internal radio and his gear's external mikes. One corner of his mind reminded him how happy he'd be when he wasn't the new guy and had a proper nickname. Then the next new guy would be "Fresh Fish" until christened by the squad.

The atmosphere in the lock was evacuated and replaced with inert nitrogen. There'd be no backdraft when the door was opened. He dropped to his knees and scrambled forward as the emergency charge blew the door halves back into their slots in the jamb. He was conscious of someone behind him directing a heavy stream of CO_2 and soda above him through the door as smoke billowed in to mix with the lock's atmosphere. Vision being useless, he relied on the heads-up display on his visor's interior for his view of the shop. It occurred to him that he hadn't noticed what sort of shop it was. Well, if anything had been explosive or oxidizing, he would have been warned forcefully by dispatch.

The picture produced by his radar showed a body on the floor to his right. The thermal overlay showed it as well above 37 degrees C. He sighed as he grabbed it and began to back out, dragging the body behind. He'd hoped his first experience would be a rescue instead of a recovery.

Outside, he cracked his visor and turned away as the med team took over his burden. He stood, looking at the mall's carpet as he felt the letdown. The heavy slap of a hand landed on his shoulder. "Why so blue, kid?"

He glanced at the squad leader's smile, then back at the floor. "Guess I just wanted the first one to come out alive."

"Oh? Well, that one never was."

Tyler looked around at the squad leader in confusion. "What?"

"You rescued a dressmaker's manikin." The other pointed to where a mousey-looking woman was putting a variable geometry dressmaker's smart-dummy through its paces surrounded by the grinning med team.

The new man cringed. *Oh, Lordy, could it get worse?*

As if reading his mind, the squad leader gave his shoulder a rough shake. "You done good, kid. That gizmo cost that lady a lot of credits. You probably saved her business." He walked over to talk to the Fire Marshal.

The lady broke away from the other group and approached Tyler. She smiled at him and he wondered why he had thought her mousey. "I want to thank you so much for saving 'Edda.' She's not covered by my policy yet and it would have taken months to replace her." He couldn't decide whether her eyes were blue, gray, or green—and, for some reason, this suddenly seemed very important to him. She colored slightly and looked down. "I was wondering if...if I could thank you with dinner and a vid? Oh. I'm Amy." She smiled that smile again.

As he helped break down the lock, a blond firefighter jerked on his bunker gear's rescue strap and grinned at him. "Hey, 'Dollman,' great work."

"Dollman" Takku returned "Bucket-Head" Schmidlap's grin, as Squad Leader "Rabbit-Tooth" Morgan looked on with a smile and "Fancy-Pants" Brenan continued knocking down the lock's other side.

97.   ANYA
FRED WARREN

John checked the door locks twice, then ripped off his tie and loosened his collar. He was drenched in sweat, and his hands were shaking. *Had to be a trick. Gamer's stunt. The fat slugs are probably laughing at me on the sim-net right now.*

He flinched as his cyborg valet slipped into position behind him and began to remove his jacket. "Did you enjoy the party, sir?"

"No."

"Shall I turn down your bed?"

"No!" John ran clammy fingers through his hair. "No...All I want right now is a drink."

"Very well. Your usual vodka?"

"Never mind. I'll get it myself. Just...go. You're dismissed."

He pushed past the valet, who watched with an expression of mild interest as he opened the liquor cabinet. "As you wish. Good night, Mr. Milton."

"Good ni...Hold it. Wait. When was the last security sweep of my quarters?"

The valet froze and his eyelids fluttered. "Two days ago. No microphones, cameras, or other surveillance devices were found."

"Good. Has anyone else entered since then?"

"No one but you, sir."

"Excellent. You may return to your alcove and cycle off for the night."

"Thank you, sir."

John shoveled ice into a glass and began to pour. There was a musical tinkling sound as the bottle rattled against its rim. Some of the vodka splashed on the floor. The blue-eyed woman's final words were still echoing inside his head...

I'm dying, John, and I have no heir. I'm inviting you to take my place. Join us. Become a Dreamer.

No one had ever directly interacted with a Dreamer. No Dreamer had ever manifested an image within the living space of Avenir. Maybe one of his competitors had arranged this little show to trap him somehow, make him look ridiculous. It wouldn't be the first time they'd tried. He gulped his drink and stared through the window at the bilious face of Eclectia as the liquor burned its way down his throat.

"The invitation has a time limit, John."

He whirled around. The valet was still standing there, smiling at him.

Smiling?

"Yes, it's me again."

John rubbed his eyes. It usually took several drinks for the alcohol to disorient him, but he'd had a few at the party. "I told you to cycle off. Get out of here!"

The valet didn't move, but his smile widened. "I'm not finished with him yet. I need to be sure you understand what I'm offering you."

That voice. The wistful lilt and soft soprano tone. Hers.

The glass slipped from John's hand and shattered on the floor. "Who are you?"

"I am Anya Sherikov, direct descendant of Mikhail Sherikov, Avenir Communications Officer. My family holds command authority over the information systems of this colony. I have unrestricted access to every computer, every commlink, every camera, and," the valet tapped his head, "every electronic and cybernetic device on the Avenir network, including Eclectia's undersea cities. Even among the Dreamers, it is a formidable power."

"But if what you've told me is true—and I'm still not convinced this isn't an elaborate prank—I'd have to surrender my humanity to accept your offer."

"Only the inconvenient, tiresome parts. You will, of course, have to be integrated into the network, but your body will be kept in perfect health, and you will experience a life infinitely more rich and meaningful than this dull, enclosed existence. You're languishing here, John. Tell me it isn't so."

"I'm not…It's just that…" John took a deep breath and straightened his shoulders. He'd been on the defensive long enough, and he knew better than to negotiate from a position of weakness. "I need proof. All you've given me is a fairy story and a few parlor tricks."

The valet beckoned with a crooked finger. "Follow me."

98.   DON'T PLAY NICE
KAYE JEFFREYS

Penny knocked on Kinsee's door and steadied herself.

The door opened and a friendly looking woman peered out.

"Hi, I'm looking for my friend, Jereth." Penny worked hard to follow the script closely. "He said he might be here."

"Jereth? No. He's not here. He went landside over a week ago."

"Landside?" That wasn't part of the script she'd have to improvise. "What's he doing landside?"

The woman laughed. "That's a good question. He doesn't belong landside, now, does he?"

"Where did he go? Landside, I mean." Penny shifted her weight from one foot to the other.

"I'm not sure where he is right now. I haven't heard from them in a few days. An earthquake knocked out communications."

"They? Who is he with?"

"With my daughter and her aid team. They had to go back toward some mountain range to check up on an independent miner."

"No communication, though. How will you get hold of them?"

"They will contact me when things are back up. Do you want me to take your name and contact info and give it to them?"

"No." When the lady started asking questions about her, it was time to go. "No. I'll try back later. Thanks."

~~~

147

Penny ran to the Benji Frank store. Gus leaned by the door waiting for her. "Well?"

"I got something." She was out of breath.

"Take it easy. We've got time." He chewed his toothpick.

Penny nodded and waited a few minutes to catch her breath. "He went landside, aid work."

"Landside?"

"That's what she said."

"That doesn't make sense."

"It's all I could get."

"It's more than anyone else could get." Gus smiled at her great big. "It's better than nothing, right? And the boss is getting tired of nothing."

"Do you have anything else for me to do?"

"No, go on home. I'll take it from here."

"But we need the money and I want to help."

"If I need help, I'll call you. Otherwise stay away from me when I'm working. The people I work for don't play nice."

99. BEDTIME STORIES
GREG MITCHELL

"Daddy? Tell me about the angels."

Dressler pulled the covers to Edilyn's neck, red light from the small bunker window painting her face in harsh contrast. The sound of dirt and grit scraped against the pane glass, a constant white noise that Dressler had all-but tuned out.

"Come on, Lyn," he sighed. "Not tonight. You really need your rest."

Through bleary eyes, she beseeched him. "I feel fine, Dad."

A sharp pang pierced his spirit.

Three Foundings old and she's braver about this than I am.

"I don't really want to," Dressler grinned, his nose and eyes burning with tears that he kept barred.

"*Please*, Daddy," the little girl begged, reminding him of all the tiny things in life she'd begged for. New toys, a special treat. A million trivial things he'd taken for granted. Things that would be left behind when she was gone.

Dressler cursed in his heart. *Better do it. Better savor these moments. You won't have much opportunity before long.*

"Okay," he relented, and the girl's feet squirmed under the covers, her face brighter than 94 Ceti. "The angels are beautiful creatures that live in the ocean depths."

"How did they get there?" she immediately asked her usual question.

"I don't know. Maybe they've always been there. Maybe they came from somewhere else."

"A boy in my class said they have magic," she nodded eagerly. "Is that true, Daddy?"

"That's what I hear, but I've never seen one for myself," he chuckled. "I guess that's why we have stories. Sometimes believing in a thing is more important than the thing itself. Does that make sense?"

She shook her head no.

"Yeah," he huffed. "Doesn't make a lot of sense to me most of the time, either."

Pausing, Edilyn furrowed her brow, the soft *shush-shushing* of the windswept sands comforting, even in Eclectia's tumultuous storms. "Daddy …Could the angels make me not sick?"

Dressler's chest tightened, his breathing short. He bit on his lip, forcing his emotions back. He'd cry later, after Edilyn was asleep. He'd cry 'til morning. "I don't know, Lyn," he whispered in a raw croak. "But I'd like to believe."

100. NEXUS
FRED WARREN

It's a trap.

As his possessed valet plodded ahead of him, leading the way to who knew where, John Milton ran down the list of his enemies—a roster of considerable length that grew with each successive Founding. One of them had to be behind this. *Chamberlin? No…he's a vindictive thug, but far too stupid to coordinate such an elaborate deception. Chun Hee? She has the technical skills, but she'd rather eviscerate her rivals publicly. Mkembe? Too craven. Sanchez? Busy fending off his own enemies. Jaworsky would rather haggle. Torrance just steals what he wants when nobody's looking…*

"Cheer up, John. It's not as if I'm leading you to the gallows."

It still made his flesh crawl to hear Anya Sherikov's voice coming from the cyborg butler's mouth. "I'd be less tense if you'd tell me where we're going," he muttered.

"We're going to the place where all your questions will find their answers. Here's the door."

The air was uncomfortably hot. They'd been walking for what seemed like hours through a maze of twisting corridors. By now, they must be somewhere close to the heart of Avenir, near the power core. The metal bulkheads resonated with eerie sounds—clanks, hums, whistles and gurgling. The valet stood before an oval hatch at the end of the corridor and palmed a square glass plate set into the left side above a recessed handle.

John's head snapped up at a high-pitched whine overhead. Two laser turrets emerged from the ceiling, one trained on him, the other on the valet. The door plate glowed green, and something clicked within the hatch. The valet tugged on the handle and motioned to John as the door silently swung open, releasing a welcome rush of cool air.

"Please, come in. I'll leave your man here for the return trip," Anya said, then the valet froze in position, eyes blank, jaw slack, bent slightly forward at the waist. John edged past, through the hatchway, and the door swung shut behind him.

The corridor continued, but it was rounder, more tunnel-like, and sheathed in some soft material that silenced John's footsteps and the other ambient noises of the station. He could see the end of it, a brilliantly-lit opening painful to look at after so much time spent in semidarkness. He had to cover his eyes with one hand as he drew closer, pressing the other hand against the corridor wall until he felt it give way to open space.

Anya's voice came from within, and the sound reverberated through what sounded like an immense emptiness. "Your eyes will adjust in a few moments. Welcome to my home, John."

Tears dribbled from the corners of his eyes as he strained to open them in the blinding light. Shapes began to form, white within white, darkening to vague shadows, then taking form and focus. The room was huge, as big as any concert hall on Avenir, and lined with ovoid structures, each at least five meters high and twice that in diameter, connected to each other and to the walls of the chamber by an array of pipes and conduits. Cyborgs shuffled about at the margins, inspecting panels and adjusting controls. John staggered into the room, head swiveling, trying to comprehend what he was seeing.

"Thinking of buying the place? I'm afraid I'm too attached to it to sell outright, but I might consider letting you move into one of the spare rooms."

He spun around. She stood before him, eyes blue and laughing, golden hair tumbling across her shoulders, resplendent in crimson—the same dress she'd worn at their first meeting.

Anya Sherikov, scion of Mikhail Sherikov, Avenir's original communications officer, heir to his power and authority.

Dreamer.

John struggled to gather his wits. He was a businessman—the best of his generation. He couldn't blindly accept Anya's proposal, no matter how overwhelmed he felt or how beautiful she looked. He needed evidence of her good faith. He needed *collateral*.

She smiled. "Now I can formally introduce you to the community. We rarely have visitors, but there is provision for a temporary connection to our virtual space. There's a comfortable couch in the alcove, over there. My drones will make the necessary attachments. The resolution doesn't compare to a hardwired link, but…"

"No. First, I want to see *you*, Anya."

"I don't understand. I'm standing right here. Perhaps your eyes still need time to adjust."

"The *real* you. No holograms, no video, no illusions. Otherwise, there's no deal. You'll have to find yourself another successor."

"The real me? Ah, the stories. You're afraid I'm a mutated horror, or a disembodied brain immersed in a nutrient vat. Believe me, I'm as human as you are. This hologram is a true image…well, perhaps with a few cosmetic enhancements for vanity's sake. Besides, John, a lady values her privacy, and Dreamers even more so. This is a rude request. Most of us wouldn't grant it. Some would destroy you for merely asking."

"If you're my future, I need to see with my own eyes exactly what that means."

"Silly boy. The body is only a reservoir for the spirit. In a few weeks, you won't care about it at all. You'll barely remember what it was like to be so limited."

"You want my trust. This is the price."

She sighed. "Very well." A drone turned from his inspection of a data panel and took John by the arm. "Follow him," Anya said, "but I'll tolerate no gawking. My dignity still matters to me, even while floating naked in a preservation chamber."

"Naked? What...wait!"

Anya chuckled and shook her head. "No, you idiot, I'm not naked. You make it far too easy, John Milton. Have your look—I've no more time for these ridiculous superstitions."

The cyborg guided John to one of the white ovoids and passed a hand over a glass plate on its side. A circular panel irised open, revealing a small porthole. The interior illuminated, and after a moment's hesitation, John looked inside.

Anya's body lay motionless within the liquid-filled chamber, nestled in a spiderweb of thin cables and tubes. The hologram was a true image, and yet...beneath the white gown and skinsuit her body looked thin and fragile, emaciated. A cascade of blond hair framed hollow cheeks. Her skin was sallow and her eyes shadowed.

Her voice whispered over his shoulder, and he thought the pale lips of the woman sleeping within the chamber might have moved along with it. "Satisfied?"

John nodded. "You're beautiful, even now. Your illness...how much longer will you live?"

"A few months. Perhaps a Founding, if I'm fortunate. Time enough to teach you all you need to take my place."

"I'm so sorry."

"Don't be. I've had a full life—several of them, by your standards. The preservation technology is very effective at easing the ravages of time, but death finds us all, eventually."

The drone closed the panel, and John turned to find Anya's hologram watching him with a faint, sad smile, eyes bright with an illusion of moisture so vivid, he had to restrain the impulse to reach out and touch her face.

Logan came up out of his chair and leaned heavy over Tuskagin's metal desk. "Are you trying to cheat me?"

"No, no. It is a fair price." Tuskagin backed his chair against the wall.

"You think I started hunting diamonds yesterday? Give them back. I'll take them to Spring Plant Valley where they will pay me what they are worth."

"You know the market fluctuates, Logan."

"It's your devotion to drink that makes you think you can rob me. Your father would be ashamed to see you. Now there was a fair man, God rest his soul." Logan fisted his hand over his heart as a sign of respect.

"All right, I'll give you what you ask." Tuskagin counted out credits. "You will ruin me."

~~~

Reece walked at Logan's elbow down the street. "Dad, I never heard you talk to Tuskagin like that before."

"He pushed me too far. You must never let the assayers take advantage of you. It's a matter of survival."

Reece nodded his agreement then whispered, "You see the guy following us?"

Logan didn't look back, he'd already seen him. "This is turning into a really bad day."

"Do you think he's from Avenir?"

"He's too tall to be from around here. His clothes are too new. He's probably some station-slicker con man who thinks he has found an easy target in a couple of outlanders."

"Hide out in the alley?"

"Yeah, we'll give him a surprise."

~~~

The two miners turned into an alley.

Jereth picked up his step. What he would say when he caught up with them, he didn't know. He just couldn't lose them. Not now.

Jereth made it to the corner and turned.

One of the miners grabbed his jacket, pushed him up against the wall and glared up into Jereth's eyes. "What do you want?"

"I'm...I'm looking for the miners."

"Well, you found them." The man held Jereth against the wall with compacted strength. As he studied Jereth he brought his eyebrows together. "Who are you?"

"Jereth Davis, sir. My mother was..."

"Deirdre..." The miner's expression softened and he looked through Jereth to a far away place.

"Yes, Deirdre..." Jereth thought he better talk fast. "She was Deirdre Lewis from The Miners of the Five Rims. That's who you are, right? The Miners of the Five Rims?"

Sterness returned to the man's face. "Did your father send you?"

"He doesn't know I'm here."

The miner smiled, released Jereth's jacket, and stepped back. "Doesn't know you're here?"

"At least he didn't know when I left. Who knows what he knows now?" Jereth smoothed out his jacket.

"Well, Jereth Davis, my sister's son, welcome home. We've been watching for you."

102. GRADUATION
JOSEPH H. FICOR

Shouhei Fiko stood proud with the other recruits in their crisp gray uniforms. There were twenty-four in his graduating class. The last six weeks had been a nightmare, but this moment made all of the sweat—and blood—worth it. Soon, he would receive the single chevron that marked his transition from Enforcer Recruit to Enforcer First Class.

Enforcer Command Chief Romero stood in front of the recruits. His face showed pride in their achievement of graduation. Rumor had it he had treated his own son no differently than any of them when he had passed through this training last Founding—both in being tough as it was ongoing and in taking pride afterward. "Recruit Platoon 74R. Attention!"

All boots clicked together as one. They were a well oiled machine.

Romero had seen to that. These were the successful candidates who had excelled where thirty-six of their comrades had washed out. Shouhei was proud to be among the ones who had finished. His parents would have been proud, but they could not make the ceremony. They could not afford the trip from Adagio to Avenir. He knew that they were here in spirit.

Peacekeeper Colonel Pietrov personally pinned the chevrons on each recruit.

After all of the chevrons had been given, Shouhei joined the others in reciting the creed of the Avenir Peacekeeper Corps:

"We swear by the honor and blood of the Founders

That we will faithfully execute our duties

As Enforcers of the just and righteous laws of Avenir.

We will carry out our duties with honesty and honor.

Deceit and greed will be far from us.

Death before the dishonoring of the Corps.

On our honor and that of our forefathers, we swear."

Romero then turned to the former recruits. "Recruit Platoon 74R, Dismissed!"

The voices—and caps—of the recruits rocketed to the ceiling of the assembly hall.

103. GAMER
FRED WARREN

The velociraptor tore Melanie's leg from her body, showering her in blood, heedless of her screams. Her finger convulsed on the trigger of her submachine gun, but the bullets found no purchase on the dino's armored hide.

"Should have loaded AP rounds, Mouse. Maybe next time you'll listen to your big brother."

"Shut up, Carson. And quit calling me Mouse."

"That's *Rhino* to you, *Mouse*. Would you please hurry up and die so we can restart the level? Man, I hate team survival criteria. I could have plowed solo through this lame scenario in five minutes, tops."

"Stupid lizard's still chewing on my leg. Aaagh, why does it have to hurt so much? If you'd laid down some covering fire, genius, I might have made it across the clearing. Using your teammates as bait...Ouch! Ouch, ouch, ouch...doesn't inspire confidence in your leadership."

"Not a scratch on me. Maybe if you could learn to follow orders, you'd live longer."

"There's no 'I' in 'team,' Carson. Ohmigosh...here it comes again."

"Heh. Nope, no 'I,' just 'meat.'"

The raptor's jagged teeth ripped into Melanie's torso, causing her simsuit to generate a convincing impression of her body being chewed in half. Her vision went full red, then black. "All right, that's it. I'm logging, if only to reassure myself that all my parts are where they belong."

"Aw, c'mon, Sis! One more run, please! I promise I'll watch your back this time, and I'll let you have your pick of the loot."

"50-50 split."

"70-30."

"60-40."

"Okay, okay. 60-40, you harpy. I should have locked you out of my circle when I had the chance."

"Yeah, right. Who else would get your hardware upgrades for half-price and install them for free? Well, *mostly* free."

"Chiseler."

"I love you too, big brother. Give me five minutes...it still feels like my guts are hanging out somewhere."

"Your guts are right where they belong, Mel. See you in five."

Melanie smiled. He was a jerk, but he could be so sweet, when he wanted to.

She groped around with her right hand, found the bailout switch, and slapped it. After her visor cleared to pink translucence, she pulled off the tri-D helmet and ran her fingers through her hair. She hurt all over. The games were fun—when she wasn't getting stabbed, shot, torched, or eaten—but she didn't share her brother's obsession. There were too many interesting things to do in the real world, and there was no way she'd ever let her body degenerate into a flabby sack of lard like Carson and his pals. *Slugs*, everyone called them. Carson wore the name like a badge of honor.

She sighed, levered herself up from the gaming couch, and staggered to a basin set into the wall where she could take a drink and splash water on her face.

Carson was the only reason she played at all. She'd promised their mother she'd look after him the day he'd filed his Writ of Independence, after he'd locked himself into a gaming suite with two caretaker cyborgs. Now, she was his only contact with the world beyond the game servers. It helped being a computer tech. She understood the games and could do depot-level maintenance on his simsuit and interface hardware. He couldn't dismiss her along with the rest of Avenir Eclectia as an irrelevant distraction from the virtual world he loved.

So he wasn't lost to her. Not yet.

Melanie stretched her cramped muscles, luxuriating in the relief it granted from the ache and burn of the simsuit's lingering effects. She owed herself a hot bath later, and that thought was incentive enough to hop back on the couch and don her helmet one last time for the day. She checked her chronograph and swore—eight minutes since she'd logged out. She swatted the login switch, steeling herself for a lecture.

Her vision tunneled, expanded, and refocused, and a flood of sensations from the simsuit rushed through her body. She was back at the rally point for *Chrono Marines*, surrounded by leafy, steamy jungle, the air alive with the calls of exotic wildlife and insects. A dino roared in the distance—probably a tyrannosaur. She gripped her weapon tightly and scanned the undergrowth. She was safe from attack here, but the sensory immersion was so complete, she couldn't help feeling as if something might pounce on her at any moment.

She checked her ammo, then swapped the default magazine for a clip of armor-piercing bullets. It stung her pride, but she wasn't going to be some overgrown lizard's chew toy twice in one day.

Where was Carson? By now, he should have been giving her an earful for being late. Melanie keyed her mic. "Car...Rhino, this is Mouse, in position at the rally point. Do you copy? Over."

There was no response, just a faint static crackle in her headset. "Rhino, Mouse. I'm at the rally point, awaiting orders. Please respond."

There were two short beeps, indicating a connection from outside the game. "Mel, something's come up. Log out of CM and jump to Conference Room Seven." Carson's voice was strained and shaky.

"What's the matter? Are you okay?"

"I'm fine. Better than fine. I got a call from Orca a couple of minutes ago. Jumbo's Folly just went hot."

104. ONLY THE STRONG
GREG MITCHELL

"It's just a fact of nature," Trebs said in a hush, watching through his set of green-tinted binocs over the ashen terrain.

Dressler kept his eyes forward, likewise watching the battle from the safety of the makeshift roost. Up ahead, two dominant beetles tore apart their weaker brother. Even from here, Dressler heard the shrill cries of the thing, and felt pity.

"It's the Rule of the Strong," Trebs added as one of the larger bugs tore a leg off the smaller. "Those that are strong make the rules, you get me?"

"I get you," Dressler grumbled, wishing Trebs would quit talking. That was always the worst part when their shifts fell together. Despite the dangers, hunting bugs for meat was usually a time for quiet reflection—a time Dressler desperately needed since the doctor diagnosed Edilyn with ash lung.

"If you can't hack it," Trebs droned on, as the lesser insect finally fell in a spray of yellow gore, "You don't *deserve* to live, know what I'm saying?"

A warbling shriek filled Dressler's ears. He clutched at his head, startled. Trebs did the same. Deadly pincers pierced the scrap metal roof and tore it back, red sands and heat pelting the humans inside. Another bug—one they'd not previously seen—reared up on its back crawlers, its throat emitting a high-pitched rattle.

Trebs screamed, "It's calling the others! We—"

The beetle that towered over them dropped its foreclaw like a pick axe, piercing the meat of Trebs' thigh. He fell back, blood gushing everywhere, and hollered in anguish. Dressler reached for his spear and jabbed at the thing, searching for the exposed underbelly.

With its other claw, the monster slapped him away and Dressler crashed through the rough wall of their roost, landing in a plume of sand. He stood, disoriented, no clue where the spear had gone. Fear took hold of him and shook hard, the sounds of Trebs struggling for his life mere feet away. Dressler dropped to one knee and brought out the scythegun rifle slung on his back. A thunderous crack echoed across the canyon as Dressler's shot struck the beast in the eye. It howled in pain, raining yellow blood on the ruined roost, and backed away.

The gunshot had scared off the other bugs, a prime reason why most

159

hunters used spears. Even though they lost their catch for the day, Dressler was relieved. He rushed to the rubble, where Trebs was alive and in pain.

It'd be a long, miserable hike back to camp.

105. ASSIGNMENT
JOSEPH H. FICOR

After the graduation ceremony, Enforcer First Class Shouhei Fiko went away from his classmates clutching the small gray envelope.

He had refused to open it until after the ceremony. His classmates had opened their assignment orders as soon as they received them. Shouhei was afraid that he would jinx his chances if he opened the envelope early. His apprehension eased a little after making the decision to wait.

The night before graduation was spent praying—and pleading—for his desired assignment. He even forsook the traditional congratulatory beetle steak breakfast given to graduates on the morning of the ceremony.

He wanted to join the space division. To be among the emptiness and infinity of space was heaven compared to the dust and heat of Adagio. He loved his family deeply, but he desired to fly in the dark coolness of space. He wanted to feel a closeness to sky from which his ancestors had descended. He desired release from the family's Eclectian prison.

A millennium of time passed before he made the final tear in the envelope.

He removed the paper and unfolded it carefully.

His dream crashed like a beetle that had been struck in the underside by a meat hunter's spear.

His destination was Sheba.

106. EXAMINATION
FRED WARREN

"This interface provides much less fidelity than a fully-integrated network connection, but we've found it useful as a means of conferencing with outsiders from time to time."

Cyborgs assisted John as he shuffled to a contoured couch and lay down. The full-immersion helmet permitted a narrow, foggy, green-tinted view of the room, and of Anya's holographic image standing to one side. "It's like a gaming rig, but it's a lot heavier," he wheezed. Tubes and wires ran from the suit to a conduit in the ceiling, high above. He felt like a life-sized puppet. "I can barely move in this thing."

"I think you'll find this simsuit is more sophisticated than the ones you're used to. Of course, when you experience the hardwired connection, you won't be able to distinguish it from real life." She turned away. "I have a few more preparations to make, but I think you're ready to enter our virtuality now. I'll see you inside."

"Wait. I still have questions…"

Anya motioned to a cyborg sitting at the control panel. "Activate the interface."

John's muscles convulsed, and a wave of vertigo tunneled his vision, then expanded it to infinity in a rush of color and light. As focus returned, he found himself standing in a bare, white room containing a table, a chair, and washbasin with a mirror. There was a single door, closed, and the doorknob didn't turn when he tried it.

He looked down at himself. He was clad in a thin blue gown that tied at the back. His arms and legs were stylized , smooth and hairless, like a doll's, but the hands and feet had the proper number of fingers and toes. Turning to the mirror, his own face gazed back at him. It wasn't a perfect image, maybe a shade more lifelike than the virtual-reality games he had played as a teenager. Dark brown hair, parted at the middle, green eyes, prominent cheekbones, a trace of stubble at the chin.

"Hello, Mister Milton. Welcome to Paradise!"

He spun round. Smiling up at him was a little girl wearing a pink-pinstriped dress, white pinafore, and a square cap emblazoned with a wide, red cross. A stethoscope was tucked into a pocket on the pinafore.

He couldn't help but grin back. "Paradise, eh? I thought it would be bigger. Who are you, and where's Anya?"

The girl tilted her head, light-brown curls bouncing with the motion. "I thought you would be taller. I'm Doctor Vicky. Miss Sherikov is arranging your meeting with the other Commanders, and she said I should see to your examination in the meantime."

"Anya said nothing to me about an examination. Is this some kind of joke? You're just a kid."

Her smile vanished, and her eyes narrowed. "I'm ten Foundings old, and I'm the Avenir Medical Officer. Sit on the table so I can begin your examination."

"Listen, Doctor…Vicky? Nobody's examining anything on me until I see Anya."

"Hmm. I guess Miss Sherikov forgot to tell me you're a moron. Get on the table. We can do this the easy way, or the hard way. Makes no difference to me."

John slid himself into a sitting position on the table, clutching the gown tightly around him. "This can't be right. It's…it's indecent."

"Mister, if you've seen one avatar, you've seen 'em all, and that goes double for this piece-of-junk interface you're using. I've got stuffed animals with more physical detail." She pulled the stethoscope from its pocket, set the prongs into her ears, and pressed the diaphragm onto his chest.

"Hey, that's cold!"

"Shut up. Lungs clear, heart function good, slight hypertension, minor plaque buildup on the aortic wall." She reached up on tiptoe and set the diaphragm against his throat. "Some narrowing of the carotid artery, but that's easily reamed out."

"What do you mean, 'reamed out?'"

"Do I have to tape your mouth shut? Bend over so I can reach your head. EEG recording…complete. Hmm. A couple of freaky spikes. I'll take a closer look at that later. Mm-hmm…intracranial pressure normal, pituitary normal, thyroid normal. You can sit up straight now." She moved to his stomach and frowned. "Wow, you've got the liver of a sixty-Foundings man. What have you been drinking?"

"Vodka, mostly."

"It's killing you. Stop it. Now, turn over."

"This thing is open at the back. There's no way I'm letting you…"

"Okay, the hard way, then." Vicky began rolling up her sleeves.

The door opened, and to John's great relief, Anya entered the room, cradling a large datapad. Like his own image, her avatar wasn't nearly as realistic as the hologram he was familiar with. She was dressed like a secretary, in a burgundy suit, and her red hair was pinned into a conservative bun. "Ah," she said, "I see you've met our Doctor Remsen. Victoria took charge of Medical and Life Sciences after her father's death, two Foundings ago. We would have liked her to have more time to ease into her responsibilities, but she's doing a fine job. She's extraordinarily bright."

"I wish you'd call me Vicky. Victoria makes me sound like an old lady."

"You're an officer now. We must maintain decorum."

"Whatever." Vicky pointed at John. "He won't cooperate with the examination."

Anya laid a hand on her shoulder. "Victoria, do you remember what Captain Aziz said about your bedside manner?"

"Yeah, yeah, I know." Vicky sighed. "Less attitude, more professional." She produced a huge syringe, with a disturbingly long needle, from somewhere behind her back. "Ahem. Mister Milton, I will need samples of your blood, bone marrow, and cerebrospinal fluid to complete your physical examination and obtain the necessary data to prepare for your integration into the Avenir Command Network. Please roll onto your stomach, as the necessary control points for your simsuit are located on your avatar's back."

"Wait...bone marrow? Cerebro-what?"

"This will hurt."

Over his shoulder, John could see Vicky's cherubic face grinning from ear to ear as the needle descended.

107. DARK (FLASHBACK)
GREG MITCHELL

Shuffling. I can hear him outside, trying to find me, but I'm good at hiding. A loud clatter. Something falls over and breaks on the floor. He shouts my name, like it's my fault. Everything's always my fault. He's been drinking again. I don't want to blame him. He's a miner, trapped in the dark for hours. Sometimes days. The dark does things to you, but I won't be like that. I'm going to grow up and stay outside, where I can see the light. I don't care about the storms. I'll gladly face all that grit and heat—even the coldest day—just so long as I'm free. I don't want to be alone, in the dark.

I'm alone in the dark now. He shouts my name again. "Trebstidium! Where are you, boy? Get out here, *now!*"

I'm alone in the dark, but I won't be forever. I won't.

108. THANKSGIVING
JOSEPH H. FICOR

The trip from Avenir to Sheba was uneventful. Shouhei sulked in his cabin. The dream of serving on a security cruiser in the Space Service was dead. He just knew that the rest of his time with the Enforcers would be spent breaking up payday saloon brawls between miners on that cracked rock.

A memory came to his mind. He was around fourteen and he had failed an opportunity to be part of the soccer club sponsored by the Countess Barslow Memorial Charity. Anger and juvenile despair had a stranglehold on his heart. His mother told him about an old saying that people should give thanks to God in all situations, especially the bad ones. She said that people needed to release their pains and disappointments to Him. This gave the Big Man an opportunity to make the situation right. The advice and resulting prayer of thanksgiving lifted his heart.

Shouhei gave a prayer of thanks for his current disappointment.

The peace that followed relieved his mind and spirit.

109. FOLLY
FRED WARREN

Melanie swayed as her equilibrium adjusted to the sudden transition from prehistoric jungle to corporate briefing room. Carson was standing beside a tri-D map of the Avenir cyberspace projected in midair, arguing with his buddy, Orca. He hadn't even changed out of his camouflage battlesuit.

Wow, this must be important.

Orca was stabbing at the diagram with an index finger. "Don't do it, Rhino. It's a really bad idea. There's a reason we call that place Jumbo's Folly."

"Jumbo was my friend. I have to follow through on this for him, or his death won't mean anything."

Death?

Melanie staggered around one arm of the U-shaped conference table and grabbed her brother's arm. "What are you talking about, Carson? What's

164

Jumbo's Folly?"

"It's the big one, Mouse. The ultimate access...the door to Paradise."
His eyes were shining with an excitement she hadn't seen for a long time.

"Paradise. You mean that storybook land where the Dreamers are
supposed to live?"

"It's real. Here, look at the map." He flicked at the image with two
fingers and it spun slowly clockwise. Nodes and connections illuminated.
"Avenir is only using 40% of its server capacity, but we keep bumping up
against storage limits. Where's the other 60% going? The network addresses
are indexed, but we can't access them." He pulled the image to a halt and
waved a hand across it. A thick, black line lifted up, encircling a large sector
of space. "They're protected by the thickest firewall anyone's ever seen,
right here. Jumbo tried to hack his way in, and he almost made it." Carson
pointed at a red dot glowing at an edge of the black circle. "That's it.
Jumbo's Folly...and it's active again."

"He died there?" Her brother's lean, chiseled avatar towered over her. It
bore little resemblance to the genuine article. She wondered if his real body
could still stand at all.

"That's what I've been trying to pound through this idiot's thick skull,"
said Orca, who must have jumped in from a sports simulation. He was
wearing a blue uniform with thick shoulder pads and a silver helmet with
bars across its face. There was a blue lion stenciled on the helmet, and the
number 74 was emblazoned in white on his jersey. "Whatever lives behind
that firewall caught Jumbo when he broke through, and it fried his brain."

Carson slapped Orca's helmet. "But the point is, he *broke through*. And if
what's behind that firewall is important enough to defend, it's important
enough to investigate."

"I think Orca's right," Melanie said. "I don't want you going anywhere
near that place."

"Listen, guys...I loved Jumbo like a brother, but he only played the
games one way: full power, straight ahead. I don't intend to go pounding on
that wall where he left off. I'll take a look, assess the break in the firewall,
and if it looks promising, we'll come up with a plan to exploit it without
killing ourselves."

Orca took a step back. "Hold on a minute. Who's this 'we,' Rhino?"

"You, me, and Mouse. She can rig our hardware to give us more
protection against power surges. We still don't know what's behind the

wall, so can't risk taking an army in there. Not *yet*."

"No way, Carson." Melanie shook her head. "Mom would never forgive me if I let you do this."

"I'll go in with or without you, Mel, but I'd rather have you watching my back. Come on, Sis." He gently squeezed her shoulders. "This is important. If it wasn't, I wouldn't ask you. Please. For me."

She squirmed and pushed her brother's hands away. "All right, already. But we do the recon *together*, and *I* take point."

"You? Why?"

She grinned. "Because I have an idea how to poke the beast without waking him up."

110.   CONTACT
GREG MITCHELL

"Somebody help! We need help over here!"

Trebs was growing pale, his lips turning purple, his skin sallow and thin. Dressler struggled under the other man's weight, barely able to breathe after their long journey. After the beetle attacked out on the field, Dressler had done his best to make a tourniquet for Trebs' pierced thigh, but without medical attention his co-hunter was going to die.

"We need a doctor!" Dressler shouted once more.

"No, Daddy..." Trebs mumbled through cracked lips. "It's too dark, Dad...too dark..."

By time they reached the infirmary tent back at the Palmer camp, another sand storm had picked up. Waves of hard grit felt like needles on Dressler's face. He had his goggles on, his kerchief over his face, but the heat was blistering. Trebs slipped in and out of hysteria, sometimes whimpering like a child, other times shouting at the air, cursing his father.

Medics hurried out of the tent, fighting against the high winds to reach Trebs.

"He got hit by a bug," Dressler shouted over nature's roar. "He's lost a lot of blood. He's delirious."

Two strong medics, decked in thick coats, caps, and goggles, hefted Trebs between them and dragged him toward the tent. Dressler followed, feeling like he'd just lost a hundred and seventy pounds. His arms tingled as

166

he moved them again, and he looked down to see he was covered in Trebs' blood.

Dressler pushed his way through the tent, instantly relieved of Eclectia's cruelty. His hearing returned, his breathing slowed, and he removed his goggles and facemask. Surgeons apprised themselves of Trebs' condition, cutting away his pants and stripping them off of him with a wet slap. Dressler glimpsed the wound, pumping blood like a volcano. Doctors hurried to stop the bleeding, beginning their operation.

"You're going to have to leave," one of the doctors ordered Dressler. He obliged, feeling unwanted, and retreated back into the storm.

Against the harsh winds, he crossed the camp to another, larger tent. Entering, he saw other dirtied bug hunters eating, drinking, laughing. Dressler dragged himself through the slop line, craving a little R&R at Maddie's Pub over toward town, but the mess tent would have to do. Nobody said anything to him as he gathered his plate of goop and found a seat at a nearly vacant table. Nobody knew what he'd just been through, the attack, that Trebs was fighting for his life.

He and Trebs weren't friends, not in the traditional sense. He knew almost everything about the man, but that came from Foundings together chasing beetles for meat. Alone out in the sands, there was little to do but talk. Get to know one another.

Except, Dressler hadn't told Trebs about Edilyn. He'd not told many, except his sister. Dressler's daughter Edilyn was diagnosed three weeks ago with ash lung. Only three Foundings old and the "experts" had given her two to six months to live. Edilyn was holding up, putting on a brave face for her dad, or perhaps she didn't realize what she was facing. Only a child, she didn't know the things she'd miss—school, growing up, making friends, falling in love, starting a family. Common human experiences that nearly everyone took for granted, but Edilyn would never have that chance. Dressler knew that even after she was gone, he'd celebrate every birthday, imagine every milestone that would have come. He'd continue to think about her life and what it could've—should've—been, long after she'd stopped living it.

It was his curse to bear.

One other hunter sat along the table from him. They were alone, the two of them. Jax was a strange one. He seemed different than the others. Quiet, withdrawn, like he was always thinking about something. The other hunters had given him a wide berth ever since his recent arrival, whispering about where he came from or who he was before he became a hunter. Most of Dressler's ilk were born into this trade, learning to use a spear and rifle as soon as they could pull a pacifier out of their mouths. It was their culture—the mark of true manhood. Bug hunters took great pride in their work, telling stories of daring adventures against bug-kind. They were a loud, conceited sort, and Dressler might have joined with them not too long ago. He would have laughed and drank and shared wild tales, but Edilyn...

"Hey," Jax spoke, breaking Dressler's thoughts. Dressler regarded the other man, surprised. Jax's face was pensive, his tone soft but distant. "You okay?"

Dressler remembered he was painted with blood—both human red and bug yellow. But he wasn't the confiding type. "Yeah."

Jax gave him a doubtful look then resumed his fabled deep thinking, continuing to eat. Dressler stared at the mound of nutritional slush on his plate, but had a hard time bringing himself to consume it. He thought of Trebs, of Edilyn, of his life on this ruined rock, and held his face in his hands.

"Excuse me," a timid voice interrupted.

Dressler saw one of the Palmer camp nurses standing over him, her gown splattered with blood. It was then that Dressler realized how quiet the mess hall had grown all of a sudden, as everyone watched her and, by proxy, him. The nurse wrung her hands and Dressler prepared himself for the news that Trebs was dead. He'd have to tell the man's family.

"Your friend wants to speak with you," the nurse said, biting her lip. Her face was a mix of worry and fear.

Dressler stood. "He's alive?"

She nodded. "We'll talk more...in private."

The nurse left him there, throwing conspiratorial glances over her shoulder. The men watched Dressler, mumbling gossip amongst themselves. Dressler felt out of place and looked to Jax for support, though he had no idea why. At last, he followed the nurse outside. She waited for him at the side of the tent, away from the hunters. The storm had subsided now, the breeze caressing the desert sands.

Dressler approached the woman, and she whispered, "He's...he's healed."

"Okay," Dressler said. "I'm glad the doctors were able to get to him in time."

"No," she corrected. "He's healed. The wound is gone. It's like he was never attacked."

Dressler's mind went blank. "I…I don't understand. He lost so much blood."

"He died on the operating table and then he just…woke up. The wound closed up on its own. There's not even a scar. Not a scratch."

"How is that possible?"

The nurse leveled her eyes at him. They were filled with a quiet terror. "It's not. But…he wants to speak with you."

At once, Dressler tromped across camp, headed for the infirmary. With force he pushed open the front flap, and gasped. Trebs was in a gown, sitting up on the bed, the medical staff pressed to one wall of the tent, talking heatedly, their voices low. Trebs turned to Dressler and smiled.

"Hey, Dress."

Doctors and nurses halted in their debate, eyeing the visitor. Dressler wanted to talk to them, to find out what had happened, but Trebs was focused on him, his face passive and full of light.

"Hey…Trebs," Dressler greeted awkwardly, not knowing what to say. Hesitant, he walked closer to the hunter on the cot. "They, uh, they said you wanted to talk to me."

"Not me," Trebs chuckled softly. "Through me, but it's someone else who has something to say. Come here." He lifted his chin towards the professionals huddling in the corner. "It's not for them."

Dressler did as requested, a foreboding dread gnawing at his gut. As he drew near, Trebs leaned forward, excited. "I saw them, man."

"Who?"

"The angels."

Dressler shook his head. "No."

"Yes. I was dead. I was in the black…Then one of them came to me, glowing and warm. He, it, whatever, said that he would send me back. He'd heal me. He said I had good to do in my life. Hah, can you believe that? My old man," Trebs trailed off, his eyes glistening with tears. "…he never thought I'd ever be any good…but I've got work to do, the angel said. And the first thing to do is talk to you."

Dressler exhaled, realizing he'd been holding his breath. "Why me?"

Trebs looked to the floor. "Is, uh…is something wrong with Edilyn?"

Dressler felt as though a weight had slammed into his stomach, punching out his breath. "What?"

"The angel told me. He knows she's sick, man. She's dying. Why didn't you tell me?"

"I…"

"It doesn't matter. The angel wants to help. He said that he knows your kid believes and that 'believers get rewarded'."

Feeling faint, Dressler braced himself on the cot, trembling.

"You gotta go down there, though," Trebs said. "I'm just the messenger. He said he can help you, but you've got to go down there. Under the water."

Dressler wanted to protest. Why? How? The angel had healed Trebs—brought him back from the dead—from all these kilometers away. Why did Dressler have to brave the waters in order for Edilyn to be saved? It wasn't fair. "Why can't he heal her like he did you?"

Trebs shrugged. "I don't know, Dress. I should've asked, but I was so grateful. You don't know what it's like when you're around those guys. I felt it, man. It was like…joy. Pure joy. But you've gotta go to him."

Dressler considered for a long moment, his mind filled with doubt, confusion, but most of all, hope. He spotted the doctors waiting on him, to hear his decision, and he would not keep them waiting any longer.

"Yeah. Okay. Where do I start?"

111. PROMOTION
JOSEPH H. FICOR

Shouhei exited the shuttle. Sheba's orbital spaceport, Carlston's Cove, handled all incoming and outgoing traffic. Most of the station's space was devoted to shipping the precious ore mined from Sheba to Avenir and Eclectia. The upper levels of the station housed exact copies of the luxurious staterooms of Avenir. Here, the masters of Sheba relished in the wealth that the broken world brought them.

Shouhei mentally prepared himself for a life of policing the mining settlements on the surface. He had not told his parents about his assignment to Sheba. Fear and humiliation restrained him. His folks were so proud that he had been accepted into the Enforcers. It was a rare chance to leave the dust of Adagio for a better life. Sheba was not a better life.

The enforcer at the customs checkpoint smiled when he saw Shouhei. He looked for a moment at the crisp new uniform of the "shiny."

"Welcome to the dump of the system," he said with that irritating smile. "You must have pulled someone's chain the wrong way to be sent here."

Shouhei said nothing. He gave the cynic his ID card.

Cynic inserted the card into a slot in his terminal.

The cynic's smile melted into a scowl as he read the screen.

He pulled the card from the computer and thrust it and a station map at Shouhei.

"Follow the map to Upper Level Six."

"What?" Shouhei just stood dumbfounded. *I'm not going to the surface? Why?*

"Upper Level Six, Shiny!" Cynic shouted.

Shouhei's confusion blazed like the exposed interior of the world below.

Cynic clarified, "You've been assigned to Governor Bokkasa's personal security detachment. Now move along! Next!"

Shouhei moved along.

112.   ORCA
FRED WARREN

Melanie closed the maintenance access panel on the contoured platform that supported Hamsa El-Hashem's—Orca's—swollen body. Swathed in a black simsuit and matching helmet, the nickname was apt. He looked like a baby whale strapped to a slab in some deranged zoologist's lab, awaiting dissection.

The two cyborgs keeping silent vigil at the foot of the table only reinforced the mental image. Even the air in the narrow compartment smelled faintly of formaldehyde.

She shuddered as she moved to the control console on the opposite wall and toggled the comm circuit. "All done. You now have industrial-strength surge protection between the network and your sim interface. Nothing short of a lightning bolt is gonna get through that."

The reply was deep and raspy—and it came from the blob on the table, not the console. Orca reached out toward Melanie with one hand. "Thanks, Mouse. I hope it's enough."

It took both of Melanie's hands to enfold his. "Enough? Weren't you listening, Hamsa? I told you, nothing short of…"

"You never saw the vids of what happened to Jumbo, did you?"

"No. I didn't. You guys said he took some electrical feedback when he cracked the firewall, and it killed him."

"It didn't just kill him, Mouse. It *cooked* him. His simsuit melted into his skin."

"Don't worry. This mod will give you enough time to bail before anything gets through." Melanie hoped her voice carried more conviction than she was feeling now. *Shells. What's hiding behind that firewall?*

He pulled his hand back, giving one of hers a squeeze as they separated. "You better go suit up. Rhino's getting itchy. The Folly's been hot 30 minutes now, and it's never stayed active more than an hour."

"Keep him on a short leash until I log in. I'm on point for this op. You both promised."

"Yeah, and we both still think you're crazy. This plan of yours better be something special."

"It is. Count on it." Melanie gathered up her tools and moved toward the door of Orca's apartment, taking care not to touch the cyborgs as she passed them. It was totally irrational, but they made her skin crawl.

Orca called out after her. "Hey, Mouse, how's Rhino looking? I mean, for real?"

She didn't turn around. "I don't know. Carson…wouldn't let me in. I had to pass the parts through a slot in his door and upload instructions to his Franks over the net. I'm praying they didn't screw up."

"That's too bad, but I can understand why he wouldn't want you to see him like this. Like me."

"Well, *I* don't understand. He's my brother. I don't care what he looks like. I want to hold his hand. I want to feel him breathing. For all I know, he's already dead, and I've been talking to some souped-up A.I. the past two months."

Orca chuckled—a metallic, rattling sound. "No, you'd know the difference, Mouse. Better than anybody."

"That him?"

Trebs led the way through the clatter and chatter of Maddie's Pub. Dressler trailed behind uncertainly, nodding a friendly "hello" to the madam of the bar. She was a mother to all the rugged workers who came here after hours and Dressler usually spent a while visiting with her, but today Maddie would have to wait.

They were here to save Edilyn.

At Dressler's question, Trebs answered, "Yeah."

In the corner of the pub, a bear of a man sat alone. He had an old prospector's hat on his head, a pair of dark green goggles over his eyes, and a great bushy white beard covering his cheeks, chin, and the better part of his chest. Presently, his head was leaned back against the wall, his mouth agape. A foul odor emanated off his gargantuan bulk and flies buzzed around him.

He didn't appear to be breathing. Dressler hesitated. "He's...not moving."

The two inched closer to the old man. Not a snore escaped his lips. His chest did not rise or fall. *No, this isn't happening.* Dressler worried. *We need him to save my daughter.* Dressler reached one hand towards his throat, intending to check his pulse. "I think he's dead..."

"Nope," the man barked, sitting straight up, suddenly alive. Dressler jerked his hand back, startled. "Just *playin'* dead. Tryin' ta keep the lowlifes away. You the guys got a job for me?"

Dressler shared a hesitant look with Trebs, but his partner simply nodded with a knowing grin. Trebs seemed a lot giddier since his brush with death and the angels of the seas. He had a perpetual glow about him these days that Dressler had to admit was a little creepy at times.

"I need someone to take me below," Dressler said, still standing.

The burly man raised his goggles and eyed the bug hunter suspiciously. "Let me guess. Angels, huh?"

"Yes."

"You one of them jelly rollers? This some kind of spiritual thing to you?" Before Dressler could answer, the man banged the table, carrying on. "Used to be a time folks stayed away from those critters. Now every Tom,

Dick, and Harry wants to take a box a'candy down to them squid heads and learn about 'em.'"

"No," Dressler corrected. "That's not why I want to go."

The scruffy brute swatted at one of the flies hovering by his nose. He snorted and glared. "Then what is it yer after?"

"I was …invited."

"By *who*?"

Dressler shifted uncomfortably. "By them. The angels. They want to cure my daughter. But, I need a tub to take me down there. Trebs says you're the best pilot."

"Ha!" The man threw his head back, roaring. "The best. The *cheapest*, you mean!"

"That, too. I don't have a lot of money, but if this saves my kid, whatever I've got is yours."

The pilot snickered a bit more. "Angels don't often take too kindly to our kind poking around in their habitat, invite or no. It'd take a *crazy* man to drive you down there to the deep to find 'em."

Dressler nodded. He knew the risks. But Edilyn was worth it.

The other man looked him up and down, but Dressler remained determined. "Will you take me?"

After a moment's pause, the pilot stood to his full height; the hairy ogre was more monster than man. He swelled his barren chest, looking down on the two tiny mortals that sought his help on their foolish quest. At last he thrust out a hand the size of Dressler's face, offering a shake. "Call me 'Crazy'."

114.   CHARITY
JOSEPH H. FICOR

The enforcer at the checkpoint, just off the elevator at Upper Level Six, smiled after he cleared Shouhei for entry.

"We've been expecting you." He said while maintaining that ominous smile.

Shouhei just said, "Thank you," as he passed the still-smiling enforcer.

The orders that had been printed out at the checkpoint stated that he was to proceed to Stateroom 14. He was there in five minutes.

Two guards, both Peacekeepers Level Two, stood on either side of the door leading into the stateroom. They wore immaculate navy blue uniforms with white berets and broad white sashes extending from their left shoulders to their right waists.

Shouhei saluted and the salute was returned. The PKL2 on Shouhei's right inserted Shouhei's ID card into a portable reader. He showed it to the other PKL2 who just grunted and mumbled something about Shouhei being the one.

The ID card was returned to Shouhei. The door opened and Shouhei entered a large office with white walls and red carpeting. Many abstract paintings hung neatly on the wall. A large luxurious Zirconian desk made of smoothed black coral stood four meters in front of the young enforcer.

A large man with skin as dark as the desk and wearing a robe of bright orange and red came from behind the desk and greeted Shouhei.

"Welcome," the man bellowed, "Enforcer Third Class Fiko! I have been looking forward to meeting you for a few months now."

Shouhei's training brought him back to his place. He straightened and saluted, but his face betrayed his confusion at the Governor's greeting.

The Governor just smiled. "My boy, I can see that you do not understand that I'm your benefactor."

Shouhei's face betrayed more confusion.

"I am your sponsor. I chose you from the dregs of Adagio to become an enforcer. You are my act of charity."

"I'm sorry sir. But I don't understand. I thought that I was accepted because of my scores on the entrance exam."

"Don't be silly," the Governor said, and laughed. "The test was just a formality. You were already in by my word. You see, I had a small wager with some of the members of my club that I could choose anyone from that waste on Eclectia and sponsor him through the enforcers. They doubted me, but you proved them wrong…"

Each of Governor's words was like the beating of a hammer driving a spike into Shouhei's heart.

"…and my boy, you paid handsomely—two platinums. So I've decided as a special reward to make you a member of my personal security detachment. What do you think about that?"

Professionalism—and his faith—prevented him from expressing the words.

175

Dressler stepped over a scrambling child, Edilyn in his arms. The shrill screams of her four tiny cousins cut through his mind like a hot poker. He winced. Edilyn's chubby hands cupped her ears.

"It's loud here, Daddy."

"I know, sweetheart. It's only for a couple days, though, okay? Then we'll be back home to the peace and quiet."

One of the ankle biters charged, a toy spaceship carved from a bug's antenna in his hand. The boy made aggressive laser sounds, orbiting Dressler in a strafing run. Edilyn looked at her father, helpless. She'd always been a shy child, but ever since getting sick, she'd been rendered nearly invisible by other children. She never felt well enough to play, and Dressler knew dropping her off here was a mistake, but he had nowhere else to go.

Maybe this whole thing is a mistake. Angels underwater want to give me the cure to Lyn's ash lung? I must be nuts to go down there.

But he'd already spent a small fortune hiring Crazy—the sub pilot. Along with Trebs, they'd made the preparations. He was locked into this course of action now, and could only hope it paid off.

For Edilyn's sake.

Or maybe just for my own.

Meryl stepped in between two warring children shouting over who had a powderbug fiber doll first. She looked flushed with embarrassment, or perhaps just exhaustion. "Hey, little brother," she exhaled, beaming. "Hey, Lyn."

Edilyn just buried her face in Dressler's shoulder.

He stroked her hair, his heart breaking. Meryl rubbed the little girl's back sympathetically. "It'll be fine, kiddo. We'll have lots of fun. You'll see."

Dressler appreciated his sister taking Edilyn in. Especially since he'd not told her what he was going to do. He'd only said that the bugs were migrating and they had to move with them for a couple days—just enough to bring back his quota. She'd accepted that. Meryl's husband was a miner and knew that sometimes the job called for sacrifices. This whole blamed planet did.

Nothing comes without sacrifice. That's what their father had taught them. Dressler wondered what sacrifice he'd be called on to make to appease these angels. Benevolent creatures or no, he didn't think for one moment they were just going to hand over Edilyn's cure out of the goodness of their squishy hearts.

No, they needed something.

But for Edilyn …he'd pay any price.

He kissed his daughter on the head and set her on her own two feet. Her arms tightened around him, breaking his heart. "I won't be gone very long, I promise."

"I'll miss you," she muttered, her eyes sparkling with budding tears.

He tried to hold in his own emotion. "I love you."

She hugged his leg as he stood. "Thanks, Meryl, for doing this."

His sister smiled, a bit sad. "She'll be fine, Dress. Just take care of yourself."

Then Meryl rubbed his arm. "We'll say a prayer to the angels for you."

Dressler grinned for his sister's benefit, though in his heart, her words felt ominous and filled him with dread. "Yeah …thanks."

116.   EXPANSE
FRED WARREN

"Good grief. Took you long enough to wake up."

John blinked and groaned as the leering face of Victoria Remsen gradually came into focus above him, framed in dangling brown curls that bobbed and waved like a collection of springs—or snakes.

"Where am…oh, right. I remember. Doctor Vicky's House of Horrors. It feels like you ran over me with a forklift."

The discomfort was real. John had to keep reminding himself he was immersed in a virtual reality simulation, and Vicky was suspended inside a life support pod somewhere nearby, practicing medicine by remote control, her brain hardwired into the Avenir computer network. She wasn't a little girl play-acting at being a doctor. She was a Dreamer, part of the legendary, hidden community that watched over the entire Avenir Eclectia colony from cyberspace—and wielded more control over it than anyone imagined. She knew what she was doing, and she was very, very dangerous.

She winked at him. "Good idea. Let's save that for next time."

The cartoony nurse costume she'd worn at their introduction had been replaced by a modest red party dress and a white lace shawl that draped across her shoulders. She began unfastening the restraints that held him to the examination table. "Well, you may be a moron, Mister John Milton, but you're no coward. I expected you to scream like a baby when I took the spinal tap, but you didn't make a sound. Impressive, but boring. Instead of letting the pain drive you into unconsciousness, I sedated you."

"How kind. Thanks."

"You earned it. It also gave me a chance to start attacking your liver problem, so the time wasn't completely wasted."

"What did you do to my liver?"

"Programmed some nanobots and set them to work reconstructing the right lobe. They should be finished in a couple of weeks. Don't worry...it won't hurt, but you can expect a little nausea mornings and evenings. Okay, maybe a *lot* of nausea. Anyhow, you're lucky. Without the repairs, you would have been dead inside five Foundings. As rich as you are, I'd think you could afford better hooch than that battery acid you've been drinking."

"I only buy the best vodka on Avenir."

"It's battery acid, and if you drink any more, I won't fix you. I don't warranty my work against stupidity. Now, get up. We're running behind."

"Behind what?" John sat up, and nearly fell off the table as a wave of vertigo washed over him, setting the entire room awhirl.

Vicky grabbed his arm, somehow managing to keep him upright and stable. "Whoa, guess I overdosed you a little on the sedative. Take it easy. Slow breaths, in and out. You'll get your balance back in a minute."

The oscillations subsided. John cautiously set his feet on the floor and stood up. He was fully dressed, the thin hospital gown exchanged for an expensive-looking formal suit in pinstriped gray with silver buttons, a starched white shirt and bow tie, and shiny black shoes. He tugged at his sleeves. "Why am I wearing a tuxedo?"

Vicky sighed. "The same reason I'm wearing a fancy dress. The command staff is honoring you with a welcome banquet. They're all waiting for us, and Captain Aziz isn't known for his patience. C'mon, *this* way."

She guided John by his elbow to the examination room's single door and unlatched it. Bright sunlight flooded through the opening, and John could hear strange twittering sounds and a low, repetitive rush of air. He stepped through the doorway onto soft, verdant grass that carpeted a broad clearing ringed with tall, thin trees. They swayed in a warm, gentle breeze that smelled faintly sour and tangy. The leafy foliage at their crowns danced in the wind, dark green fronds that stood in sharp contrast to the brilliant blue sky. Tiny winged creatures with indigo, crimson, and vermillion plumage fluttered among the treetops. *Birds.* He'd only seen pictures before, on his computer display or in old, old books.

In the distance, visible between the trees, was an expanse of translucent blue, tipped here and there with frothy white. The door had vanished behind him, and as he turned first to the right, then to the left, then all the way around, he could see the water encompassed the land on all sides.

It was an ocean. A real, living ocean.

He was on an island.

There was a long table at the center of the clearing with people seated around it, half a dozen or so, talking and laughing.

Vicky jabbed his shoulder with a manicured fingernail. "Quit gawking, and start walking."

117.   PRIZE PUPPY
JOSEPH H. FICOR

The Governor gave Shouhei many trivial errands to run, mostly taking things to the other aristocrats of Carlston's Cove. Everyone praised Shouhei for being so favored by the Governor. The young man's discipline was pushed to its maximum tolerances every time he heard a greater-than-thou exclaim "Here is the symbol of Bokassa's benevolence" or "Here is the epitome of rich charity."

The other members of the security detachment chose to call him the "prize puppy."

His "cuteness" began wearing off after a month on board the station. The Governor and other higher ups started showing disdain and boredom when he came around on official business.

Fear seized him when an Enforcer Second Class shouted at him as he passed a guard station on the Governor's level, "Hey, prize puppy! You're going to play with the big dogs soon."

His soul forecasted ill times ahead.

AVENIR ECLECTIA
SPLASHDOWN · MICHAEL L. ROGERS

Dressler settled in the seat of the sub, his thoughts a jumble. He was really doing it—going down to the depths of Eclectia's waters. Trebs sat beside him in the cockpit, uncharacteristically quiet. A serene smile stretched across the resurrected hunter's face, one that Dressler didn't understand. He didn't share Trebs' newfound faith or security.

At the controls of the underwater vessel was Crazy. His hands roved like wild over the console as he chewed a fat wad of actual tobacco. Music blared from the sub's speakers, some long lost ancient genre called "hip hop", Crazy said. The hairy man bebopped his head, but the rattle gave Dressler a headache. That the man had enough money for such tobacco and music players showed his submarine business had been doing pretty well.

"This is the classic stuff!" Crazy guffawed. "This was back when folks knew what music was all about. Now it's all just noise and dreck."

"If you say so," Dressler replied loudly to be heard over the bass.

Crazy chanted along with the music, and Dressler's eyes wandered to the viewport to his left. His ears popped as they descended deeper into the ocean and wondered how long this would take. How long did it take to speak to some angels and get a cure for Edilyn?

"You're nervous," Trebs seemed to pick his thoughts. The man leaned over with a knowing nod. "Don't be. Believers are rewarded."

Yeah, Dressler worried. That was the problem. *I'm not a believer, not as such.* Would the angels find him wanting? Would his doubts and Sheba-blamed practicality steal away the love of his life? He saw his daughter's face in his mind's eye, left behind on the surface with her aunt. Meryl, his older sister, with four screaming, joyous, healthy children.

He only had Edilyn.

What was he saying? That'd he rather see one of his sister's children die than his own? Was he saying Meryl had some to spare?

I'm horrible.

"Whoa!" Crazy bellowed. At first Dressler thought he was injecting some flavor into his sing-along, then he glimpsed it. Glowing, ethereal, vaguely humanoid, but wrong somehow. Fish-like. Alien. Other.

An angel.

She—he assumed it was a she—filled his port, startling him. But she was not alone. More joined her, swimming around the sub. Suddenly, he felt words worming their way through his mind. Words of warning. *Turn back now*, and *You don't belong here.*

"Told ya!" Crazy snapped, shaking his bushy mane. He must have been hearing them too. "Told ya they wouldn't want us poking around."

"It'll be fine," Trebs said, still calm. Still smiling. "It's a test, that's all. Scaring off the unfaithful."

"It's working!" Crazy said.

"No!" Dressler snapped. "I paid you for a job. Keep going."

"I am, I am, relax. And hold on!"

The sub lurched forward, evading the angels, swirling down into the dark abyss of the Boatic Trench.

119. GOVERNOR'S DECREE
JOSEPH H. FICOR

Peacekeeper Major Stotter, head of Governor Bokkasa's personal security detachment, stood at parade rest before the great black desk of the Governor.

"Thank you for coming as such a late hour, Major. I know that you had just finished your duty shift about an hour ago—around two?"

"Yessir, I did," replied Stotter. "You said that you wanted to discuss your pet, Enforcer Fiko."

"Yes." Governor Bokkasa leaned back in his chair. "I'm bored with him. The excitement of my charity is waning. I want you to take him and have him do some real work."

"Forgive my bluntness sir, but wouldn't it look bad for you to throw him away so easily after only one month? I've heard of officials planning to visit Eclectia to find even lower scum than Fiko. They want to outdo you."

"Let them." Bokassa waved his hand dismissively. "I'll always be remembered as the first to have lifted a coffee ground to the level of cream."

Stotter's face remained expressionless. The Governor's attempts at creative witticisms always fell short of their mark. "What do you have in mind, sir?"

The Governor immediately brought himself back to the main topic. "I want you to take Enforcer Fiko and some other expendable on a collection run to Docking Bay Five. Dear Artimus hasn't paid his station tax in four months."

Stotter's expression cracked. A smirked formed across his lips. "Artimus Rawlings is a difficult man to find. He usually manages to avoid our enforcers. We can only collect when he is overpowered and his cargo confiscated. And he said that the next time we came..."

Bokassa finished the sentence: "...to collect, he'd kill our enforcers. I know. I know. My sources have confirmed that he is now at a Docking Bay Five. He won't leave until tomorrow afternoon. Besides, this run will be an excellent opportunity to kill two birds with one stone."

"What do you mean, sir?"

"Easy. Rawlings has outlived his usefulness. He never realized that the ore that he has been smuggling out of here was my way of making a little extra profit without concerning the aristocrats on Avenir. They have enough wealth. I thought that it was time for them to share a bit more of it with us. Now Artimus needs to be eliminated."

"And Fiko is the second bird?"

"Exactly. He has outlived his usefulness. It is time for him to go out in a blaze of glory. I've proven my charity. He can serve as some kind of example of hope for the dustbugs on Eclectia."

"I'll see to it, sir."

"Thank you, Major. Please send Enforcer Second Class Hicks as the second expendable. He's annoying me."

"Yes sir. Good night, sir."

"Yes, yes. Good night, Major."

Stotter thought to himself after he left the Governor's quarters. "A very unusual execution decree. And a triple besides. Very original."

Stotter went to his quarters for a good night's sleep.

"Ninja outfits, Carson? Seriously?" Melanie wrestled with the black mask shrouding her head and face. The eye slit had somehow gotten turned around the wrong way and she couldn't see anything. Virtual reality could be amazing, but she still didn't see the point of the sort of realism that simulated clothes going askew.

"You said we have to be stealthy. And how many times do I have to tell you to call me Rhino?"

She gave the mask a final yank and glared at her brother. "This isn't a game, Car...*Rhino*. We're not going to sneak up on the firewall and stab it with a knife. I mean, *look* at it."

The firewall manifested in the simulation as a towering range of obsidian mountains spanning the visible horizon—enormous, black, jagged teeth poised to devour the twilit sky. Melanie, Carson, and Hamsa crouched behind their rally point, a low hillock that felt profoundly inadequate to screen them from any observers watching from the heights.

"All right, fine! It makes me feel less...visible, okay?" Carson shoved the dagger he'd been fiddling with into the belt of his shozoku and turned away.

"Skitterbug."

Hamsa chuckled. "You're on point, Mouse. What now?" Even in ninja garb, his avatar looked more like a sumo wrestler than an assassin.

"Where's Jumbo's Folly?"

"It should be right in front of us," said Carson. "Look for a glow at the base of the mountain. There should be a crack where Jumbo broke in."

"There!" Hamsa pointed to an indentation in the obsidian wall, about 200 meters away and slightly to the right of their position.

Melanie squinted in that direction. "I don't see...wait. You're right. There it is...that hazy green patch. Good eye, Orca."

"How are we going to get over there without anybody seeing us?"

"I don't think there *is* anybody. From what you told me, Jumbo didn't encounter any resistance until he started his hack. The defenses don't kick in until they sense an intrusion." Melanie stood up. "Follow me."

Carson didn't move. "Uh, Sis...how about Orca and I wait a few paces to make sure they don't have some kind of death ray aimed at you?"

Hamsa grabbed Carson by the arm and hauled him to his feet. "C'mon, Rhino. Mouse is in charge. We have to follow her orders."

They trotted in a loose column toward the green glow. She'd die before giving Carson the satisfaction of betraying her own fear, but Melanie found herself checking the mountainside every few seconds from the corner of her eye. There were no signs of life, yet she could feel a kind of *pressure* from it, a massive power, coiled and waiting.

But nothing happened. Nothing moved on the silent monolith of ebony glass. No alarms sounded; no death rays flashed out to meet them.

As they drew nearer, the glow coalesced into a zigzagging crack that traveled 10 meters diagonally upward from the mountain's foot. There was a pile of rusty scrap metal with bits scattered across the ground, and something that looked like a huge, twisted drill bit wedged into the obsidian where the crack began.

The remains of Jumbo McLaren's security hack, left behind by its incinerated creator.

Hamsa shook his head. "It's too narrow. We'll never fit into that."

"We don't have to." Melanie fished around in a pocket of her shozoku and pulled out a short length of fabric, a few centimeters wide.

"What's that?"

"Not what. *Who*. Gentlemen, meet Flat Audrey."

"It looks like a piece of tape." Hamsa bent down to take a closer look.

"Audrey is a sophisticated micro-AI, optimized for information collection. A flatworm. She was my tech school graduation project. Say hello, Audrey."

The fabric curled up into an S shape and warbled, *HELLO, AUDREY.*

"Oh, yes," Carson sneered, "*Very* sophisticated. Does it tell jokes, or does it just sit there, *being* a joke?"

I GATHER INFORMATION. I DO NOT TELL JOKES.

Melanie swatted Carson's head. "Pay attention. Audrey will go into the crack, follow the data leak, merge with the network inside the firewall, and camouflage herself as a diagnostic subroutine. She'll collect information for a couple of days, then return to us. She's got 20 teras of storage. I've instructed her to pinpoint weaknesses in the security protocols, analyze their encryption scheme, and collect access keys. With that information, we can find our own way in."

185

"You're an impressive little bug, Audrey," said Hamsa, nudging Audrey with a finger.

I AM NOT A BUG. I AM A FLATWORM, BUT I AM IMPRESSIVE. THANK YOU.

Melanie smiled inside her ninja mask. "Audrey also enjoys compliments."

She drew a katana from the sheath strapped to her back and gently placed Audrey on its tip. "All right...if we get any reaction at all from this, everybody logs out immediately. Understood?"

"Understood." Hamsa took a step back.

Carson hesitated a moment. "Be careful, Mel."

Melanie extended her arms, slowly pushing the katana's blade toward the crack in the mountain. She inhaled sharply as it entered the aurora of green mist surrounding the crevice, but there was no change in the glow, or any other sign of trouble. She positioned the blade's point as close to the opening as she could without touching the obsidian. "Audrey, deploy. Recovery in 48 hours."

DEPLOYING. The flatworm extended itself and slid into the gap like a tiny snake, its skin instantly matching the color and texture of the volcanic glass, and vanished.

Melanie pulled back and returned her katana to its sheath with a sigh. "She's in. Now, we wait."

121. WAKE UP CALL
JOSEPH H. FICOR

Shouhei struggled to stay awake in the elevator as it traveled to the docking bays of Carlston's Cove.

The loud voice—and hands—of Enforcer Second Class Damon Hicks had forced him out of his rack only twenty minutes before.

The young enforcer had just fallen asleep after serving a fourteen hour shift when Hicks stormed into Shouhei's quarters. Hicks ordered him to get back into uniform and to bring his sidearm. Peacekeeper Major Mao Stotter, commander of the Governor's personal security detachment, had personally ordered Hicks and Shouhei to accompany him on an assignment. They were to apprehend a star pilot named Artimus Rawlings.

Rawlings had not paid his station docking fees for several months. He was also suspected of smuggling large amounts of ore from Sheba. Shouhei had heard his name thrown around by the veterans of the security detachment. Rawlings had earned the nickname of "Bakemono." It was an old Earth word for ghost. He was the given the moniker because he had always managed to avoid being tracked down by the authorities. That is, until now.

"Fiko! Wake up!" Hicks's booming voice—and sharp slap on the back—jolted Shouhei back into conscious focus.

Even the granite face of the Major winced at the high volume in the small space of the elevator. Shouhei had the feeling that Hicks was more hated by the other members of the detachment than himself.

The elevator stopped, the display showed Docking Bay Five, and the doors opened.

Hicks's hand made contact again. "Showtime, Prize Puppy."

Shouhei swallowed hard and followed the Major and Hicks into the wide space of the docking bay.

122.   ON THE EVE OF THE END
GREG MITCHELL

The sub was on autopilot. Crazy had since outmaneuvered the angels at the top of the Boatic Trench, hiding within a series of underwater coral caves. It'd been tense for nearly twenty minutes as Dressler, Trebs, and Crazy nestled in the coral, no lights on, running on minimal power. The sub had been quiet as a tomb, filling Dressler with dread. At last, the angels moved on and the sub resumed its underwater quest.

Now they were lowering their way towards the meeting place, where Trebs' angel contact was leading him. It occurred to Dressler more than once to ask why, if the angels had invited him to the ocean depths, the ones closer to the surface were so intent on keeping them away. The couple times he'd posed that same question to Trebs, his co-hunter had simply said, "Trust me."

It was a lot to go on trust, but every time Dressler thought of returning to dry land, he only had to think of Edilyn.

Crazy sipped at a mug of steaming drink, the same as Dressler and Trebs tended. The three of them sat around a small card table in the sub's hold, taking a moment for themselves while the autopilot finished its journey. The coffee break was equal parts celebration that they'd dodged the angry angels and a time of quiet reflection. A strange sort of bond had been formed through the experience, and Crazy was feeling chatty.

The large man went on, pleasantly enough, talking about his various adventures piloting the oceans. Dressler nodded in and out of the conversation, enjoying the man's stories when he was listening, but mostly thinking of home and how much he stood to lose if this little sojourn went south.

"So you're a bug hunter, huh?"

Dressler blinked, realizing that Crazy had addressed him. "What? Oh. Yeah."

He sipped at his drink. "Thought only criminals took that job."

Dressler shrugged. "That's not always true."

"I don't mean to offend," Crazy quickly added. "If that's the case, then that's your own business. Just saying you don't look to me like much of a criminal."

"No, it's okay," Dressler said. "I...served some time."

Trebs blanched. "You never told me that."

Of course he hadn't. He didn't tell anyone, save his employers. "It was about three Foundings before Lyn was born. My daughter," he added, realizing he'd not told Crazy her name. He felt as though the man had earned that much—risking all he had to escort Dressler on this fool's errand. "It was a bar fight. I was lit up and mad about something. Guns got involved...I got a lenient sentence on account that we both were drunk and no one could tell who started shooting first. But..."

Crazy nodded, listening with a sympathetic ear. "You're not that man now," he said, not asked.

Dressler felt a thin smile emerge. "No. My daughter changed all of that."

"Kids have a way of doin' that." Crazy buried himself in his mug again, thoughtful.

"You have any kids?" Trebs asked the pilot, suddenly, and it felt as though the man was a third wheel, butting in on a private conversation, though he'd been there the whole time.

"Used to," Crazy answered, and left it at that.

Proximity alarms bathed the cabin in red. Crazy simply rose, slow and steady.

"What's that?" Dressler asked, his heart starting to race.

"We're here," Crazy announced, like they'd reached the end of a leisure tour. "Now it's time to see what the fuss is all about."

"Yes," Trebs stood, solidly. "It is."

That's when Trebs pulled the knife.

123. BANQUET
FRED WARREN

Vicky tugged at John's arm as they walked up the broad, grassy slope to the clearing where a group of people sat around a long table laden with flowers and exotic food. John was still gaping at the rainbow-colored birds, swaying palm trees, and most of all, the turquoise-blue water that surrounded this tiny island. When he didn't respond, she pulled on his ear with enough force to make him double over.

"Keep your mouth shut and smile a lot," she whispered, "Talk only if somebody asks you a question. When you do talk, don't be boring, if that's possible."

"Thanks." John rubbed his ear and straightened his jacket. "I'll try to remember that."

A low burble of conversation coalesced into intelligible words as they approached the banquet table.

"In my opinion, they've become far too dangerous. How long do you intend to let them run on?"

"Teriyaki chicken? I've never heard of it."

"Levitation? You're joking. That's impossible."

"Oh, a while yet. The scheme amuses me, and their blundering draws attention away from our activities. After they've been exposed, it should be easier for us to proceed."

"Take a bite. It's one of the formulations I recovered last week. Since I incorporated my new algorithm into the core recovery utility, I've repaired fifteen teras of memory I thought was lost forever."

"I watched it happen. If only I'd thought to initiate a recording. There's more going on here than meets the eye."

"Just don't wait until they've wrecked the entire station and decimated the colony. Pineapple?"

"Mmm. It's heavenly. I may eat nothing else for days."

"Next you'll claim they're conjuring apparitions of the Holy Virgin."

"Don't mind if I do. Thank you. How goes the refit?"

"Wait 'til you taste the lemon meringue pie."

"Don't scoff. You should peruse my predecessor's archives sometime. Avenir Eclectia's history is chock full of unexplained phenomena. He was convinced there's a spiritual element to it."

"Poorly. There's nothing for it but to completely strip and resurface the radiation shield. I can jigger the nanofactories to produce the necessary materials, but I'll have to move at a snail's pace to avoid attracting attention. It will be at least one more Founding before we can think of proceeding to the next step."

"I'm hoping our new recruit can help us expedite that. Ah, here he is now." The man at the head of the table rose from his chair. He wore a white, military-styled cutaway jacket trimmed with gold braid. Wavy black hair fell almost to his shoulders, and his brown eyes and dark complexion made the brilliance of his smile that much more striking. "I am Captain Kagan Aziz, and these are my friends and advisors."

A burly, redheaded man wearing a uniform similar to Aziz stood up and seized John's hand in a crushing grip. "Otherwise known as 'The Staff.' I'm Colin Finn, First Officer, in charge of colony liaison and human intelligence."

The other officers arose in turn and moved around the table to greet John.

"Girard LeBeau, Engineering."

"Yeong Soo Min, Astrophysics and Navigation."

"Nigel Cromwell, Security."

"Jiro Sukahara, Chaplain."

John nodded at each one, accepted and returned a firm handshake, and tried to maintain an expression of polite interest, the only way he could think to follow Vicky's instructions without looking like a complete idiot. *So these are the Dreamers.* It beggared belief. The descendants of Avenir's original command crew, living in a virtual world but still influencing the colony their ancestors helped found so long ago. Not a legend. Real, powerful, and active.

But there aren't very many. Are these all of them?

Aziz finished the introductions: "You're already well acquainted with Anya Sherikov, Communications Officer, and your lovely escort, Victoria Remsen, Medical and Life Sciences. Please, join us. I must apologize in advance…the food and drink will have little taste due to the limitations of your interface, but once you are fully integrated into our network, I promise you flavors and sensations beyond your wildest imagination."

"So Anya has told me, but I haven't actually decided whether…"

Cromwell interrupted in a rumbling voice that matched his scowling, craggy face. "Anya, I thought we agreed not to use the visitor interface until the firewall was repaired."

"This is a situation of some urgency, Nigel." She flicked her fingers in an airy wave, as if she was shooing off an annoying insect. "Don't worry, I'm monitoring the fracture. There have been no attempts to probe or penetrate it, only some idle chatter on the Gaming net."

He tapped the table with a stubby finger. "I will not tolerate any compromise of the firewall."

The carefree mirth vanished from Anya's countenance. "Oh, I'm certain all the Gamers are still shivering in terror after what you did the last time. It was excessive, and it compounded the damage. You probably drew more attention to our existence than any number of data leaks."

"I'll do it again, if necessary."

Anya pushed up from her chair and slowly leaned across the table, coming almost nose-to-nose with Nigel. "The Command Network firewall is *my* domain. You will *not* apply active countermeasures without my consent."

"I won't need consent if I void your security clearance."

"Ha! I'd like to see you try."

Aziz raised a hand. "That's enough bickering, both of you. This is no way to behave in the presence of a guest. Anya, continue to monitor for intruders. If Nigel thinks countermeasures are necessary, I would like input from the *entire* staff before I decide whether or not to respond. Is that clear?"

The two combatants remained silent, eyes locked.

Aziz steepled his fingers beneath his chin and sighed. "*Is. That. Clear?*"

"Yessir." Anya flopped back into her chair and turned it sideways.

"Yes…*sir*," Nigel growled.

"Excellent. Now, to business. Mr. Milton, we have been observing you for some time, and are very impressed with your business acumen and technical expertise. Most of all, you appear to share our vision for the future of this colony. Anya thinks you would make a worthy replacement for her when the time comes, and I concur."

Vicky piped up. "Miss Sherikov doesn't need replacing. I'm going to make her well."

"Your father spent many years studying Anya's ailment, without success," said Aziz. "We must prepare for the worst-case scenario."

"Father was close to a cure. I *know* I can finish it."

"Victoria, now is not the time."

Her face flushed. She fixed her eyes on her plate, but her shoulders were trembling. "No! If I don't figure this out, we're all…"

Aziz's voice cracked like a whip. "Victoria!"

There was silence all around the table for several long moments, then Vicky murmured, "I'm sorry, Captain."

He reached across the table to grasp her hand, and John was surprised she didn't pull away. "We are all very fond of Anya, but we must also acknowledge the reality of her situation. It may be that you will identify an effective treatment, but we cannot risk a gap in transition for the Communications function. Many things depend on its smooth operation."

Anya gently encircled Vicky's shoulders. "I have confidence in your skill, dear one, but the Captain is right. We must be prepared. Anyway, it's a long while yet before we have to worry. In the meantime, our new friend has many things to learn."

Vicky sniffed and rubbed her nose. "That's for sure."

Aziz leaned back in his chair and gestured toward John. "As you may have noticed, despite living in this virtual paradise, we are not a community of lotus eaters. We are passionate about a great many things, and it keeps life interesting, at the price of an argument or two along the way. Now, I'm sure you have many questions about us. Proceed."

John didn't hesitate. "I've at least a hundred, but there's one thing I'm particularly curious about. You said I share your vision for the colony. I don't understand. I don't *have* a vision for Avenir Eclectia. In my opinion, it was a mistake for us to settle here."

"Precisely." Aziz smiled and twiddled a tiny cocktail umbrella between his fingers. "We are convinced the colony is no longer viable. It must be relocated."

"Move!" Crazy hollered, his meaty fists wrapped around Trebs' wrists. The knife in Trebs' left hand wavered centimeters from the pilot's gray-white beard. Dressler stood back, hardly able to comprehend the order of events. In a span of seconds, Trebs had pulled a knife and lunged for the sub pilot, just as they reached the meeting place with the angel that had Edilyn's cure. Crazy held his own—and rightly so for he was three times the size of Trebs—but the bug hunter was nearly superhuman in power. A sweaty sheen draped over his face and his eyes were glassy and mad.

"Trebs, stop!" Dressler shouted, futilely. "What are you doing?"

Trebs didn't answer, his beady gaze directed on Crazy. Unrelenting, he leaned on the blade.

"A gun..." Crazy grunted, struggling. "Cockpit...Under the pilot's seat..."

Dressler thought to run across the sub to find it, but acted instead, lunging on his co-worker—his guide down here into this aquatic hell—and wrapped around his arms. Pulling with every ounce of strength hard work had given him, Dressler roared, "Let go! Get off of him!"

"The jelly roller's...snapped!" Crazy barked, his thick arms visibly shaking, giving in.

Dressler put Trebs in a chokehold and pried him off the pilot. Trebs merely flexed his trim arms, and Dressler was thrown backwards, hurtling across the card table where they'd shared drinks moments ago. He collapsed the table, dashing the ceramic mugs to the floor where they popped. Dazed, he pushed himself to his knees, feeling warmth spreading down his temple. Blood dripped from his stubbled chin, dotting the floor.

Getting his senses together, he looked back to Crazy still bravely wrestling with the knife. The ogre was on the floor now, on top of Trebs, trying desperately to turn the blade back on his attacker. Trebs never faltered, his face blank and expressionless, his eyes distant but intelligent. Like a machine.

"Gun!" Crazy shouted once more. This time Dressler did not hesitate. He clattered out of the small cabin, bouncing against the handrails, clanking down the hall, racing for the cockpit. His heart rammed hard in his chest and he thought of Edilyn.

I'm never going to see her again.

He tripped into the cockpit, falling face-first on hard metal. From his vantage point he glimpsed the simple handgun holstered underneath the pilot's seat. Scrambling on hands and knees, he undid the latch and drew the gun. Checked to see it was loaded. Cocked it and rushed back to his friend.

Re-entering the cabin, he saw Crazy, spread on the floor.

Unmoving.

Trebs stood over him, bloodied knife in hand, barely breathing hard.

"Dress," he stated simply, Crazy's life dripping off the knife's edge.

A blossom of red spread on Crazy's barrel chest, intermingling with his frizzy beard. The man's eyes were cold, lifeless.

No...

"Dress," Trebs said once more, snapping him to.

Dressler ignored the man. Bared his teeth and raised the gun, firing. Trebs ducked impossibly out of the path of the bullet and it ricocheted off the wall deeper into the room, throwing sparks. "I'll kill you!" Dressler screamed.

He shot again, but Trebs moved fast and leapt, tackling Dressler backwards, smacking his head on corrugated flooring. He saw stars, then only black.

125. A FORTUITOUS STUMBLE
JEFF CHAPMAN

Another gust pelted Elihu Simmons's goggles with ash grit, each tiny speck clicking against the translucent saucers of scuttlebug shell and gouging a new pit that he would have to polish away. He thanked the good Lord that Sarah had chased after him with the goggles he had forgotten. He made a mental note to thank her—passionate kisses or watching the baby—when he got home, if he got home. He hadn't seen this storm coming. It might exhaust itself in an hour or expel its fury for days.

The gray dust cut his vision to a few steps. The scuttlebug shell blurred what remained, reducing his perception to shapes and shadows. *Got to find shelter*, he told himself, *before you're hopelessly lost.*

A bandanna woven from powderbug bristles wrapped his mouth and nose. Dust clogged the fabric where the moisture from his breath dampened the cloth. Grit stung his left ear. Another blast scratched the sliver of cheek exposed above the bandanna. He cursed creation and then asked forgiveness before he'd sucked another bitter-tasting breath through the bristle cloth. Struggle, curse, and beg forgiveness, his daily mantra and all for what: to keep Sarah and the baby alive and offer a few souls a grain of hope. If this was the Lord's gift, He could have it back. Elihu begged forgiveness. "Service and humility over pride. With humility comes wisdom," he repeated. "The Lord sustains the humble but casts the wicked to the ground."

Elihu held his spear in the crook of his arm and reached behind his head to adjust the knot and raise the cloth to shield his cheeks. The next gust caught him standing straight and off balance, punching him in the chest. He stumbled backwards and to his right and then took an extra step to regain his balance, but the ground he sought was not there. He tumbled over, thinking his appointed day had come. Sharp rocks, a cluster of beetles. He saw them both in his mind's eye and both would tear him to shreds.

Twigs snapped as they poked his hands and arms. He landed in a prickly bed of lavabushes, on his stomach. The impact knocked the wind out of him. Perhaps the Lord had more for him to do. Something moved beneath him. He ripped off his goggles to see a horde of scuttlebugs burrowing into the ash beneath the bushes, kicking up plumes of dust as their wriggling bodies disappeared. About the size of his palm, the critters lived off lavabush seeds near the bottom of the food chain.

Walls of black lava rock, rippled with vertical crests and troughs, towered on either side of him at least seven meters and tapered until they met five meters ahead of him like the prow of a boat, an ark of shelter. Ash swirled into the crevice, but the deep, narrow crack offered protection from the blasting wind. Behind him, the crevice extended as far as he could see. In a cave here he might wait out the storm, protected from the wind with plenty of lavabush to fuel a fire and its seeds to roast and eat. If he conserved his water, he figured he could last for days.

Elihu found his spear lying atop the tangle of lavabushes that had been tumbling across the waste into this crack for tens of Foundings. Already a layer of dust coated the shaft and blade of his spear. He strapped his goggles across his forehead. He needed all his vision to watch for signs of a cave. With his spear thrust forward, he crunched through the knee-deep lavabushes, which stuck to his pants, requiring him to stop every few meters to knock the bushes loose. He crept forward, listening and studying the walls. "Though I walk through the darkest valley," he whispered, "I will fear no evil, for you are with me." If he ever needed to believe those words, it was now. An occupied cave could be worse than none at all.

126. STANDDOWN
JOSEPH H. FICOR

The trio stepped off the elevator and looked at the motley array of ships. It was a collection of all shapes and sizes.

Shouhei's heart leapt in joy at the sight of so many spacefaring beauties. How he greatly desired to step aboard one and fly among the blackness. He made sure that his emotion did not show on his face.

"Look for a ship that looks like a long, gray needle." Major Stotter added, "Deadly force is authorized if you deem it necessary."

Everyone unholstered their pistols. Shouhei fought to suppress a smile at the sight of sweat beading on Hicks's brow. He never thought that he would see the day when Hicks would be silent.

The ship in question was found within a few minutes. Stotter motioned Hicks and Shouhei to take up positions around the ship while he covered the main hatch.

"Artimus Rawlings," Stotter called out. "Come out and surrender peacefully. You are under arrest for delinquent docking fee payments and suspicion of ore smuggling. If you just come with us quietly, I assure you that this matter will be cleared up very easily."

A bullet narrowly missed Stotter's head. Stotter dived behind a stack of nearby ore containers before Rawlings fired another shot.

Shouhei followed his superior's example. He took up a position behind the control panel of a loading crane.

More shots were fired.

Hicks was not so fast. He lay on the deck, his head surrounded by a steadily growing crimson puddle.

Stotter feigned rage. "Rawlings! I'm going to deep space you for that!"

"Shut up, Stotter," Rawlings screamed back. "You have as much feeling for your men as a whale has for its dung."

Stotter and Rawlings exchanged verbal barbs—and occasionally shots.

Shouhei caught sight of the suspect. He was sheltered behind a landing strut of another ship. The strut's cover provided excellent protection against Stotter's pistol.

Shouhei fired some rounds that startled Rawlings more than anything else.

He returned fire.

Shouhei ducked as the rounds sounded on the control panel in front of him.

Shouhei got back up to return fire, but he could not see Rawlings.

The hot barrel touching his temple alerted him to Rawling's new location.

"I'm going to send you into early retirement, Enforcer."

"Rawlings," Stotter shouting as he pointed the pistol at Rawlings. "Stand down!"

Rawlings turned his head. "Or wha…"

Shouhei took quick action and shot Rawlings in the left knee. Then he hit Rawlings in the jaw with his pistol. Rawlings fell to the deck. He was out cold.

Stotter rushed over. "Are you okay, boy?"

"Yessir," Shouhei responded.

"Why didn't you kill him?" Stotter demanded.

"I don't know, Sir." Shouhei responded as he looked down at Hick's dead body. "It just didn't seem right. I know that he had killed one of our own, but I couldn't do it, Sir. I'm sorry."

Stotter pointed his pistol at Shouhei's head. "Me too."

127. DOWNLOAD
FRED WARREN

Melanie stood in the shadow of the obsidian mountains, alone this time. No ninja outfit, no dodging and weaving her way from boulder to bush, trying to hide from an enemy that wasn't there. Most of all, there was no Carson and no Hamsa. She'd catch hell later for doing the retrieval without them, but they'd just slow her down. This place, deserted or not, gave her the creeps. It felt haunted. The twisted drill bit embedded in the fractured cliff ahead was Jumbo's Folly, the headstone of a reckless gamer who died trying to break into whatever was protected by the mysterious black wall. Carson thought it was Paradise, the fabled home of the legendary Dreamers. Melanie thought he was nuts.

He'd abandoned life beyond his simulation couch, but he was her brother. She'd never abandon *him*.

Whatever it was, it didn't want visitors. Two days ago, Carson and his friends had detected a data leak here, and she'd sent a reconnaissance AI into a crack in the firewall. By now, the chameleon program should have filled its memory with the information they'd need to penetrate the enclave without triggering a lethal response.

It was time to recover Flat Audrey and get out of here.

"Audrey, return."

The slender black ribbon that dropped from the gash in the cliff lay in the grass for a moment, then curled up on itself like a tiny serpent, whistling in a reedy voice, *MISSION COMPLETE.*

Melanie picked it up and set it in the palm of her right hand. "Welcome back, Audrey. How are you?"

I AM FINE. I AM FULL. I DO NOT LIKE THAT SYSTEM.

This was an odd status report, even from Audrey. "What don't you like about it?"

MANY HOSTILE SECURITY PROGRAMS, ALL PURPOSED TO DESTROY INTRUDERS. WE SHOULD LEAVE NOW.

"No argument here. Were you detected?"

NO. I AM EXTRAORDINARY.

"Yes, you are. Let's go home."

It was a relief to get out of the gaming rig. Melanie used the suite's interface to transfer Audrey from the network into a memory stick, then she returned to her own room and plugged the stick into a stand-alone workstation. She didn't want anybody else seeing what Audrey had discovered behind the firewall.

She opened the first archive and groaned. It was encrypted.

"Audrey, why didn't you decrypt this data?"

UNABLE. MILITARY-STRENGTH ENCRYPTION. I AM NOT THAT EXTRAORDINARY.

Melanie chuckled. There weren't many AIs that could make a synthesized voice sound sad. The developers usually didn't bother. Audrey, however, was a labor of love.

"It's not your fault, baby. I programmed you."

YES, IT IS YOUR FAULT.

"Saucy girl." Melanie could still hack the encrypted files, but she'd have to call in a favor from one of her tech school classmates who had a bone to pick with the Peacekeepers. "Is anything you collected *not* encrypted?"

YES. OPEN ARCHIVE 8034-A. INTERFACE DATA AND ID OF GUEST USER EXTERNAL TO NETWORK. ARCHAIC ADAPTER SPILLED DATA THROUGH GAP IN FIREWALL.

"Do tell. This must be the guy who lit up Jumbo's Folly. Let's take a look." Her fingers flew across the touchpad, and lines of data, *readable* data, flowed across the screen. Technical specifications of the user's simulation rig. Network addresses. Data volume and rate of flow. At the end of it all was a standard colonist identification code cluster. And a name.

Melanie blinked. "John Milton?"

She knew the name. Milton was a celebrity, a big-shot businessman, an import-export broker. It didn't make sense. This guy was too busy making money to waste any time on sims. He played his games in the real world with real people. What possible connection could he have with the Dreamers? Why would he care?

He wouldn't.

Melanie smiled. *That* was the answer. There *weren't* any Dreamers. The obsidian firewall was there to protect records of shady business deals, or embezzlement, or bribes paid to government officials. That would make a lot more sense than a play world for disembodied relics of a bygone age. If she could prove it, her brother would lose interest in Jumbo's Folly, and the firewall, and the missing memory blocks in the network servers. He'd go back to his friends and his games and stop risking his life sticking his nose where it didn't belong.

It was time to pay a visit to Mr. John Milton.

128. SUDDEN TURN
JOSEPH H. FICOR

Shouhei turned to see the muzzle of Stotter's pistol only a few centimeters away from his face.

"Sir," Shouhei fought to keep a professional composure, "why are you threatening me with your firearm?"

Stotter tilted his head to the right in mild surprise and smiled. "Are you so naïve? I thought that your short time with us would have wisened you up to real life."

Shouhei maintained his composure despite the fear that flooded his mind like a tsunami torrent. "No sir, I'm not naïve anymore. I guess the Governor is tired of his prize puppy?"

Stotter nodded his head in acknowledgment. "You got it. Not bad for a piece of dust." His smiled broadened. "You see, here's how life works on Carlston's Cove: Your life span is equal to your usefulness. Yours just hasn't been very long."

"How are you going to explain my death to my family?"

"Any spacing way that we want," Stotter shouted. Then he relaxed and calmly resumed. "I guess we can just say you died in the gunfight. You'll get a nice medal—posthumously, of course. And maybe a nice funeral. Maybe your parents will get a nice… What are you doing?"

Stotter stopped as Shouhei's eyes widened. The young enforcer raised the pistol in his hand and aimed it at Stotter.

Stotter grinned at the sudden turn of events. "If you intend to shoot me…"

Shouhei cut him off. "I don't intend to." And fired.

129. AFTERLIFE
FRED WARREN

"Move the colony."

It was a throwaway line, something John would toss out for a few cheap laughs at a cocktail party, a bit of cynical commentary on the state of Avenir Eclectia. It wasn't a call to action. No one but the lunatic fringe would seriously consider it. The Avenir space station might have been born an interstellar transport, but in the hundreds of Foundings since its arrival at 94 Ceti, it had added a panoply of pods and modules and bays and docks, like a hermit crab adorning its seashell home with bits of flotsam and jetsam, until its spacefaring origins were obscured beyond recognition.

But the Dreamers had not forgotten, and they were working patiently, incrementally, and invisibly to make Avenir a spaceship once again. John had no doubt they would succeed, and his business instincts screamed at him to seize their invitation to unlimited power and leverage. They controlled the nanofactories, the computer network, and who knew how many key government officials. Their virtual world was amazing, even when experienced through an obsolete interface. Part of him longed for the full experience. Sensations, smells, tastes, sights beyond his wildest imaginings, so vivid as to make the distinction between real and virtual irrelevant. Islands, and birds.

And there was Anya.

Something still held him back. All dreams came at a cost, and this one was no exception. He'd never thought much about his fellow colonists, other than as human resources or business competitors, but now as he wandered the station, ranging farther than he ever had before, he found himself looking at their faces, pondering their fate. From the idle rich of the upper levels to the desperate poor begging for scraps in its depths. Aristocrats and merchants, Peacekeepers and Enforcers, dockworkers and technicians, fishmongers and beetle butchers, pickpockets and orphans. Who would be taken when Avenir shed its encrustations and blasted away to a more hospitable star? Who would be left behind? Would they find a way to survive without the station's technical resources? Would the colony devolve into barbarism, a handful of scattered tribes clinging to life as both hunters and prey of Eclectia's giant insects, slowly suffocated by the planet's corrosive atmosphere?

What did it matter? The colony was dying anyway. The Dreamers knew this. The only way to save any of it was to move along with whatever they could salvage. From that perspective, his choice was either to remain as he was, gathering wealth and gilding his own pleasures as best he could until the end, or to join the Dreamers, where he would have a voting stake in the colony's future—and the power to shape it.

When John thought about it that way, there wasn't any choice at all. He found an observation gallery in an obscure corner of one of the station's lower levels and gazed out at the feverish countenance of Eclectia and beyond to shattered Sheba and the leering glow of the Whale Star itself. It might be the last time he saw them face to face, with his own eyes.

"You've made up your mind." The image of Anya Sherikov stood beside him in her shimmering red dress, her eyes merry.

"I can't even have the privilege of a quiet moment with my own thoughts?"

"You will succeed me as Communications Officer. No one can intrude upon your privacy without permission, save Captain Aziz. Even he must knock first."

"That's reassuring."

"We had wagered among ourselves how long it would take you to deliberate. Captain Aziz thought you would decide within the first day. Victoria was less optimistic."

"How much less?"

"She said I'd probably find you dead drunk in a dockside bar two weeks from now."

"Vicky is one scary little girl. What about you? What was your guess?"

Anya smiled. "You're right on time."

"Congratulations. So, what now?"

"Look over there." She pointed toward the window. A Hawthorne-class VIP shuttle had just cleared its moorings and was falling away from the station toward Eclectia.

It exploded in soundless flash of white light.

"The official records will state that all occupants, including one John Milton, were lost when their spacecraft suffered catastrophic engine failure en route to Adagio. Your personal assets have been dispersed and controlling interests in your various business ventures transferred to your partners. It's time to take up residence in Paradise, John. Welcome to your afterlife."

Melanie checked the address again. It had taken a little digging, but she was certain this was where he lived. She smoothed her tunic and trousers and brushed a stray wisp of hair from her eyes before ringing the chime.

A thin, pale man wearing a plain black suit opened the door. His face was void of any emotion as he examined her. "May I help you, Miss?"

"I...my name is Melanie Hunt. Are you Mr. Milton?"

"No, this unit served as Mr. Milton's valet. I await re-purposing."

It was a Frank. Melanie swallowed hard. She had to see this through, for Carson's sake. "I need to speak with Mr. Milton. It's urgent. Tell him it's about the Dreamers."

The cyborg butler was still for a moment, then it blinked twice. When it spoke again, its voice was higher in pitch, almost feminine. "Mr. Milton died early this morning."

"What? Oh...oh, no. I'm so sorry. I had no idea. Thank you. I...I hope they find you a good job." She had to fight an impulse to flee. *Turn away and take one step at a time, like a sane person.*

"Wait."

She spun around. The impassive face wore a softer expression. It was smiling. There was just enough curve in the mouth to make it certain. Franks weren't supposed to feel emotion. Was this a new feature, special for rich owners?

It opened the door wider and bowed. "Come in, Miss. Perhaps I may be of assistance."

130. SHELTER FROM THE STORM
JEFF CHAPMAN

Elihu poked the oval shadow with his spear, but unlike the other shadows, which had been indentions or shallow fissures, this one swallowed his spear head and all the shaft he fed it. The cave entrance rose from the crevice floor to his waist. Maybe it ballooned farther in or tapered to a crack. He couldn't tell without crawling inside. Much too small for a mammothbug, but he had once seen a black spider with orange splotches dotting its abdomen lunge from one of these holes to snatch a powderbug that he had been stalking.

The pastor-turned-hunter swallowed hard, jabbed his spear into the hole twice and then jumped back to a crouch, holding his breath, listening, his spear poised to skewer anything that emerged. Nothing came. Only the soughing wind overhead and the settling ash pecking against the dried lavabushes disturbed the quiet. No skittering legs or clicking pincers against rock.

He broke three of the thickest branches from a lavabush and then stripped the lower branches until he could hold the three together like a bouquet. Taking a lighter from the inside pocket of his coat, he clicked the trigger, igniting a mixture of burnweed and fish oil that flamed yellow and blue. Burnweed grew in the ocean shallows and, in bulbs that studded the long olive-colored leaves, held an oil that was toxic to eat but highly flammable. Strange, he reflected, that sources of fire came from the sea.

The dried bush caught and crackled, bathing his face with heat and yellow light. The smoke scent and flames reminded him of drinking tea with Sarah after supper. She would nurse the baby and he would talk and when he stopped to sip his tea he would ponder his child's future. Sarah would worry, but he had been gone overnight before. He thrust the torch into the cave. Bugs feared fire.

He expected smooth walls fading to blackness or a pair of eyes the size of his head retreating from the flames that glittered and repeated across purple and yellow compound eyes. A bristle blanket, or something like it, hung across the tunnel no more than two meters in. Could be spider silk, he thought, some sort of trapdoor or cocoon. He lit another torch, laid it on the tunnel floor and prodded the flaming bush into the tube with his spear, following behind on his hands and knees. The weave in the cloth stood out, a beacon of friendship or at least common species. He sighed, letting go the tension. "Thank you, Lord," he muttered. "Thank you."

"Hello?" The flames collapsed to orange embers. "Anybody in there?" He listened. Nothing. "This is Elihu Simmons, pastor at Tube Hill. Just need some shelter for a bit, from the storm. Hello?"

He crawled backwards out of the tunnel. The gloaming weighed on him with its uncompromising edict, the doom of darkness when the biscorpiabugs woke and unfurled their bifurcated tail and stingers, and all the other bugs he couldn't see pushed out of their holes. The ash-gray sky had faded to charcoal overhead and black along the eastern horizon. This tunnel had to be the one, he told himself. Might still be a spider or bug inside—only the cautious survived in this world—but already he was thinking how this ordeal might complement a Bible story. David found refuge in caves.

He entered the tube with a larger torch clutched in his left hand and in his right gripped his spear together with two more unlit torches. Heat singed his face and smoke stung his eyes in the cramped tunnel. He poked the blanket with his spear tip and lifted the edge. Minerals glittered in the rock wall opposite the entrance. A cavern. He might be able to stand up. He thrust the torch past the threshold into the chamber, following close behind.

A domed ceiling sparkled with flecks of minerals embedded in black rock, stars in a night sky, as the Milky Way galaxy would shine down on Eclectia if the curtains of ash fell aside. The lava here held riches of minerals the likes of which he had never seen. Elihu shook his head to clear his thoughts.

The stars dimmed as the flaming bush starved for fuel. He stuck the other torches into the embers of the first and they roared orange and red. To his left a lone table fashioned from fist-sized chunks of dolerite and a slab of stone held a lamp and a hodgepodge of bowls, and to his right a pile of blankets covered the floor. A niche in the wall appeared to serve as a hearth.

Liquid sloshed inside the lamp when he picked it up and held his torch over the wick, which caught and burned at the center of an orange halo, the same halo that lit his wife's face when she checked on the baby long after dark. Her face would be creased with worry tonight. Hunting was no job for a family man and no work for a pastor.

He stuffed what remained of the torches inside the hearth. A crack the width of two fingers snaked up the wall from the hearth and disappeared into the ceiling. He gathered more bushes from outside. The woody stems at the base of the plants, some as thick as Elihu's wrist, burned slowly, and in the light from the lamp and hearth fire, he plucked seeds from the lavabush branches, dropping the kernels into a blackened carapace bowl for roasting. A hymn of thanksgiving thrummed at the back of his throat and the repetitive picking and hulling lulled his mind.

A groan snapped his senses awake.

131. THE LAST FIGHT (PART II)
GREG MITCHELL

{*Awake*}

Dressler opened one eye. The other felt tight. Swollen shut. *Crazy's dead.* Would he be next?

Boots clanked on metal and he drew his head up, feeling it pound—full of thoughts, but not his own. He saw Trebs circling him, wiping Crazy's blood off his knife. The killer bore no satisfaction on his face, in fact very little recognition that he'd murdered a good man *at all.*

{*Welcome, believer*}

"Trebs," he muttered. "I'm gonna kill you…"

When Dressler wavered to weak feet, he realized Trebs had not addressed him. Beyond the killer, through the front viewport, Dressler beheld a crimson-colored fleshy mass, adorned in writhing tentacles. Large suckers from one giant appendage were fixed to a corner of the glass. A single baleful eye held him in place. Dressler's mind pulsed and swelled. He gripped at his temples, gnashing his teeth.

{*Welcome, believer*}

"Why…do you call me that?"

{*It is what you are*} the Beast thought to him.

"*You're* the angel?"

{*Your kind must name everything*}

Woozy, Dressler got out through grit teeth, his heart burning from betrayal. "Why did you bring me here? My daughter's cure—"

"Don't let the fish look fool you," Trebs spoke up, and Dressler wondered if he were somehow hearing what the "angel" was speaking to his mind. "This thing is the *real* fisherman."

He would kill Trebs. He'd settled that in his mind now. He'd killed a man before, out of anger and booze. He'd never killed clear-headed, but for Trebs, Dressler knew it was worth a try.

"You got me down here," Dressler spat. "*Why?* What now?"

{*Your faith feeds me*}

Dressler massaged his forehead, the throbbing blood vessels there, and thought he might pass out. "Faith…what? I don't…I don't have faith."

{*No? Wasn't it faith that led you down here?*}

"You lied to me."

{Faith is faith}

A deep chuckle rumbled from Dressler's throat, passing his clenched teeth. "You went to all of this...why? For a *snack?*"

It was Trebs who answered, "Do you realize how many people it's lured down here? The angels up top, they try and keep this place sealed up, to keep guys like *this* from getting out. The angels, they can influence your mind—project thoughts, Dress. But that's not the only tricks they got. They can *siphon* thoughts, too. Emotions. Memories. Good ones, *or* bad."

Dressler leveled his good eye at the monster outside the viewport, seething in contempt for the creature that had toyed with him, dangling Edilyn's life before him as bait.

Trebs continued, "All that anxiety you got for Lyn, it was like a *beacon* to him!"

{Your misery called to me}

"So, I'm the delivery," Dressler snapped, cutting hard eyes at Trebs. "And what were *you*, the delivery boy?"

Trebs smiled, opening his mouth to answer, but the Beast cut through.

{He is the entree}

Trebs quickly closed his mouth, swiveling to face the monster. "What?"

{You have pain, too, human. Fear of your father. It drives everything you do. It always has}

"Wait, wait!" Trebs waved his hands, stepping closer to the glass. "We had a deal! I was supposed to bring you Dressler and more!"

{I healed your body by stimulating your mind. Stopped your bleeding. Sped up your body's natural restorative properties. Your life belongs to me, to do with as I see fit. Your faith has fed me, human, but I find it lacking. I am done with you now}

"Wait!" Trebs commanded once more, his voice shrill. At once, the seam in his leg that the bug had inflicted days before—the wound that would have, *should* have, cost him his life—opened up as though someone had pulled a zipper on it. Blood cascaded down the grievous rip and Trebs collapsed, gasping in pain and fear. "No! No, no, no!"

Dressler closed his fists, finding that, when once he held nothing but hatred for the bug hunter, now he felt pity. Undone, Trebs passed out from shock, and died in silence.

{He was but a tasting. Your faith is much stronger. I will gorge myself on it. Or...}

Infuriated, and feeling increasingly helpless to do anything about it, Dressler ventured, "Or what?"

{I could dine on your mind all at once, or feed off your pain a little at a time, allowing you to continue in your pitiful existence. Better yet, perhaps…you could fulfill the other human's role…bring other faithful to me. Offer their minds to me in your stead and sate my thirst}

Images of Edilyn flashed before his eyes. When she was born, crying and naked and vulnerable, needing him to cradle her in his arms. Protect her from the terrible world she'd been born into. That's all he'd wanted to do—save her life to bring some purpose to his own.

{Return to the surface, human. I will fulfill my promise and heal your daughter. You can live out the rest of your days with her…only do not forget our arrangement. Bring me others with strong faith like yours. Feed my hunger}

Edilyn would be safe, while Dressler would be damned. A monster, dragging jelly rollers into the ocean, to the consumptions of their minds— their very souls.

But Edilyn would be *safe*.

"No," Dressler said, praying his daughter would understand. He wouldn't be there to explain it to her. He would be long dead by then, unable to tell her that there were things worth fighting for.

Worth dying for.

Edilyn was worth dying for.

But the destruction of this leviathan was worth more.

I'm sorry, Lyn. Don't forget your old man.

{What are you doing?}

Dressler hopped over the back of Crazy's empty chair at the deck, his hands hovering over the strange consoles. He'd never piloted before, but he only needed to know enough to charge. Following the instructions the best he could, flipping a number of toggles, Dressler finally powered the sub to life.

{You can't run from me}

"Not trying to."

In the process of rummaging through controls, music blasted through speakers. More of Crazy's "hip hop". Something called "Power" by K-West. He didn't know if K-West was a great composer of ancient days or not. Dressler didn't know much about culture. Didn't know much about a lot of things.

He'd done the best he could.

Dressler pulled back on the yoke, arcing in the water. He felt the monster roaring furiously in his mind, but he pushed it aside. His brain hurt, swelling with rage, blood running out of his nose. The Thing was ever-present in his thoughts, drowning out his own, but he focused on Edilyn. Her laugh, her smile, her hand in his, her arms around him.

Tentacles snapped, slapping the sub. Glass cracked, alarms screamed, and sparks and hissing steam shot out of paneling. Dressler ascended higher and higher, then slammed against the yoke as one of the alien arms snatched his propeller. The sub lurched hard to the right and he was thrown from the seat, crashing to the floor next to Trebs' lifeless body. Poor Trebs. All talk, and too dumb to know when to shut up.

Dressler picked himself off the floor and slid back into the seat, juking the sub, breaking loose of the tendril.

{*You will not escape*}

"You don't seem to get it," Dressler huffed, wheeling the sub around, aiming his viewport at that single glaring eye. "I'm not going anywhere."

Reaching across the console, Dressler cranked the music up, its thumping beat moving in time to his heart. He grinned, eyes squinting back tears—

—and flooded the throttle.

The beast grew larger in the viewport as Dressler plummeted hard and fast. He screamed, cried, shouted, and laughed all at once. A female automated voice warned him the ship was in danger of exploding, and he was glad for it.

"You wanna feed on my faith? I hope you *choke* on it!"

The Beast screamed in his mind, as the ship pierced the eye. Dressler heard a pop, a sizzle, and was thrown backwards when the cockpit exploded. Water punched through the glass, carrying him away as the ship tore apart, carrying him into black oblivion.

132.   SAVED
JOSEPH H. FICOR

Stotter stood shocked. Shouhei's shot came close, but missed. Stotter fired his own weapon. He hit Fiko in the left shoulder. His sudden surprise at the Governor's prize puppy suddenly turning aggressive ruined his aim.

Shouhei collapsed on the ground. He held his bleeding shoulder.

An eternity passed before Stotter heard the thud behind him.

Stotter turned to see who had been Shouhei's true target.

There was not much left of the face, but the slim body and the curved, saw toothed knife in the corpse's right hand was enough to identify him. Jing Laforsé. Even more wanted than the smuggler. He was a professional hitman who favored stealth and his knife to any sort of firearm. He sometimes traveled with Rawlings on runs.

Stotter's hard exterior returned. He kicked at Shouhei. He held his pistol at the young enforcer's head. But he could not bring himself to pull the trigger. He lowered his weapon.

"Get up, Fiko!"

Shouhei obeyed and the two walked past the corpses to the elevator.

The only speech in the elevator was Stotter using his communicator to request a clean-up crew to come and collect the bodies.

133. THE HERMIT'S CACHE
JEFF CHAPMAN

Elihu Simmons's eyes darted from the blanket hanging across the cave's entrance to the hearth. That groan didn't sound like the wind. He sat perfectly still, holding his breath, listening. He knew he should grab his spear and prepare to fight whatever might be coming, but after finding some comfort from the storm, the last thing he wanted to do was fight. The struggle to keep his family alive weighed on his soul and the addition of his congregation's troubles nearly crushed it. He'd stumbled into a black pit with no bottom and no rope. Every day he fought the good fight and every time he coughed and saw the ash in his phlegm, the circle of light at the top of the pit contracted, but somehow he held everyone up.

Strength swelled in his core, as it always did, thank God. His fingers curled around his spear.

The pile of blankets stirred, a faint ripple, but enough to trip his tightly strung senses. Another groan. He saw it now—the feet, the bent knees, the torso—a human form curled beneath the blankets. He folded back the top edge of the covers. White hair streaked with gray crowned an old man's head and brushed his shoulders. A white beard covered his face and neck, trailing down to his chest. Something hard and cylindrical rolled beneath

Elihu's knee, the old man's spear. Of course, he would sleep with it, thought Elihu. There was no more need to worry if someone would come back.

Elihu gently shook the man's shoulder. The old man groaned. Some kind of hermit, Elihu thought.

"Hello? Are you sick?"

The old man's forehead felt hot and dry. Elihu poured some water from his canteen into a bowl. Cradling the hermit's head in the crook of his arm, he dripped water on the man's cracked lips. The hermit licked the moisture. Elihu persisted in dripping water until the old man opened his mouth enough to drink in short sips.

"I don't have much water," said Elihu, "but you're welcome to what I have."

The hermit's eyelids fluttered across steel-gray irises. He nodded then sank back into sleep.

Elihu sighed. He possessed the will to help without the means. He decided to make a travois with the two spears and the blankets and drag the hermit to Tube Hill when the storm passed. Not that they could do much for him there, but he couldn't leave him here. Elihu folded a blanket into a pillow and placed it underneath the wadded blanket on which the old man's head rested.

Elihu's eyebrows knitted in surprise when his fingers brushed a bag of metal pieces that moved and clinked under his touch, coins. "What's this?" he whispered. He pulled two items out from beneath the old man's pillow. A drawstring cinched the pouch whose bottom bulged with the coin's weight. He pulled it open. Gold, silver, and platinum coins—more money than he had ever seen, more than would pass through his hands in a lifetime—winked at him in the lamp's dancing light.

He glanced at the old man whose chest rose and fell with the shallowest of breaths. Was this the cache of a lonely bug hunter? His gaze passed over the glittering walls and what at first escaped his notice, the gouges of a chisel, shouted at him. "What have you found out here?" he said to the old man.

Elihu remembered Elsa begging for scraps at his doorstep. With these coins he could feed his family and Elsa's family, his congregation, his entire village for many Foundings. He could move his family to Zirconia, buy his children hope, and rekindle the sparkle in his wife's eyes.

What sort of man sleeps on a hoard like this in the midst of such suffering? Stories of dragons came to mind. If the old man died, he thought. And then he recalled what happened to those who coveted a dragon's hoard and took the dragon's place atop its pile of shiny things. Elihu cinched the pouch and flung it against the rock wall. It landed on the second item from beneath the old miser's pillow.

He picked up a sheaf of stiffened bristle fabric cut into rectangles and knotted together with twine along the left edge, a homemade book. The beige cover, splotched with darker shades of brown, was blank. Elihu turned back the cover. Small squiggles in a dark-yellow ink—bug blood, he well knew that stain—sprawled across the pages. Thumbing through the book, he found page after page of tightly packed markings. The last three pages were blank. He laid the open book on the cavern floor in front of the hearth and knelt over it, puzzling over the characters which flowed across the page in an unbroken stream, line after line. The script could be very ancient or very new, he thought, or nothing. Someone at the university or the monasteries might know.

Elihu studied the old man, wondering what sort of man creates a book that no one can read. One of the traveling ministers could arrange passage to the Abbey of Francis. And what would become of the rest of those coins, barring a miraculous recovery? He knew better than to hope for a windfall for Tube Hill. Brother Trollope might direct some back to Elihu's congregation, but not the others. The whiskers on the old man's lip trembled with his breathing.

Elihu bit his lip in anger. "Perhaps I should throw lots to see who gets your money and possessions?"

Better to remove temptation than struggle to fight it. That's what his father always used to say. He tucked the coin pouch under the hermit's pillow, to remind himself of its owner.

After leaving the elevator, Stotter and Shouhei went to the Governor's quarters.

The Governor listened to the story told by Stotter—with Shouhei's attempted execution omitted. After Stotter finished, the bulk of the Governor lifted from behind his desk. He smiled. "Fiko, my boy. You are a credit to the Corps—and especially to me. Now go and see the medics for your shoulder and get some rest. The Major and I have some business to discuss."

Shouhei got his shoulder fixed, returned to his room, and collapsed on his bed. He slept for twelve hours.

He was awakened by a knock on his door. He straightened his uniform as best as he could. Enforcer Second Class Yuri Jao stood at the door.

He was scowling more than usual. This scared Shouhei because Jao was one of the most vocal in his contempt for Shouhei.

"Come on," Jao shouted. "We need to hurry. You don't want to miss the ceremony."

"Excuse me?" Shouhei was still half-asleep and bewildered by Jao's sudden appearance. "What ceremony?"

Jao sneered. "Your award ceremony."

Shouhei and Jao entered the large auditorium on the fifteenth level. The auditorium was large—three hundred seats. It was usually for live entertainment like plays or—as in this case—pomp and ceremony.

The seats were full of the elite of Carlston's Cove. The Governor's entire security attachment had been assembled also. The Peacekeepers and Enforcers stood in two neat lines down the aisle leading to the main stage.

Shouhei stood confused and dumbfounded. Jao indicated for Shouhei to go to the main stage by jabbing him in the back.

As Shouhei walked down the aisle, the Enforcers and Peacekeepers saluted him as he passed. The young enforcer searched for signs of genuine respect in the faces of his comrades, uncertain if he saw any. Peacekeeper Second Level Stalinsky—one of the Peacekeepers who had been standing in the front of the Governor's office when he first reported for duty—smiled as he passed.

On the main stage were the Governor and Major Stotter.

Shouhei stepped onto the main stage and stood before them.

The Governor grinned, showing all of his teeth. Stotter remained utterly stoic and unreadable. "Ladies and Gentlemen, I present to you the hero who not only stopped the piracy of Artimus Rawlings, but also the assassin Jing Laforsé. We are greatly indebted to you, Enforcer Fiko."

Applause thundered in the auditorium. Apparently genuine.

Governor Bokkasa waited for a few minutes before putting his hand up as a signal for the applause to stop so that he could continue. "So it is with great honor that I bestow upon you the silver Avenir for bravery. Congratulations."

Applause broke forth again as the silver award, in the shape of Avenir Station, was pinned just above Shouhei's left breast pocket. Shouhei felt his pulse pound at the honor of getting the award. But he couldn't help but wonder if this was another of the Governor's little games.

After the applause died down, Bokkasa broke into a long and dry speech entailing duty and honor. Shouhei hardly heard a word. Fear gripped him as he looked at the icy cold face of Stotter. The Major's words in the docking bay resounded in his mind: "...on Carlston's Cove: Your life span is equal to your usefulness."

Shouhei silently—and desperately—prayed for future courage and divine protection.

135. MORE BEDTIME STORIES
GREG MITCHELL

Dressler awoke on rock. Vision blurry, he heard the drip, drip, drip of water echoing in a cavern. Above, he glimpsed wet stalactite, glistening with reflected ethereal light.

Am I dead?

His head ached, but his thoughts were his own. Private once more, as they ought to be. The monster in his mind was dead—he could feel that. He'd done it. He'd killed the blasted devil.

But where am I?

Groggy, he stood, covered in cuts and bruises, sopping wet. Looking about, he saw he was in a cave, a giant lagoon at his feet. Was he still underwater? Had he floated up into some kind of air pocket after the blast? Kneeling to the edge, he peered into the water—

"Ah!"

A host of fish-like "angels" floated just below the surface, all of them staring back at him. He fell back on the seat of his pants, backing away. "No, no!"

{*Wait*} a soft voice implored him psychically, patient and kind.

"Where am I? What do you want?"

{*You were foolish to come here*}

"Yeah," he said at length, standing again, feeling in no immediate danger. "I know. I'm...sorry."

{*We guard the Trench. There are many secrets in the depths that man should not know. We were trying to warn you when you evaded us*}

"It was a mistake...I didn't know..."

{*The dark can be deceptive and alluring. We understand how weak you can be, more than you do, it seems*}

At the time Dressler was about to take offense, the angel's soft voice soothed his heart. {*But we also see how strong you can be. You have killed a terrible foe. And you did it at great personal sacrifice*}

"How did you know?" he asked, then shrugged it off. "Forget it. I don't want to know."

{*You have impressed us—one most in particular*} A lithe feminine hand emerged from the lit waters. In its scaly palm, a tiny mess of tentacles, dark green in color, and squirming comfortably.

"What is that?"

{*He doesn't have a name. He believes in being defined by one's actions. By your act of bravery, he recognizes you as kin. As family*}

"He...thinks we're related?"

{*Of a sort. You would sacrifice your life to save your people from a wayward of our kind. He would like to return your generosity*}

"I don't understand."

{*Take him to your child. Fix him to her breathing port—her mouth. He will breathe into her. She will be cured of her ailment. He would consider it an honor to die so that his kin might live*}

Dressler stepped forward. "Wait, die?"

{This act will be his last. He can save her, but he will die in the process}

"I—I can't," he said, painfully.

{But you must. That is what family does and he considers you family now. Do not dishonor him}

Dressler focused on the writhing thing in the outstretched hand, gently writhing, waiting for him to accept its sacrifice.

Carefully, he extended a hand in gratitude.

"Daddy? Tell me about the angels. The ones who saved me. And Crazy!"

Dressler pulled the covers to Edilyn's neck, red light from the small bunker window painting her face in soft contrast. The sound of dirt and grit brushed against the pane glass, a constant white noise that Dressler found pleasant and reassuring these days.

"Come on, Lyn." He grinned. "How many times have I told you that story?"

"Not enough."

There had been five Approachings since bringing back Edilyn's cure. The little squirmy angel did it, breathing new life into his daughter, clearing her ash lung, and softly giving up his spirit in the process. Dressler didn't know what "peaceful" looked like on an angel, but he'd liked to think he'd seen it.

Lyn was fine, running and playing again, living life. Dressler returned to hunting, even had a new partner. Yulaura was a pistol, a rough and tumble sort that kept Dressler on his toes, and so far, had shown no signs of being under some evil angel's thrall.

He liked that best about her.

Life had returned to a modicum of normal, but Lyn still wanted to hear the stories.

"Please, Daddy," she begged, healthy and full of life, his every prayer answered.

Maybe Trebs—as barking mad as he was—had been right: His faith had been rewarded.

Dressler had never considered himself a man of faith before that day at the bottom of Eclectia's oceans, but Life had a funny way of changing things.

"Okay," he laughed easy, before kissing her cheek. "I tell you the story. One more time."

136.   REJOICING IN HOPE
TRAVIS PERRY

Elsa hauled a wooden bucket of dirty water out of the tavern. She carried it downhill and poured into a coarse gully leading to the bay. She planned to next retrieve a clean bucketful from the well and finish her cleaning, when she saw a man walking up toward her. Not many men came around the tavern in the middle of the day—they were out hunting.

The man was tall and unshaven, gaunt like he hadn't eaten in a while, with dark hair and eyes, and tattered clothing smelling of seawater. He stumbled like he'd been wounded in his right leg, while burns plainly showed themselves on his rugged face.

"Young man, are you all right?"

He turned toward her and grimaced. "I've been better."

She walked to him and put her shoulder under his arm. "I'm not that bad off," he said, but he allowed her to help. She took him to the well, sat him on its edge, and hauled up water for him to drink.

"Thanks, old lady."

"I'd do it for anyone. What's your name, young man?"

"Ernsto...last name doesn't matter."

"Of course," she answered, offering him an understanding smile. Many of the new hunters had pasts they didn't want to talk about.

"Say, old lady, you remind me of my grandma. Can you help me with something?"

"I'll do whatever I can."

He reached inside his left front pants pocket and pulled free a dark sack. It clicked with movement and she could make out shapes of round hard objects. As if it were filled with coins. "Could you take these for me? They're gettin' awful heavy. You wouldn't believe what I went through to bring them this far."

"All of them? Surely you don't mean it!"

"Surely I do."

"May I…look at them?"

"Why don' you wait 'till I leave, Grandma."

Elsa waited but she was overjoyed. It was a huge cache of copper coins, maybe fifty or more. These by themselves might be enough to pay for a trip to the orphanage, especially if there were a silver or two hidden among them. In her mind she praised God and she hummed a happy hymn as she washed Ernsto's wounds.

He rested with her a half an hour or so, but then arose and started walking inland. "I'm goin' huntin', Elsa. You take care."

"Wait! Won't you need some money to buy some gear?"

"Don' worry about me, Grandma. I'll be fine."

"God bless you, young man. And thank you," she added, rattling the coin bag.

She didn't open it right away.

Some part of her had begun to fear there must be something wrong— perhaps the metal pieces were cheap tin slugs instead of money…though the bag seemed too heavy for that and she didn't really believe that young man would trick her so cruelly.

In the evening, after finishing the tavern floor, in the isolation of the privy, she emptied out the coins. At first it seemed her fears had come true, the coins were very light colored, like tin. But then she realized what they really were.

Platinum.

She almost squealed but stopped herself in time. It wouldn't do to let everyone know what she had.

People got killed for far less.

But this would change everything. She could now afford new hunting gear. She could pay back Pastor Simmons beyond a tithe and return home with her grandchildren and teach them what they needed to know to survive—her family could live on. In freedom. In peace. And most importantly, together.

Her heart poured out into silent song, *Praise God from whom all blessings flow, praise Him all creatures here below…*

Mary leaned over the rail of the crib and kissed Jacey's tiny forehead. The peach fuzz along the baby's hairline clung to her skin, damp with sweat, but her angelic face was completely relaxed.

"If only your daddy could have seen you." Mary gazed at Jacey in wonderment over the features that looked so much like Jax. A perfect replica, even down to the arch of her eyebrows and the dimple that played in and out on her left cheek as she smiled in her sleep.

She sighed and left the room. The kids would be home any minute and she hadn't even figured out what to cook for dinner. Granted, having an old friend stop by had been a worthy excuse. She smiled as she sorted through the conversation she'd had with Tomika, recalling how good it had felt to talk to someone about Jax without feeling like "the *criminal's* widow."

As she walked across the living area, chill air hit her skin. She stepped toward the environmental control panel next to her bedroom door, but as her gaze passed the open doorway she froze. Something silvery glinted on her nightstand.

What is that?

She crept into the bedroom, chills running up her arms. Atop her journal lay a triangular piece of metal. It looked like a knife.

No, as she got closer she realized it was too wide to be a knife and had no real handle, but it looked deadly sharp. She reached the nightstand and sat down on the edge of the bed, tears burning her eyes as she read the word "Mary" carved into the metal in Jax's signature scrawl.

Jax...

She slid from the edge of the bed and landed on her knees, her hips sinking until she was sitting on her heels. Her hands found their way into her bangs and her torso rocked back, forth, back, forth, tears streaming her cheeks and dripping from her chin.

Jax....Oh, God, thank you...

The door to Maddie's pub slammed behind Jax as he exited. His head swam from too much ale. It had been an unusually good haul today—but

221

as his dust-encrusted boot caught on a rock and he stumbled to regain his balance, he wondered if maybe he'd celebrated a little too hard. But celebrations were something that came few and far between for him.

Most days he was happy just to be alive.

INSIDE
AVENIR
ECLECTIA

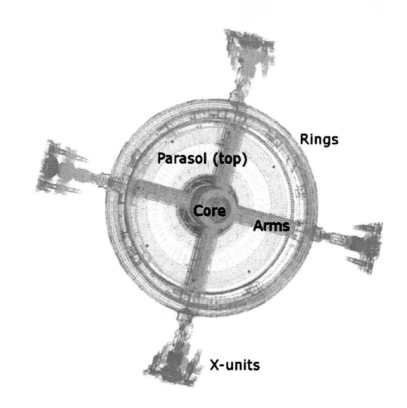

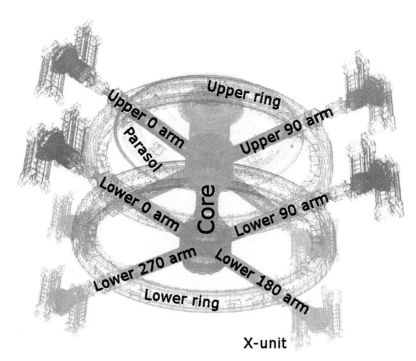

THE AVENIR STATION
INFORMATION BY TRAVIS PERRY

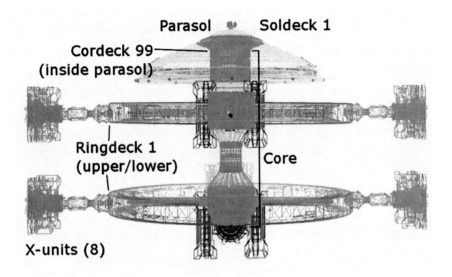

Parasol · Soldeck 1
Cordeck 99
(inside parasol)
Ringdeck 1
(upper/lower)
Core
X-units (8)

Avenir is 442 meters tall along the central core. It is approximately 100 decks high.

The station is made up of "cordecks", "ringdecks", and "soldecks", and locations are specified by numbered degrees along the arms and rings. With the 8 X-unit names as well, it is very confusing for outsiders especially when residents rattle off the deck number without stating which kind of deck it is. People familiar with Avenir know which is which by the context.

The core was the original ship that traveled here from Earth. Its decks start numbering at the bottom with deck 1 and count upward to 99 inside the parasol. Decks 80 and up contain most of Avenir's government offices and managerial office space. The richest aristocrats shuttle back and forth from their homes in the soldecks to offices in the cordecks.

Each of the arms are numbered by degrees. So there are two 90 degree arms, and two each at 180, 270 and 0. The inner ring docks at ringdeck 8 are specified by numerical degrees and letters as referenced in some stories.

The numbers are written on top of the rings in ten degree increments, 1-36, though the inner degree measurements are 0-359, one degree at a time.

Avenir rings are honeycombed into individual compartments mainly intended for residential living. Each ring contains approximately 30,000 rooms of rough inner dimensions of 4x4x4 meters—16 square meters or 169 square feet. This will allow only one or two people in each room. Larger dwellings can be linked by inner doors. Avenir's maximum population capacity therefore is between 100,000-150,000 people when other station areas are included.

Avenir ring circumference: 1778 meters.

Arm length: 156 meters. Maximum diameter including X-units: 860 meters.

The rings are 52m high—12 vertical decks. Outer ring: Seven "onion" layers of about 4.5 meters each. Inner ring thickness 32m. Habitat area, originally using centrifugal force for gravity. Inner ring, cargo area and other uses. 1 deck of 18m.

Main cargo bay in the core: 74 meter inner diameter.

Ring decks are numbered starting at deck 1 which is the outermost deck. 2 is one deck inward and so on up the arms to the center core, ending at Ringdeck 22. Decks 10-22 have docking ports.

The X-units are eight in total and extend from the end of each arm beyond the rings. These were added after Avenir developed artificial gravity and no longer needed to spin the rings. Their purpose was to expand and improve the station, providing common meeting areas for things like theater and sporting events, shops, hydroponic crop areas, manufacturing, and additional docking ports. Each unit has its own name and ambience. They are 143m wide and 145m high. 93 meters are occupied by 7 layered decks, which are about 13.3m high each, and the remaining height is taken up with docks. The large glassed decks are big enough for trees. Originally designed as park areas, some of these large decks are used for other purposes.

The Avenir "parasol" provides housing for the elite in the upper levels and some government offices in the lower levels. The parasol has 121 meters vertical rise, divided into 27 decks. The bottom ring of the 'sol is 27. The soldeck numbers start at the top, so that deck 1 is the large dome with a garden.

Avenir abounds with docking areas. The upper parasol has large landing bays generally reserved for government purposes. The inside edges of the rings are lined with docking ports around the inside of the circle. There are also docking ports along the ring arms, though not all of these are actively used. Each of the eight X-units also has a large docking area of 30 meters diameter, plus smaller docking ports facing the ring. One of these is engaged in interplanetary spaceship manufacturing, while others are raw materials processing plants.

94 CETI
INFORMATION BY WALT STAPLES,
TRAVIS PERRY, AND GRACE BRIDGES

The orbital habitat, Avenir, circles the planet Eclectia which in turn orbits the star 94 Ceti A, known to the locals as "The Whale," one of a binary star system in the constellation Cetus or the Whale, which can be seen from Earth in the southern skies. The secondary star of the system, 94 Ceti B, orbits the primary at an average of 151 AU (Astronomical Units), though the current distance during the time frame of the AE colonization is closer to 120 AUs. The entire system is approximately 73 light years from Earth.

94 Ceti A is a yellow-white dwarf star belonging to the main-sequence and has a spectral classification of F8V*. It's partner, 94 Ceti B (known to inhabitants of the system as the "Twin Whale" or just "Twin"), is a M3V red dwarf. The Twin Whale, being a relatively dim star which is more than three times further away from 94 Ceti A than Pluto is from Earth's sun, is at its brightest only a bit more luminous than the full moon on Earth. Bear in mind that during part of each of Eclectia's orbits around the sun (each Founding) the Twin will be aligned in the general direction of the Whale and will be invisible from the night sky on Eclectia, but will be barely visible during the day.

That 94 Ceti A had a planet orbiting it was discovered 7 August 2000 AD (old form). The planet discovered has an approximate mass of twice that of Jupiter and is called "b" or "Ab" to distinguish it from the red dwarf star 94 Ceti B. Eclectia shares the same orbit as Ab, but is 180 degrees from it along their shared orbit. In other words, 94 Ceti Ab is never visible in the night sky from Eclectia—as a result, human colonists of the system have no special word for it.

Eclectia is larger than Earth and is in turn orbited by two moons of greater collective mass than Earth's moon. Sheba and Quatermain together are approximately the mass of Mercury and pull Eclectia into a rapid "wobble" of its axis. A planetary disaster of unknown cause divided the moons from each other less than 200 standard Earth years ago, leaving much of their surfaces severely fractured and covered with hot magma, but still inhabitable in places. The split of these moons, already collapsed back into separate spheres, has created numerous asteroid-sized moons that orbit both Sheba and Eclectia in thin rings of rubble.

* A word about stellar spectral classifications:

Stars are classified by their color and size. The color of a star gives an idea of its temperature. The color of a star is denoted by a letter as follows:

O   Blue
B   Blue-White
A   White
F   Yellow-White
G   Yellow
K   Orange
M   Red

The number in the designation denotes how close the star is to the next coolest type. There are ten units between each type. Thus, 94 Ceti A is 8 tenths of the way to being a "G" type star (Sol, our star is a yellow G2V type star).

The "V" in the designation is actually the Roman numeral for number "five." This denotes that 94 Ceti A and 94 Ceti B are both dwarf stars or main-sequence stars like our Sun.

This means that the Whale Star is somewhat hotter than our Sol. But Eclectia orbits at a greater distance than we do, putting it on the inside edge of the inhabitable zone.

OF DAYS, MONTHS AND YEARS

INFORMATION BY GRACE BRIDGES
AND TRAVIS PERRY

The differing time calculations between Earth and Avenir Eclectia have the potential to be quite confusing, so let's explain how to keep them straight.

A day on Avenir is 25 hours, based on the human Circadian rhythm. But a day on Eclectia varies between 20 and 30 hours due to the planet's wobble, which is maintained by the orbits of its large moons, Sheba and Quatermain.

This wobble also creates the speedy changes in season. At the beginning of a five day (or four and a half day) period there is a "winter" in the Northern hemisphere, the pole pointing away from the sun. Within two and one quarter days the pole shifts back to pointing at the sun for a brief "summer." Two and a quarter days later the pole is back into a "winter" position. So every fiveday (the Avenir Electia equivalent of a week) there are two "winters" with a "summer" in between. Each brings extremes of cold and heat, and short/long days. Like Earth, the Southern Hemisphere has the opposite pattern, so that fiveday that begins in the Northern winter begins in the South's summer.

There is a pattern to the seasons that repeats every fourteen days, with the second seven having the opposite pattern to the first. The pattern goes like this:

Day 1: Winter, morning
Day 3: Summer, afternoon
Day 5: Winter, overnight
Day 8: Summer, morning
Day 10: Winter, afternoon
Day 12: Summer, overnight
Day 15: Winter, morning (restart)

This rapid wobble and temperature differential creates powerful winds that sweep the planet at high speed in most regions. The speed of the seasonal changes is too rapid for the full effects of winter to be felt, for example, the oceans do not freeze over, and snowfall is rare, even though temperatures are briefly cold enough to freeze water. Since large bodies of water store and release heat very efficiently, the effect of the rapidly changing seasons is less pronounced near the North and South Polar Oceans than it is inland. Local conditions vary greatly depending on specific topography, but some inland places may heat up to as much as 40 degrees or more Celsius in summer, only to briefly plunge to minus 40 only sixty hours later.

Six fivedays make a month, so there are thirty days to a month. An Eclectia year is called a Founding to avoid confusion with the shorter Earth year. A Founding marks every fifteen months and serves the purpose of a year-type time period for expressions of history and age, except in certain figures of speech that cling to the use of the word "year." The names of the months originate partly from the Founders' own names and partly from Earth terminology fallen into disuse in this new world. So people might talk about the fourth fiveday of the month like we talk about the third week of the month, as well as specifying dates such as the 29th of Celeste. The year is designated A.F. or After Founding and the current timeframe of the Avenir Eclectia stories is 179 A.F., flashbacks excepted (that's nearly 224 years, by the way.)

So fifteen months at thirty days each gives us 450 days, but the yearly orbit of Eclectia is 454 days. The final four days are the Festival of Founding, something like our New Year.

So what does it mean when Ave is 14 Foundings old? That's a good bit more than 14 Earth years, because an Avenir year is 3 months longer than ours. Let's do the math...to make it simple let's assume an equal month length. 14 Foundings x 15 months = 210 months. Divide that by 12 and you have your Earth years: 17 and a half. Another way to think of it is that each Founding is one and a quarter years.

It works the same the other way, of course. If you want to say "five years ago" in Earth terms, that is 60 months = 4 Avenir Foundings.

LAW AND LAW ENFORCEMENT IN THE 94 CETI SYSTEM

INFORMATION BY WALT STAPLES, KEVEN NEWSOME, AND TRAVIS PERRY

No society survives long without a generally respected set of laws. To ensure that laws are respected, they must be enforced in such a manner that the perception within the society is one in which the system is seen to operate consistently. Whether the laws are fair or not is of a lesser importance to the members of that society in comparison to the expectation, that given the same situation, the law will produce the same or near same results each time. The Peace Council on Avenir makes the laws in use within the 94 Ceti System. The Council along with local temporary tribunals see to the maintenance of the law.

A secondary requirement is the inculcation in the majority of the society's members of a mindset that accepts that the law will successfully be applied by the forces representing order whenever the need arises—that basically, "you can't get away with it." In most societies, there is a percentage of the populace who, for whatever reason, disbelieves this. Through most of human history, this percentage seems to have hovered around 10 percent. The peacekeepers and their enforcers exist to deal with this 10 percent.

The Peace Council came into existence after a brief but bloody war between the land and undersea colonies of Eclectia and the orbiting space station Avenir and its allies, the spacers. Avenir won the war, which is why the Peace Council meets on Avenir and primarily makes decisions for the benefit of the station. The Council appoints law enforcement and all other regional governmental officials throughout the 94 Ceti system. Local government officials, at the level of mayor and below, are usually chosen by a local process, such as a general election. But all regions of the system accept the authority of the peacekeepers and enforcers, some grudgingly.

Peacekeepers work as plain clothes investigators and command uniformed enforcers. On Avenir and in other large population centers, the Investigating peacekeeper is in charge of all facets of an investigation including oversight of assisting peacekeepers and enforcers, preparing cases against suspects, and the supervision of the execution of sentences involving capital punishment. In these settings, most peacekeepers specialize in one or more areas of criminal investigation such as homicide, robbery, corruption, etc. In more remote areas, a peacekeeper travels a circuit of his assigned area and dispatches enforcers to keep order, investigate crimes, and apprehend suspects. The peacekeeper is then responsible for empanelling a three person tribunal, prosecuting the accused, and insuring that the accused receives a proper defense. The accused has the right to appeal the verdict to the Council on Avenir. The best analog of this role of the peacekeeper would be the Texas Rangers of 19th century North America (both during the Texas Republic period and after statehood). For the use of the peacekeeper's enforcers, the best analog is the Federal Marshals and their Deputy Marshals operating in the Indian Nations (later the state of Oklahoma) in the late 1800s.

Enforcers, with their gray uniforms, are trained at the Academy on Avenir. On the habitat and in population centers, they fulfill a role reminiscent of the patrolman or bobby found throughout Europe, North America, the Indian Subcontinent, and the Pacific Rim in the 20th century.

The Revenue Service is charged with the collection of duties and taxes, the maintenance of trade, and the safety of intra-system shipping. To do this, the service operates a number of revenue cutters whose duties include inspection of all space-going vessels and cargoes, rescue outside the sphere described by the orbit of the asteroid Assisi (within this sphere, rescue is a concern of the peacekeepers), and the suppression of piracy wherever discovered. They also maintain a presence at transit centers to and from underwater and land-based colonies, under the newly-minted title of "Customs Service."

Punishment of crime takes a number of forms. Depending on the local circumstances, fines, humiliation, incarceration, and corporal punishment may be levied. In the case of capital crimes, three forms of capital punishment are in force. In the jurisprudence in effect on Avenir, those convicted of a capital crime are allowed to pick their own punishment from a selection of three:

1. Death by spacing (rarely enforced).

2. Exile to Eclectia as a bug hunter for the rest of their life (this may

be reduced by a quota of kills met or the convicted person is remanded to one of the other two sentences).

3.   Transformation into a cyborg and labor for the rest of their life.

Those judged by the Council to be of too much of a danger to their fellows are sentenced to the first.

THE ABBEYS OF JEROME AND FRANCIS
INFORMATION BY WALT STAPLES AND TRAVIS PERRY

Shortly after the first library disaster, as a result of the so-called "Great War" between Avenir and the Eclectia colonies, when 60% of the holdings existent on arrival of Avenir in the 94 Ceti System were lost, the Catholic hierarchy (headed by an Archbishop) decided to launch the Byblos Project. This consisted of the various Christian and Jewish texts, and those of some other religions, still in the collection being printed out on hard copy (plastisheet) and archived in libraries and caches in a number of places in the 94 Ceti System. This was done in spite of assurances from Administration and the Council that it was impossible that such a loss would again happen in the future. At the time, St. Gunther of Sheba, then Bishop Juan Hiro Gunther, remarked that his own experience and that of most people taught that it was highly unwise to believe in the concept of "impossibility" or to use the word, "Never." As the library crashes of the next several decades showed, the churchman proved correct. After the second crash, part 2 of the Project was set in motion.

The Abbey of Jerome was founded by the Order of Friars Minor (OFM) in the worked-out shafts of a platinum mine on Sheba by St. Gunther, who stepped down from his diocese to become the first Abbot. As the platinum veins were exhausted, the Abbey grew to fill the empty space. The reason for the Abbey's existence was to train young men to memorize the various versions of the Bible that had been rescued before the final Terminal Crash.

In the Abbey, each boy memorizes a single version of the Bible, for instance The King James or the Ignatius, to mention only two. The students are referred to as "Manuscripts." Upon entry to the Abbey, they are given or pick a name that they will be known by as long as they are in holy orders. After the required years of study, when they have mastered their Bible's version, they are graduated as "Bibles" in the Rite of Publication. At this point, they will be known by the name of their Bible and their religious name. Later, after retirement—some to return to teach manuscripts at the Abbey—they will be known as "Brother" and their religious name. Once "Published," the new Bibles are sent into the outside world, to carry the Word of God to all who wish to hear it. Most are teamed with a priest trained in the seminary at the Abbey of Francis on Assisi. Others' services are rented by some Protestant churches—usually, the King James Versions, New International Versions, and Jerusalem Bibles.

The Abbey of Francis, founded on the asteroid, Assisi, by the Third Order Regular (TOR), produces priests in its seminary for the missions and some dioceses. The Abbey shares the asteroid with a Jesuit operated observatory complex noted for the massive optical telescope and radio telescope of the St Joseph Cupertino and Consolmagno Observatories. The feature that makes Assisi extremely suitable for astronomy is that its orbit is tipped at an angle of 78.654 degrees to the plane of the ecliptic. Thus, it is able to allow observations with less regard to the location of the other bodies of the system.

ON SEVERAL PLANTS OF ECLECTIA
INFORMATION BY KAYE JEFFREYS AND TRAVIS PERRY

The plant life on Eclectia must be very hardy to withstand the extreme temperatures of the 5 day summer-to-winter cycle and the arid conditions of the planet outside of the Polar Regions. Most Eclectia plants have an outward appearance that resembles some sort of evergreen plant on Earth, such as pines, firs, holly, or boxwood, etc.

The lavabush resembles sage and like sagebrush dominates many regions of mostly arid Eclectia. For many Eclectia colonists, the lavabush is the only wild plant they have encountered. The founders of the colony made early efforts to terraform Eclectia which largely failed. One such effort involved genetically engineering the lavabush to make its berries edible and long-lasting. This effort had the unexpected side-effect of making the lavabush into an even more dominant species than it had been previous to human colonization.

Nevertheless, other plant life does exist, and in some places prospers, especially in areas more remote from human settlement. One of these plants is a succulent spiral shoot that is called a spring plant, because it is shaped like a spring. In certain isolated regions whole fields of them grow together and are called "spring fields" because the collective group of them interlace and block out other plants, including the tenacious lavabush. When it's a winter day, the plants contract down together close to the ground for protection and to insulate their roots from freezing. On more tepid days, the spring plant loosens up and becomes springy, much to the delight of the children of those few human colonists who live near spring fields, because the plants are bouncy and their fields are used for playing sports. But on hot summer days, the coils loosen even more, making them hard to walk over, tripping and snagging at the feet.

Contraction during the winter is what protects the spring plant's extensive root system. On the coldest days or nights, temperatures may harm the coils, but the intact roots are preserved and will start sending up new coils to replace the damaged or dead ones. The spring plant doesn't flower often since it does most of its reproducing by its root system. But when the conditions are just right, a few the spirals may produce seed pods. These are heavy, with a tough outer shell, and smooth. So they neither float on the wind nor attach to the hairs of a bug to be carried off. The pods usually just fall into the ground near to the ground that is already overrun by spring plants. Thus the saying that is sometimes heard on Eclectia, "The pod doesn't fall far from the spring patch." Eaten raw, spring plants are bitter, but a few spirals in a large pot of soup adds a unique flavor that makes bug meat more palatable.

The thorny fan gets its name from its two extreme phases. On summer days, the leaves spread open like fans to capture as much sunlight as possible. But on winter days the leaves fold in on themselves, then twist, forming tough, sharp thorns an inch or two long. The prick of the thorn causes an irritation like a mosquito bite and both man and animal avoid patches of thorny fan on winter days.

It is a medicinal plant gathered when the leaves are open. The leaves are either chewed fresh or dried and kept on hand to produce a tea that takes the edge off of pain. It is also a fever reducer. The plant refuses to grow on Avenir or in the undersea cities no matter how hard anyone tries to reproduce the extreme conditions of Eclectia.

Thorny fans produce an extraordinary flower. It comes up on the first summer day each month, green in color like the leaves. But rather than fan shaped, its pod bursts open in all directions like an exploded fire cracker. Then it draws in these bits and closes for a winter cycle. The next summer day it opens in brilliant colors ranging from purples and deep blues to reds and oranges, depending on the acidity of the soil. Then the flower closes again for a winter cycle. The third summer day it opens up as a parachute ball seed head. The first strong breeze or hearty wind sends the parachuted seeds flying to find new ground to sow.

The oil of the plant, when refined a certain way, has the same effect on people as an opiate. This was discovered when producers worked to extract the medicinal qualities from the bulk of the plant for easier shipping. Unfortunately this discovery led to abuse.

The plant grew in many places on Eclectia but enforcers have destroyed most of the plants and made its oil a controlled substance, because the poor would produce the drug to ease the pain of their hard lives. Many deaths and unwanted pregnancies resulted. Deaths came from overdose or murder. Parents would abandon their children or sell them in order to get thorny fan oil or thano. The plant can be legally grown by a very few who obtain licenses to do so. And still others risk growing it illegally for either themselves or for profit. Thano drug busts remain a not-uncommon occurrence on Eclectia.

Although it is illegal to grow thorny fan without a license, in the high country and desolate places naturally occurring thorny fan is left unpoliced by enforcers due to the difficulty of law enforcement to police in remote areas and also since the nomads don't have the technology to produce thano. In any case, the nomads, along with the hermits and miners of the Five Rims, prefer to use it in its natural form for pain and fever reduction.

AVENIR ECLECTIA: THE HISTORIANS

Grace Bridges owns Splashdown Books, an indie press that publishes speculative fiction. She is also a science fiction author and has two published books: Faith Awakened (2007) and Legendary Space Pilgrims (2010). Grace is a New Zealander of Irish descent and a multilingual do-it-yourself force to be reckoned with. Often found staring into trees in search of a tui, she is a mystic wordnerd, urbanite hermit, and a writer of futuristic dreams that mess with your mind. http://grace.splashdownbooks.com

Jeff C. Carter lives in Venice, CA with two cats, a dog, and a human. His short stories appear in the anthologies *Tales From The Bell Club*, *Short Sips 2*, *Science Gone Mad* and *Frightmares*, issues of *Trembles* and *Calliope* magazine, and of course Splashdown Books' website Avenir Eclectia. He is currently developing *Mechawest*, a steampunk RPG for Heroic Journey Publishing. Visit him at Jeffccarter.wordpress.com.

By day **Jeff Chapman** writes software, by night or early morning or whenever he can sneak in some time, he writes speculative fiction that falls somewhere in the fairy tale, fantasy, and ghost story genres. His work has appeared in various anthologies and magazines. He lives with his wife and children in a house with more books than bookshelf space. You can find him musing about words and fiction at jeffchapmanwriter.blogspot.com.

Frank Creed is a housecatter, creator of the Underground cyberpunk universe, and a techno-thriller novelist. His short fiction has been featured in anthologies, and Frank has won both novel length and short story awards. He founded the Lost Genre Guild for the promotion of Christian speculative fiction, and is an advocate for the genre. Learn more about Frank at www.frankcreed.com.

Pauline Creeden is a horse trainer from Virginia, but writing is her therapy. She becomes the main character in each of her stories, and because she has ADD, she will get bored if she pretends to be one person for too long. In her fiction, she creates strong female characters who live in worlds that are both familiar and strange. Her short stories have been published in Fear & Trembling, Obsidian River, and anthologies from Port Yonder Press and Diminished Media Group. www.readers-realm.com

Karina Fabian enjoys looking at usual things in unusual ways, and writing about them. She's won numerous awards for her science fiction, fantasy, and comedic horror, but none of that compares to someone saying they snorted soda out their nose reading her book or a review that says, "Wow. Just, wow." Find her books at www.fabianspace.com.

Joseph H. Ficor hails from southern Illinois in the United States. In addition to science fiction, he has a major love of history. He currently lives in Niigata, Japan, with his wife and ever active and curious son. In addition to his stories for Avenir Eclectia, he has published science fiction based haiku for Digital Dragon Magazine. His story, "The Timeship of Semak," was published in the Light at the Edge of Darkness anthology (Writers Café Press) in 2007. You can learn more by visiting his blog at: hoshitosakura-gificor.blogspot.com

Kat Heckenbach spent her childhood with pencil and sketchbook in hand, knowing she wanted to be an artist when she grew up—so naturally she graduated college with a degree in biology, went on to teach math, and now homeschools her two children while writing. Her fiction ranges from light-hearted fantasy to dark and disturbing, with multiple stories published online and in print. Her YA fantasy novels *Finding Angel* and *Seeking Unseen* are available in print and ebook.
Enter her world at www.katheckenbach.com.

Holly Heisey is a writer and illustrator with a lifelong love of science fiction and fantasy. Her short fiction was chosen as a finalist in the Writers of the Future Contest and has appeared in *Aoife's Kiss* and *Avenir Eclectia*. Holly is currently at work on an epic science fiction novel. www.hollyheisey.com

Kaye Jeffreys hails from the Heartland of the U.S. with husband, two children remaining at home, three cats, and a dog. She started writing stories for her friends while still in grade school. Her day job in Foster Care provides fuel for the characters in her head to multiply, keeping her entertained as she conspires with them on how to best unleash them upon unsuspecting society. She's jazzed about writing microfiction for Avenir Eclectia where some of her characters can escape the confines of her head and explore the expanse of the Whale Star system.

Greg Mitchell is a screenwriter and novelist, and the author of *The Strange Man* and *Enemies of the Cross*—the first two installments of *The Coming Evil Trilogy*. In 2001, he wrote the novelization for *Time Changer*. He has had numerous tales of the macabre published in various anthologies, as well as writing official tie-in material for Lucasfilm's *Star Wars* mythology and the *Halloween* franchise based on the influential John Carpenter film. Mitchell's first produced screenplay, *Amazing Love: The Story of Hosea* starring Sean Astin (*Rudy*, *The Lord of the Rings Trilogy*), was released in 2012. He lives in Paragould, Arkansas with his wife and two daughters.
Visit him online at www.thecomingevil.com.

Keven Newsome is a graduate student at the New Orleans Baptist Theological Seminary, where he is pursuing a Master of Arts in Theology specializing in Supernatural Theology. He writes stories that portray the Supernatural and Paranormal with an accurate Biblical perspective. He is the author of the *Winter* series of thrillers published by Splashdown Darkwater. He currently lives in New Orleans, LA with his wife and their two children. Keven is also the founder and administrator of The New Authors' Fellowship and produces music and video through Newsome Creative.
www.kevennewsome.com

Travis Perry is an aspiring interstellar dictator…er, I mean, "writer," who's produced a bit of military non-fiction, loves science fiction and fantasy short stories, especially those with a Christian twist, and has contributed to several collections of them, most notably Aquasynthesis (2011) and this current work. He co-authored The Crystal Portal (2011) with Mike Lynch, gets more and more fun out of editing (perish the thought), and is rather full of oddball speculations (though he's trying hard to get empty, please see http://travissbigidea.blogspot.com). A father of six and also an Army Reserve officer who has served in Iraq, Afghanistan, and now Africa, you really would think he'd write more military stuff…

Mary Ruth Pursselley is an Ozarks farm girl who, by rights, probably should have grown up to write horse stories and prairie romance. Instead - when she's not reading, teaching violin, studying (and debating) Christian apologetics, or working on the family ranch - she writes fantasy, sci-fi, and steampunk. She is one of three contributing authors at The Lost Scribes, and her work has been featured in several other places including Mindflights, Digital Dragon Magazine, and of course, Avenir Eclectia. You can get acquainted with her at enterthewriterslair.blogspot.com, where she blogs about writing, reading, her Christian faith, life with her disaster-prone family (easily summarized as "a comedy of errors"), and anything related to Christian fiction…because it's not about what you see *in* the stories, it's about Who you see *through* them.

J. L. Rowan has been reading and writing fantastic tales since childhood. Her love of far-away, magical places drew her to both personal and formal study of all things medieval. She has had fantasy stories published by Uncial Press, Pill Hill Press, The Cross and the Cosmos, and Hadley Rille Books (upcoming). An excerpt of her unpublished novel saga, To Tread Upon Kings, won the 2007 Novel Excerpt Contest put on by award-winning author Tosca Lee. When not writing, she enjoys practicing the book arts. She lives in the Pacific Northwest with two mischievous balls of feline fur. http://jlrowan.wordpress.com

Walt Staples (1950-2012) was a previous President of the Catholic Writers' Guild and contributed to their blog at http://blog.catholicwritersguild.com. He was a top writer for Avenir Eclectia and his short stories are widely published. His work has appeared in Digital Dragon Magazine, Avenir Eclectia, Wherever It Pleases, The Dead Mule School of Southern Literature, Christmas: Peace on All the Worlds, and Residential Aliens Magazine. Walt was also rumored to be a member of the Marine Corps Association and the Lost Genre Guild. His blog and a list of publications can be found at http://gkfields.blogspot.com.

H. A. Titus can usually be found spinning story-worlds in her head or with her nose stuck in a book. Occasionally, her meteorologist husband makes her emerge for a real-life adventure that includes anything from severe weather to rock-climbing to snow-mobiling. She writes steampunk, urban fantasy, and epic fantasy stories about the journeys of heroes. Her collaborative steampunk serial novel, *Falls the Shadow*, can be found online at The Lost Scribes and her short stories in the *Alternative Witness* anthology. http://magical-ink.blogspot.com

Fred Warren's short fiction has appeared in a variety of print and online publications including *Kaleidotrope*, *Every Day Fiction*, *Bards & Sages Quarterly*, and *Allegory*. His first novel, *The Muse*, debuted in November 2009 from Splashdown Books, and was a finalist for the American Christian Fiction Writers Carol Award for book of the year in the speculative genre. A collection of his short stories, *Odd Little Miracles*, followed in July 2011, and *The Seer*, a sequel to The Muse, was published by Splashdown Books in November 2011. Fred works as a government contractor in eastern Kansas, where he lives with his wife and three children.
http://frederation.wordpress.com

Read new stories at:
www.avenireclectia.com

and background information at:
inside.avenireclectia.com

splashdown

Gizile follows her mysterious teacher, Tok, as they look into the ice of an ocean pool to contemplate a series of strange and mystical visions: astonishing tales of technology and transcendence, aliens and elves, space and time, dragons and demons, prophecies and scriptures, humor and horror, the gifted and the enslaved, virtual and supernatural reality, insanity and inspiration.

Dive into the creations of the Splashdown wordsmiths. Visit the edges of story worlds you love already, and taste their delights if you are new to Splashdown's universe.

with stories by Fred Warren, Caprice Hokstad, P. A. Baines, Adam Graham, R. L. Copple, Travis Perry, Mike Lynch, Keven Newsome, Kat Heckenbach, Ryan Grabow, and Grace Bridges. Narrated by Walt Staples.

aquasynthesis

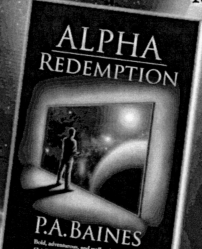

CPSIA information can be obtained at www.ICGtesting.com
Printed in the USA
BVOW081212071112

304910BV00003B/14/P